THE GREAT GENDER REVOLT

The Big Book of Feminization ~ Volume Two

Seven erotic stories of men who dress like women!

COVID Feminized My Husband

Dominated by a Gang of Women

The Feminization of Jackson

My Husband the Model

Being a Woman

I Changed My Nephew into a Girl

The Great Gender Revolt

Grace Mansfield

THE BIG BOOK OF FEMINIZATION ~ VOLUME TWO

ISBN: 9798509560958

Do you have all six of the Big Books of Feminization?

TABLE OF CONTENTS

1) COVID Feminized My Husband	5
2) Dominated by a Gang of Women	38
3) The Feminization of Jackson	71
4) My Husband the Model	103
5) Being a Woman	137
6) I Changed My Nephew into a Girl	173
7) The Great Gender Revolt	207

BOOKS BY GRACE MANSFIELD!

My Husbands Funny Breasts
Too tough to Feminize
I Changed My Husband into a Woman
The Emasculation Project
The Feminization Games
A Woman Unleashed
The Stepforth Husband
Revenge of the Stepforth Husband
The Sissy Ride
Feminized by a Ghost
The Curse of the Werefem
Silithia
The Big Tease
Womanland
The Man Who Abused a Woman

COLLECTIONS BY GRACE MANSFIELD

Woman on Top
Ration of Passion
Achy Breaky Naked
The Girl in Me
The Secret is Out
Stories to Pump Your Heart
Dirty, Rotten Nasty Smut
Tainted Love
The Electric Bone
The Shivering Bone
The Whisper of Flesh
Quivering Buns

COVID Feminized My Husband

Published on Kindle,
appeared in 'A Ration of Passion.'

PART ONE

The accident, if it was an accident, happened in my lab.

As far as accidents go, it wasn't much. Just somebody left their lunch in the wrong refrigerator, then discovered it and put it in the right refrigerator. Unfortunately, nobody ever found out, and what happened happened.

Janey and I eat lunch at 11:00. We go in an hour early, eat early, and leave early. And, we share our lunches.

Now Janey is a knock out blonde. Wears glasses to read, but when she takes those lenses off, zowie! Baby blues knock those boys right out of the park.

I'm married, so I don't care. And, to tell you the truth, I've sort of let myself go. Kids, work, my lazy ass 'house husband' does a few dishes and a load of laundry and calls it a week.

So I'm about 5'6", 200 pounds, and haven't had sex in a half a year.

In fact, I heard my bastard hubbie talking to a friend on the phone, he didn't know I was talking, and he said, "I just roll her in dough and look for the wet spot. He was referring, of course, to how he ever found my hole on my blubber laden frame.

Okay! It's my fault! But there were extenuating circumstance. His promises to love and support, backed up by endless games of football on the TV, and then, later on, suspicions.

I always sort of knew that he was stepping out on me.

'Cause he had to roll me in flower and look for the wet spot. Bastard.

Anyway, Janey and I sat down to eat. She shared her PBJ with me, and I shared my tuna fish with her. What we didn't know was that the PBJ had a little extra something. Something it had picked up by being placed in the wrong refrigerator, the refrigerator we use to keep samples of germs. And the germs had already been altered, mutated, and nobody really knew what was in some of those little babies.

So I ate half a PBJ, finished the rest of the day, and went home. The good news is that whatever was in that sack that nudged up against Janey's sack and impregnated it with the latest and the greatest in diseases...didn't effect me.

I rolled into the garage and stopped the car. I had gotten in the habit of being sneaky. I really wanted to catch Chuck. Catch him at what I wasn't sure, at first, but, as time rolled on, I caught him more and more.

For instance, this day I coasted to a stop, got out of the car without making any noise, closed the door without a click. Then I entered the kitchen, taking off my shoes when I opened the door. I tip toed across the floor, down the hall, and peeked into his office.

There he was. Pants down, dick hanging out, flacid, white goo in his hand. On the computer screen I saw a video of a Carolina Ramirez doing her thing.

His thing.

Her thing.

She was a transgender from across some border, selling videos of herself jacking off. She had big tits and a monster cock. For a tranny.

As usual, I took out my cell phone and took pictures.

He slept the deep sleep of someone who has just squirted his brains out. I risked tip toeing into the room. I got close ups of his drooling face, snorting in in happy but demented dreams. I got a far away shot that caught his dick laying on his happy lappy and the tranny on the screen moaning and shooting a monster load.

Finally, one more day of evidence done, I tip toed back through the house, into the garage, and opened closed the car door loudly. A second later I opened the kitchen door and yelled, "Honey! I'm home!"

Why, you ask, didn't I bust him?

I honestly don't know.

Maybe there was some residual love. We'd been together ten years. Maybe I was waiting for better evidence. After all, a man jacking off to trannies isn't much when it comes to divorce court.

But I didn't really want a divorce.

Somewhere inside me I think I remembered a time of love. When I had been skinny and svelte, and had world class boobs instead of these big, fatty hangers. I remembered when he used to open the door for me, when his eyes had lit up at the sight of me.

Sigh.

So, while he tucked his lazy dick into his pants and tried to look like he'd just been napping, I fixed lunch. I had a doctor's appointment the next day and I wasn't supposed to eat anything.

So Chuck entered the kitchen with a grin that concealed nothing, at least not to me, and pecked my cheek, and put his arm around my shoulder in a perfunctory hug, and asked what was for lunch.

Then I sat across from him, sipped some hibiscus tea, good for weight loss, and watched him slurp and gobble and spread crumbs across the table.

Slob.

I didn't know that the next day was going to change my life.

I took work off and went to the doctor the next day. Parked and entered his office, exchanged chattie nothings with his secretary, and was shown to an exam room.

Another nurse took my vitals. And my blood, and a few other things. I asked her if she was going to pay for all my 'vital essences,' and she just smiled. Seems like nobody has a sense of humor these days.

The Doc walked in, a skinny, bald fellow with thick glasses. He joked with me, listened to my heart, and then started asking some weird questions.

"When did you start gaining weight?"

"What is the heaviest you have ever been?"

And, "Would you like to lose all that weight? In a month?"

Blink. Open-eyed stare. WTF?

He continued. "Elle, you have been victimized."

"What?"

"Look, medicine is getting better all the time. New breakthroughs. New advances."

"No, no. go back to that weight loss bit."

He grinned, "You fall into an odd category. You are healthy. You have some rather unique readings, and we think we can wake up your thyroid."

My thyroid, the little son of a bitch that had stopped working shortly after I got married, and had slapped 80 pounds onto my once sleek body.

"We've known that your weight gain isn't because you ate too much, or exercised too little. We know that your thyroid just...stopped working. And that's why you had considerable weight gain.

Considerable, huh! He was being polite. I had inflated like one of the Spruce Goose's tires.

"So...what? You're going to give me a thyroid transplant?"

He chuckled. "No. A small firm in Germany has developed a serum that they believe will kickstart your thyroid. Initial trials have caused fat mice to slender down in a week. A couple of human trials have resulted in exceptional weight loss."

"How much?"

"Everybody is different, but from your statistics I estimate you will lose up to 80 pounds."

My jaw dropped. Eighty pounds. I would be 120. About what I was when I had first gotten married, and a hell of a lot better than 200 pounds. I would be sleek and slender again.

"Doc?" I actually grabbed him by the lapel. "Sign me up!"

So he signed me up for human trials, and I was one of the first people in the world to experience the effects of Zildo 123, otherwise known as 'The Red Pill.'

One month later—a month in which I came home no less than 9 times to take pictures of my degraded hubbie—I sat in the Doc's exam room, three suits and four doctors watching me, and the nurse put a red pill in my maw, and I sipped from a paper cup.

"That's it?" I asked.

All those suits and white coats, they seemed extraordinarily pleased with themselves. They high fived and shook hands and even hugged one another.

"As agreed, you will come here 3 times a week for tests."

"Okay," I answered. "When can I buy a bikini?"

They laughed, soon after departed, and I went home.

I felt nothing. After eight years of crash diets and boot camp work outs, I expected something. We're the world of instant results, you know?

Fast food on the dime. Infomercials promising the moon. But I felt nothing.

Sigh. Well, what did I expect?

I expected 200 pounds to suddenly shlurp away. Faster than I could gobble a french fry.

Well, I wasn't in the fast food world, really, that is just a gimmick. I was in Kansas, where fat housewives wear wallpaper dresses and the nylons swell up and can't contain all the cellulite.

I walked into the house. I slammed the door. I didn't feel like sneaking around. I wanted results. And, boy, did I get results. I heard some muttering, some weird rustling sounds, then Janey popped out of Chuck's office.

"Janey?"

She stood there, looking nervous. Her hair blowzy and her make up slightly mussed. Her lipstick, specifically, was smeared around her mouth.

"Uh, hi."

She looked away, she glanced in the office, she looked desperate and pathetic all at the same time.

I stomped down the hallway, it's impossible not to stomp when you weight as much as I did.

"I dropped by to see you, and, uh…"

I looked into the office. Chuck was desperately buttoning his pants. He turned and stared at me. His eyes were dark and haunted, like a thousand yard stare. But he hadn't been in combat…he had been in my best friend.

"Chuck?" And I turned to Janey. "Janey?"

"I'm sorry," Janey burbled.

"It doesn't mean anything," blurted Chuck.

"Shit," I said. And then I realized…it really didn't mean anything.

And here's the weird thing.

Chuck? Janey? They were just…silly people. Insincere. Dishonest. The kind that you stay away from.

That day I packed a suitcase. Grabbed a couple of dresses. A couple of small boxes with personals in it, and I walked out the door. Never to return. I thought. What I didn't know was that I had already struck, and that I had had my revenge.

Don't let me get technical here, but here's what happened. For 6 hours after I took the pill I was contagious.

I know, a pill doesn't make for contagion. Or does it? The Red Pill was designed to grab one of my organs and strangle it into motion. And the things that went into that little bit of packed powder...I still don't know, but I was contagious for 6 hours.

I didn't infect Janey. She was a woman. And she was the wrong blood type.

But. I infected Chuck. I didn't even have to have sex with the bozo to give him a...'disease.'

What was going to make me lose more weight than a blimp shot by a cannon was going to something to him. And, oh baby, it was REALLY something.

The first ten days I lost 20 pounds. I was taking in my dresses, buying new bras and panties, and my hair was even turning lustrous. Lustrous hair, what a side effect, eh?

The people at work all marveled, asked me what my secret was. "Oh, nothing. I just finally got serious with the weight lifting."

A lot of the over sized gals at work started shaking the iron after I made the comment.

And my thyroid was just getting started.

The second ten days I lost 40 pounds. 40 FUCKING pounds!

Oh, the doc was worried, that much weight leaving my obese frame at once, he was worried.

But I was healthy, and, if anything, The Red Pill had made me healthier.

Now I couldn't just take in a dress. I had to buy new clothes. And, here's the good part, I had to buy them so they'd still fit when I hit 120 pounds.

Every day I woke up, feeling fresh and full of vim and vigor.

Every day I jumped on the scale, without the fear of breaking it, and took note of the pounds dwindling away.

Every time I stepped into the doctor's office the secretaries cheered.

One day they even opened a bottle of champagne.

Ten more days, and…20 more pounds.

80 pounds in a month. And here's the really good news. What extra fat I did have was in my boobs.

I have always been healthy in boob department. A solid C cup. But then I had gone to fat city. But, now that I was back, my boobs were bigger than they had been before I had gained all that weight. I don't know if it was just the fat accrued when I had been obese, or whether The Red Pill did this to me, but I had to get bras for double D. And I was skinny as a boy. I had some fanny, but not much. I had abs. The results of all my exercise regimes was now being revealed.

The only weird thing was that I had to do all sorts of exercises for excess skin. I mean, 80 pounds in 30 days, that stuff would have hung off me like drapes over a window.

But I exercised, took some other pills, and the Doc even cut some of it off me.

Bottom line, day 30 I was back to being world class knock out. Big tits. Long, shiny hair. A body to die for.

And, I had not only lost 80 pounds of ugly fat, I had lost 140 pounds of cheating bastard.

I thought.

It was day 31, I had just gone out and gorged on clothes. I had flimsy bras, thongs, nylons for my now sleek legs, and fresh make up.

And I had several dresses, boots and sandals and high heels, and everything that a gorgeous babe needs.

Ding a ding a ding.

The phone.

I frowned. I wanted to take a bubble bath and then try on clothes. Maybe have a drink, maybe even go out to a bar and look for an honest man.

I know, an honest man in a bar? That's an oxymoron.

I certainly didn't feel like yakking on the phone.

Besides, I didn't really have many friends. I hadn't seen cheating bastard in a month, and I ignored Janey at work.

I gave a sigh and I picked the phone up.

"Elle? Elle?" Chuck's voice was hurried, actually sounded a little frantic.

I hung up. I said a few bad phrases. You know, things like, 'fucking cheater. Bastard,' as I walked away from my cell.

It rang again.

I went back and looked at the number. Chuck. Fucker. I walked away.

And the damned thing stopped ringing. And started. And stopped. And…I picked up the damn thing and snarled, "Don't call me any more!"

"Elle, please!" And I knew he was crying. His voice was strangled, choked up, and his tones, he was sobbing like a baby.

Now, truth, I didn't much care for Chuck, but there was just the teensiest concern. You can't live with a man for eight years and not care something.

I didn't say anything.

He blubbered, "Elle, something has happened to me. Something bad. There's something wrong with me."

"Sure," I quipped manly. "You're a cheating bastard who wants to beat off to trannies. That qualifies as 'something wrong.'

"Honey! Please. It's not that. My body. Something's happened to my body. I need…I need you…I need help."

I listened, and frowned, but there was a spark of interest. Something had happened? Was he sick? Had he been in an accident.

That teen, little spark of concern popped. And curiosity. Though, I have to be honest, maybe I just wanted to see what was wrong with him so I could gloat.

"Okay," I spoke savagely, after 15 minutes of him wailing and crying. "I'm coming over."

So I stalled a while. Took a bath, and answered the phone. Dripping wet, rubbing my big boobs with a fluffy towel, I answered, and when he began crying I merely grinned and said, "I'm on my way over."

Then I picked out my best new bra. A shelf that would like my excited nipples poking through the stiffest of material.

And a blouse, thin, sheer, not thick.

A thong, a short skirt that showed off my freshly shaved legs. High heels that showed off my calves.

The phone rang and I picked it up.

"Almost there," I lied cheerfully.

I put on make up. Red, red lipstick, shadowy eye shadow. I put in my earrings, little springs of diamonds that swayed and gave sparkle to my face.

I walked down to the car, my ass swaying, my boobs shaking, and answered the phone. "Just a couple of minutes," I said.

I had to laugh. Here he was, crying, moaning, sobbing like a little girl, and I was going to knock his eyes out and remind him of what he had lost.

I pulled up in front of the house, not in the driveway, it wasn't my house anymore, and sauntered up the walk.

Mr. Kevins, across the street, opened his mouth so far his dentures fell out. All the way out. Landed on the lawn where he quickly picked them up and tried not to stare some more as he walked toward his front door.

"Hi, Billie!" I waved.

He waved, then tripped on his front door step.

I stepped into the house. And it hadn't changed much.

Maybe a few more dishes in the sink. Articles of clothing strewn about. Well, Chuck did most of his living in front of the computer.

"Elle?" he called to me from the bedroom.

I snorted. Bedroom. Fat chance I'm going in where he can grab me. And he would grab me. Chuck was always a horny bastard. Even when he didn't want me he was whacking off several times a day to the computer.

"I'm out here."

"Can you come back here, please?" whiney, moany Chuck. I wasn't falling for that stuff.

"No way, Jose. Get your butt out here."

"Please, Elle. Please."

And, I have to say, the way he was carrying on, sounding so pitiful. I actually took a few steps down the hallway. I stopped.

"Come on, you bozo. Get your ass out here or I'm leaving."

"Elle!" And there was something so rock bottom in the way he said my name. There was something so broken and shattered and gone to hell, I started walking down the hallway. I stopped before the end of the hallway, before the door to our bedroom.

"Chuck?"

"I'm here," almost a whisper, but a cracked and whining whisper.

"You better not try any funny stuff."

"I won't. Please. I won't." And he was openly crying again.

Just for a moment I felt concern. concern for another human being. Didn't matter that he was a no good, cheating bastard, he was a human being.

I stepped into the doorway, ready to run the other direction, and my mouth dropped.

Chuck was standing on the far side of the room. His head was hanging and he was crying, and he had boobs.

"Chuck?"

"I'm…something's happening…I'm…changing." He sobbed uncontrollably.

I couldn't help myself. I entered the room, came around the end of the bed.

He had the body of a 20 year old woman. Slender. Big tits. Almost as big as mine. He always kept his hair long, was too lazy to get it cut probably, and his hair hung down over his face.

His shoulders shook, and his boobs shook.

"Turn towards me."

He turned, and he had no manhood. No pecker. No balls. Just a wisp of hair, a landing patch, and inside that small bit of fringe he had a vagina.

"Oh. My. God!"

"I can't…I don't know what happened. Elle!"

Now that I was here I realized that he had been making himself talk in a deep voice, normal for the old Chuck. As I stood at the end of the bed and listened to him his voice went up, became feminine.

"I don't know what to do. Elle. I'm sorry. I don't know what…"

He crumpled up then, actually fainted. He half fell on the bed, slid off, and puddled on the floor.

I picked up the phone and called my doctor.

I didn't call 911 because this wasn't their purview. What? They were going to come arrest a guy for turning into a girl? what would they charge him, or her, with? Transgendering in the first degree?

I explained to the Doc that my husband had turned into a woman.

He scoffed at me. Said I was drinking, that my little joke was ridiculous, and I kept talking…and he started to believe me.

He told me to just wait where I was—what did he think…I was going to do cartwheels down the street?—and people would be coming to see me.

The people were the suits and lab coats who had given me the pill. I didn't know why them, but eventually I would find out. They represented a big pharma company. They were involved in researching an amazing number of subjects. Said subjects included COVID, kickstarting thyroid glands, and…sexual mechanisms of various animals. Animals like Clownfish, appropriate for my hubbie; Slugs, yea, that was Chuck; frogs; green sea turtles.

Animals that turned from one sex into another.

My doc knew this. He knew what they were researching, and that was why he called them instead of the CDC.

Chuck woke up and began struggling when they loaded him on a stretcher. He fought, but how much fighting is a girl capable of.

So these big, strong huskies in white coats put him on a stretcher, strapped him down, and carted him off.

I followed them out of the house, watched them put Chuck in an ambulance.

Neighbors came out. Mr. Kevins came out to stand next to me, his eyes glancing at my boobs, the old lecher, and asked, "Where are they taking him?"

I shrugged. "Don't know."

"Well, if you need anything…" and he turned to me.

Fucking Mr. Kevins. He laughed at me when I was fat, made jiggling motions to his wife when he thought I wasn't looking, and now he was hitting on me.

I smiled, turned to him, and said. "How nice of you," and I touched my hand to his cheek.

He bonered up and gulped and watched as I walked away, forever out of his reach. Let the fool suffer.

Tell the truth, I sort of forgot about Chuck then. He wasn't in my life, or thoughts, and that was fine with me. I returned to my apartment, gloried in my new looks, and went out on the town a few times. And I found out something interesting.

The world had changed.

Well, actually it wasn't the world that had changed…it was me.

I would sit down at a bar and some good looking hunk would come sit next to me, chat me up, buy me and drink, and I would see right through him. All the way through.

Shallow, insincere. Only wanting a roll in the hay.

So I stopped going out.

And I was getting horny.

The guys at work were hitting on me, but they were all old and married. I didn't want to do to somebody else's marriage what had been done to mine.

And, a month later, there I was. Gorgeous and horny. Beautiful and frustrated. No options for love. And, in a way, I cursed Chuck. I blamed him for taking away my best years, but I knew it wasn't his fault.

It was my thyroid. If I hadn't gotten so chubby maybe I could have kept Chuck interested. Maybe he wouldn't have gone looking. Maybe he wouldn't have spent his time beating off to big breasted transvestites and transgenders and trans everything.

Poor, stupid Chuck.

And, poor me. All dressed up and nowhere to go.

And that was where I was on a Friday afternoon. Off work, looking good, and nowhere to go…when the phone rang.

"Hi, Elle."

"I recognized the voice right away. "Hey, Doc. Thyroid is still working. What's up?"

"Well, uh, can you come pick up Chuck?"

"Chuck?" I have to tell you, laugh if you want, I actually had forgotten about my poor schmuck of a husband.

"Yes. He's ready for release."

"Release?" I didn't want him. "Did you find out what was wrong with him?"

"Actually, yes. Your body was doing a chemical dump for several hours after you took Zildo 123, we think, well, the egghead doing the research said that shouldn't have done anything, but…have you been exposed to COVID?"

"What? No!"

"You haven't been around anybody who has had it?"

"No. Look, I know about COVID. My company is doing research into it."

"It is?" And that interested him. He asked me for some contact info for my company, and months later, many months, I would eventually find out that it was the COVID that did it.

I had picked up COVID from a bag put into the wrong refrigerator. I had given it to Chuck. Neither of us had ever shown symptoms, and it had not effected me. But he had the COVID, then he was exposed to the changes happening to me from The Red Pill, and it was the perfect storm. Everything came together, wiped out his Y chromosome and left him with double Xs. It was the worst sort of double cross, and an accident, and what had started Chuck down the inexorable path to womanhood.

Right then, however, we knew nothing, and, even if we had…what difference would it make? It was all done, and the Doc asked me again, "Can you come pick up Chuck?"

"So he's cured?"

"Well, uh, he's not sick."

That was an evasion if ever I heard one. "What is he?"

"Well, he's doing well."

"Is he still a girl?"

Silence.

"He is."

More silence. Then: "Look, the company can't keep him anymore. They have done what they could, but they're releasing him, and somebody needs to come get him."

"Let him walk."

Silence. Then: "He really needs somebody to pick him up, to, uh, help him."

"Help him what?" I asked suspiciously.

"Look, Elle. Please. Just come see him. You'll understand then."

So, against my better judgment, not wanting to, I drove down to the hospital and walked in the front door.

"Elle?"

I walked into the hospital room and knew exactly what was wrong.

"Elle?"

He was scared. He was shivering and frightened and was scared of the world.

In a way, I understood it. He had been changed. One day he was a hunky man, sort of, if you discount the porn problem, and then he was a girl.

Well, a woman.

Some nurse had taken pity on him and done his hair up. Piled it on his head in a french bun.

And this merely emphasized how his cheeks were more hollow, and his chin more narrow, and that made his lips bigger and plumper. Real Angeline lips.

And, here's where it gets weird, I felt a warmth ignite in me. Those lips. I could imagine them all red and juicy. Ripe for kissing.

Oh, I'm not a lesbian.

But I do appreciate beauty.

And, let's face it, my whole image of Chuck was of him as a man. And there was something soft and warm for him in the way back of my soul.

Hell, I had married the damned doofus! I must have loved him. Once upon a time.

"Chuck?"

He sprang out of bed. He was a lithe 5 foot 6, my height now, he had lost 4 inches, and he had curves. I could see them under the hospital gown.

Curves like mine. Big breasts, round hips, and…and no bulge down where the dick should be.

He ran at me and hugged me. I could smell his hospital washed hair. something would have to be done about that. His armpits needed shaving, and his legs, but there was no trace of hair over his lip.

I could feel his big bosoms smashing into mine.

I let him hug me for a long minute. He was crying, getting my sheer blouse all wet. And I felt the weirdest feeling. A mix of sorrow for a fallen man, and warmth for this…this creature in my arms.

I wasn't a Lesbian, but I did feel something for a man in a woman's body.

"Please," he kept begging. "I'm sorry. Please forgive me. I'm sorry. I'm sorry."

I started saying, "Shh, it's all right."

But it wasn't all right.

A minute before I had been a proud bitch, ready to take on rather frustrating and disappointing world. Now I was saddled with a crybaby man in a woman's body. A person who had no idea what to do, who was victim to the world.

And that warm spot in me got warmer and warmer. My eyes even started to fill.

I pushed him back, held him at arm's length. "Chuckie, Chuckie. What will we do with you?"

And then, hating myself, but giving in to that warm spot in my could, I did the only thing I could do.

"Get your stuff, Chuck. Let's go home."

And the big baby cried all the way home.

PART TWO

Chuck was a mess. Apparently they kept testing him, taking samples, telling him everything would be all right, and ignored the fact that he was totally and utterly freaked out.

He had been a man, a perverted man, but he had the dick and the balls and the scratch yourself and drool mentality. Then he was a girl. Thirty days may seem like a long time to be changing, but when it is happening to you it is both fast and slow.

Fast, because every day you wake up and your boobs are growing, and your dick is shrinking, or your balls have disappeared, and you can't even look in the mirror without freaking out.

Slow, because each moment drags on forever. You are stuck in a nightmare and even though the Mummy is waddling behind you as fast as a duck hauling a car, he is catching up to you.

And with all the testing and sampling and pin pricks and hypodermics and everything, they had never bothered to send in a psychiatrist, or a transgender counselor, or anything.

I had to drag Chuck out of the car. He just wanted to lie there and sob.

I pushed him up the steps into the kitchen, and then he just stood there. Looking around. His face all wet with tears.

So I pushed him down the hallway, took his stupid hospital gown off, and shoved him into the shower.

Even then, warm water sluicing his new body off, he just stood there and cried.

I pulled him out. He was getting a bit more malleable, so I dried him off, then put him in bed and tucked him in.

"Go to sleep," I said.

"I…I…will."

But I could tell he wasn't going to sleep. His eyes were big and dark with despair. He had bags under them, which meant he hadn't been sleeping at the hospital, and they didn't care. Fucking hospital.

So I went and found some Vicodin, popped two tabs into his mouth, and made him sip warm milk.

He couldn't sip worth shit, and he only took a couple of gulps, then placed the glass on the side table and stared at the ceiling.

I waited.

He yawned, but he didn't go to sleep. A half hour later he was still staring at the ceiling.

"Crap," I said. I lay down next to him and I held him. I cuddled him. I rocked him. I soothed him. I sang a lullaby to him.

Oh, I was pissed. I didn't want to be here. I was all dressed up, and forced to babysit my brain dead husband. But I had to.

The guy was messed up! Who else was going to help him?

So. I cradled him, and rocked him, and said sweet things to him. "It's going to be all right. We'll get through this. Come on, baby."

And, an hour later, the Vicodin actually started working.

Now Vicodin isn't sleeping pills, but it was all I had. And I figured if he got a little loopy he would relax, and then maybe he could fall asleep.

And he did.

Two in the morning, I had been here for hours, and he gave a snore. Just a light one. Not a barn burner like he usually did, but it was a start.

I waited, and slowly he began to grow in volume.

"OINK SNEW! OINK SNEW!"

He might be a woman, but that was the residual man in him.

Smiling, I slithered off the bed. Thank God, he kept sleeping. If he hadn't I was going to take a mallet to his noggin.

I tip toed down the hallway, poured myself a stiff drink, then thought. Long and hard.

I could leave him, and he'd probably be in a psych ward, or commit suicide. So as much as I didn't want to, I was going to have to stick around. For a few days at least.

Heaving a dissatisfied sigh, I washed the empty glass out, and went out to the car and drove back to my apartment.

I threw a bunch of clothes into a suitcase. I put all my new sex underwear into one of the big shopping bags I had accumulated, grabbed my make up kit, and headed out the door.

My mind wasn't in a good place. I wasn't pissed so much as resigned, and there was a dark blot sitting right in my forehead.

Yet, inside that dark blot, hidden so well I wouldn't admit to it, was a spot of warmth.

Truth was, I was already tired of being single. I didn't want Chuck back, I didn't think, but…I was tired.

I drove back home, checked on Chuck, lugged my stuff in, poured another drink, and face another problem. Where would I sleep?

I wasn't about to sleep in the big, comfy double bed in Chuck's room. Chuck was in that, and I didn't feel like cuddling up to him. And I didn't like the guest room. The bed hurt my back, and a street light outside the window made it too bright to sleep.

So where?

Sigh. The living room. On the big, old comfy couch.

I stripped out of my sexy duds, pulled a blanket over, fluffed up a pillow, and gave up for the night.

Daylight struck me in the face. I grumbled something, and turned over. But now I was awake. I was still tired, it had been a rough night for me, but it was time to get up and join the human race. Or, at least put up with the human race. The human race, in this instance, consisted of Chuck.

I didn't bother to get dressed. I just walked down the hallway and into the big bedroom.

He was laying on his back peaceful, his eyes closed.

The curtain was a little open, and the light was going to hit his eyes, so I tip toed over and pulled it shut. When I turned around his eyes were open.

Open and staring at the ceiling. Filled with misery and despair. This was a guy who was going to kill himself. I could see it all over him.

"Good morning," I said.

He said nothing.

I sat on the edge of the bed. "Chuck."

Slowly, slowly, he turned his head, focused his bleary eyes on me.

"I said 'good morning.' What do you say?"

Oh, Lord, it was pulling it out of him. But he mumbled a slow and dull, "Good morning."

"Excellent. It's time to get up."

He just lay there.

I stood up and pulled the drapes. Light flooded the room.

I turned around, about to say something, and he was staring at me.

He had never actually seen my new body. At the hospital he was so out of it he wouldn't have noticed if an elephant shit on him. But now, a new day, the first real sleep he'd probably had in weeks, since his 'change,' he noticed.

I felt naked then. He was my husband, but I had written him off. And here he was, staring at me, my nakedness, studying my tits.

"You've changed."

Tell the truth, I should have celebrated. This was the first coherent thought he had had, and he had actually said something, me, in the real world. But I was feeling pissy, so I snapped, "So have you."

He turned back to the ceiling, and I realized maybe I should be a little more gentle and understanding.

Oddly, the comparison of Chuck to Chuck happened in my mind.

Chuck, the pervert watching trannies and jacking off. A handsome man, but a sad man, trapped in perversions with no hope of controlling himself.

And Chuck, the sad shell of himself. The bozo who cheated on me, and was rewarded with a brand new body. The king is dead. Long live the queen.

"Chuck, time to get up."

He lay there.

I went to the bathroom and got a glass of water. I returned and threw it in his face. So much for compassion and understanding.

He sputtered, and he sat up. Yippy.

I pulled the covers off him, I pulled on his arm. He was light, easily handled. The old Chuck I couldn't move with a tractor. this Chuck weighed about as much as me, 120 pounds, and he didn't have my exercise improved muscles.

"Stop," he said. A dull protest which I ignored.

I pushed him into the shower and turned it on. Cold.

He shivered, looked around, and then stepped to the side and turned the hot water spigot.

Good. He was starting to move.

"Can you come to the kitchen if I leave you alone."

He stared at me. He was standing quite motionless.

I sighed, jumped into the shower and began scrubbing, first myself, then him.

I soaped his body. I paid attention to his long hair, using lots of shampoo and conditioner. Damned hospital were a bunch of slackers. how could anybody feel good about themselves if nobody else cared?

Then I soaped his body. His back. His torso, and…his boobs.

I had never felt another woman's boobs, and the experience was fascinating.

He wasn't a man, I reminded myself. He was a woman. No matter what was going on in his mind, his was a woman's body. And it was a pretty good woman's body.

His tits were firm, but soft. I soaped them thoroughly, knew that I was getting carried away, but was unable to help myself.

I soaped his nipples, and I watched his face.

He was getting warmer. In fact, his boobs were actually turning red, like they were blushing, and his nipples stood straight up.

And, I was getting warmer. To handle another woman's boobs. It was forbidden, and therefore delicious. I felt myself blush.

I stopped rubbing his tits and soaped his hips, and…his pussy.

Oh. My. God! He had a real live pussy. Under my fingers I could feel the labia, the clitoris, the plump softness of the whole area.

I soaped, and realized I was getting carried away again. And he was starting to breath hard. And so was I.

I stopped soaping him, was embarrassed, and said. "Rinse yourself off, then come into the kitchen. I'm making breakfast."

I got out of the shower, toweled myself off, left a towel for him, wrapped another towel around my hair, and walked to the kitchen. I left little, wet footprints all the way down the hall.

In the kitchen I threw a dozen links of sausage into a pan. Put some hash brown patties into the toaster, then poured myself a drink.

I was drinking too much, but I didn't blame myself. Heck, I hadn't had a drink for breakfast for eight years, and it was fun.

Everything was done and ready for consumption, and I was wondering if I was going to have to go drag him out by the nipples, when he came down the hall.

He was clean, and his hair was wet and straggling—he didn't know anything about hair care—and I took the time to really look at his body.

He was slender, like me. His tits were as big as mine, but I don't think any bigger. My bras would certainly fit him. The main thing was that there was no trace of man about him…except for his walk.

"You're walking wrong," I blurted.

"What?" He looked confused. He looked at the plates on the table. I realized he was hungry. A good sign.

"Sit and eat. I'll tell you."

He sat down and picked up a sausage, got his fingers all greasy and put it in his mouth and chewed. Like a man.

I sighed.

"What?"

"Look, when you walk you walk like you still have a pair of balls between your legs, keeping them apart, forcing you to walk stump legged, like a man."

He didn't say anything, but it was easy to see what he was thinking: *I am a man!*

But he wasn't.

"You have to walk gently, almost like you have on high heels. Padding like a cat, not stomping like a pit bull.

He frowned. And ate.

"And, another thing. You eat like a pig."

He stopped eating and stared at me. but I was pissed. I had to be here and take care of him, and I felt like my life was on hold. So damn the torpedoes and full speed ahead.

"Men eat with their hands, grunting and slobbering, shoveling food in because they're in a hurry. Watch."

I picked up a fork, neatly sliced a bit of sausage, and placed that bit in my mouth. Easy peasy. No lipstick smeared. And I chewed with small motions.

"Got it?"

"Uh…"

"Do it."

Frowning, he had a lot of frowns in him, he did. He cut the sausage, put a little bit in his mouth and chewed.

"Not bad. Needs work, but we can do that."

"Do what?"

Yes. Do what? What was I doing?

I was taking care of an invalid. I was raising a retard. Or was I?

And inspiration just sort of whelmed over me, glomped down on me, and I answered, "Teaching you how to be a woman."

We stared at each other for a long time, and then a deep down sort of wail could be heard erupting from his throat.

I reached across the table and grabbed his chin. "Stop that! It's not ladylike."

He stopped.

I finished my drink. I felt like another one. But…no. I wasn't going to—

"Can I have a drink?"

I blinked.

He was recovering. He might be a girl, but there was a hint of the old Chuck in there. Beer swilling, bourbon sucking, throw a football better than the next guy Chuck.

"Sure. You can have a wine spritzer. That's what ladies drink."

Oh, the disappointment on his face.

I laughed, a harsh laugh, and I said, "Fix us each a drink. A stiff one. I'm going to show you something."

Puzzled, the frown rippling across his features, Chuck stood up and poured us a couple of drinks.

Hell, I thought. Not even ten in the morning and I'm getting sloshed.

But, you know? It felt good!

"Now, drink that whole thing, as fast as you can."

The old Chuck, brawny and in shape, could do it. And do ten more. And then do a full set of push ups and sit ups and everything.

The new Chuck drank the drink, he managed to get it down, I'll give him that much, then we sat there and looked at each other.

"What?" he asked.

"Wait for it."

"What?"

I smiled.

The booze was hitting him hard. He had a 200 pound male mind in a 120 pound female body. something had to give.

"BLURP!" He threw up.

I knew it was coming, so I got out of the way. He messed up the table, got puke in his hair, and couldn't figure out what happened.

"Women can't drink as much as men. It's not just the size, it's that we have softer bodies. We can't digest all that poison all at once.

He nodded. Miserable. Chunks of sausage and bits of hash brown littered the table and the floor.

"Now go take another shower, then come back out and clean this mess up."

Dismal, feeling like frozen turds, he left the kitchen and headed for the shower.

"And dry your hair off and wrap it with a towel."

Ten minutes later he was mopping the floor. A blue towel wrapped around his head It was a poor job, but he had tried, and I smiled as I watched the expression of disgust on his face as he mopped up the vomit.

Finally, he sat down.

"I'm hungry."

"Suffer."

"Why are you so mean?"

It was an honest question. I couldn't fault him that. But I didn't want to answer him. Heck, if I answered him I would have to admit to myself, and there was no way I wanted to do that.

By now I was dressed. I hadn't put on make up yet, but I was wearing a sweat shirt cut off at the midsection. It showed my new belly button piercing. And I had on running shorts. I liked running shorts, they showed off the legs, were just tight enough around the hips, yet loose enough to move. And running shoes.

I wasn't going to go running today, but I liked the ease of these clothes.

He said, "You look beautiful."

I ignored him.

And, unfair, the idiot started crying on me. His eyes filled up and overflowed and little trails dribbled down his cheeks. He mumbled, "I'm sorry. Whatever I did…I'm sorry."

Tears. Son of a bitch! How often had I used tears on him to get my way? And now he was doing it to me. But his were real, much more real than mine had ever been.

"You really don't know? What you did?"

"I cheated on you," he looked down, and the tears were really started to flow. And, dammit, they were working on me.

"And you looked at porn on the internet, trannies, for chrissakes, and you jacked off." I snarled, trying to get the anger up there, desperate to keep the anger between me and him.

His head was bent all the way over now. Hair was falling out of his towel, his chest was heaving, and those damned breasts were surging up and down. "I'm sorry. I'm sorry."

I just sat there, getting myself dismantled. Not knowing what to do about it. Damned women. They are so insidious. You can't trust them.

"It's okay," I finally muttered, looking away.

His tears slowly stopped. Then he stood up and trundled towards the bedroom.

"Where are you going?"

"Get dressed," he sniffed.

Huh! I got up and followed him. This I wanted to see.

He entered the bedroom, went to his dresser and took out boxers and an undershirt.

He stepped into the boxers, then pulled the shirt over his head. He looked ridiculous, and I stifled a giggle.

He looked at his own body, I think he knew how stupid he looked, but there was nothing else he could do.

He got out a pair of jeans and tried them on. Inches too long. He took a pocket knife out of the top drawer and tried to cut the pants off. He lacked strength, and he wasn't used to slender fingers, and I knew if he had any nails he would have destroyed them.

Still, he managed to shorten the pants, and he put them on. They hung around his waist and he had to buckle the belt extra tight, and he had folds of cloth inside the belt.

He sat on the bed, then realized he wasn't tall enough to just bend over and pick something up off the floor. He got off the bed, got some athletic shoes out from under the bed, and sat back on the bed, and put them on. And, of course, no matter how tight he tried to tie them, they fell off.

I giggled. Then I laughed.

He looked at me, and I stopped laughing. Yeah, he was stupid, but he was also hurting. I was reminded of times in my life when people had hurt me, and how I had felt.

"Come on," I said, and I stood up. I led the way into the living room and got out my sack with my brand new, sexy underwear in it.

"What?"

"Okay, let's get you dressed." I upended the bag on the couch and he stared at the colors, the fabric, the sexy new ways of doing things.

"I can't wear that stuff."

"And I don't want you to. But you don't seem to have any woman clothes, so…put this on." I tossed him some thigh high panties. All cute with flowery material. I loved the way they looked, and the way I thought they would look on me, and now he was going to get the look.

He sat down, like a man about to pull up trousers.

"No. Stand on one foot, balance, that's how women put their panties on."

He looked like he was about to start crying again. But he stood on one foot, then the other, and had to lean against the corner of the couch, and pulled on the panties.

"Now this."

I tossed him a wispy sort of bra. His nipples would show through the material, big time, but they were perfect for his skin color.

He tried, but couldn't. He kept getting the straps fumbled up, and then the cups were backwards. I showed him how to fasten the clasps in front, then slip it around the body and pull it up.

He took my breath away. His shape was perfect. Every bit as good as mine. His breasts, now held up, were like torpedoes, and his legs were curved and reached the ground.

"What now?"

I was getting warm now. My face was slightly red and I was breathing harder. Fuck. I didn't think he would be this good looking, and he didn't even have any make up on. And, suddenly, I got inspired. I wanted to see how good looking I could make him.

I helping him into a garter belt, then unrolled stockings up his legs, always telling him how to do things, how a woman does things.

Then I put him in a short, pink skirt and held a halter top in front of him.

Fuck! I took the bra off, then put the halter on him. His skin was creamy smooth, ready for petting.

"Come on." I led him back to the bedroom. My make up table was still there. Empty, and I put my make up kit on it and started taking out items.

"Okay, let's get to work…girlfriend."

God! I wasn't angry anymore. What had happened.

And what was happening is that the simple act of sharing make up cements girl friends. The small talk and the trading of beauty secrets, the rolling of each other's hair, it erased boundaries and made girl friends.

Was he still my husband?

I didn't know and I didn't care. I was just feeling the feelings take me, and I was following my gut.

I sat him down, and sat next to him, and began working us up.

First I cleaned and moisturized him. Then myself. Explaining about cleaning pores and making sure the face was in good shape for the creams and powders to come.

I put on foundation, a bit of blush. I worked on the eyes. Eyes require delicate work and focus. I put shadow on him, and on me, then I curled my lashes, and told him how to curl his own.

Dully, yet moving faster, certainly breathing harder, Chuck curled, and then mascara-ed, and, finally, I pulled out the lipstick.

"We're going to have to get you your own. These are my colors, though I have to say, you're so beautiful you could make anything work."

"I'm beautiful?"

"Oh, yeah." He watched me as I colored his lips Bright red, my favorite color. His favorite color on me. And now on him.

"Okay, we need to attend to this mop."

I brushed out his hair, tugging the knots out, spraying a bit here and there, making a shoulder length bob with just a hint of curl on it.

Finally, I stood him up and walked him to the full length mirror.

"Oh," he blurted. "Is that me?"

"Turn a little, show some ankle, yeah. Yeah. That's you."

He turned to me then, and I was struck by how truly beautiful he was.

"Thank you," he said.

And I realized that I had just saved his life. He had been mourning the death of the male, now he saw the true potential behind his change.

He saw what he had been lusting after his whole life. He saw the trannies he had jacked off to, and wanted to be…but….he had gone all the way. He had lost his penis, gained a vagina, had the most wonderful tits this side of me, and…and he looked like dynamite with a short fuse.

"What now?" he asked.

I smiled. "Time for lunch."

And it was. It had been hours since breakfast. And he had thrown his breakfast up, anyway. And now we were hungry, and thirsty.

I helped him slip into some heels, he walked like shit so I linked my arm in his and kept him balanced, and we went out to the car.

We drove to a fancy restaurant. And all the time I lectured him. Sometimes with short, snappy remarks, because he should have known better, and sometimes with giggling little asides, treating him to the secrets of woman.

We had chicken salads, blue cheese on top. And we nibbled, careful to keep our lips perfect. And I lectured him about men. Which was something that truly scared him.

"But, I'm a guy!" he complained.

"You were a guy," I explained. "Now you're a girl, and even if you never go out with a guy, you have to know how to act, how to move, how to hold your own. This world isn't always kind to women, and you have to learn how to survive in it.

We treated ourselves to small scoops of Vanilla with chocolate sauce. Mmm. And I lectured him about keeping his figure.

"You don't want to end up like I was, right?"

"Yeah, but you didn't get there by being a pig. You had thyroid problems, and you worked like hell to beat them."

I frowned. "Well, that's past. Shall we go get a drink?"

We found a small bar, very dark, with no men in it. And I told her about drinking. She already knew that she couldn't drink as much, and she quickly took to sipping and making alcohol last.

A few men came in, and I showed her how to use body language to fend them off, or to pull them in.

"Men really are suckers," she laughed. It was the first laugh she had given since the hospital, and it really warmed my heart.

And, speaking of being warm, I was feeling downright hot. I was flushed, slightly high, and my groin was feeling, shall we say…slippery?

We stepped out of the bar and went to the car and I drove her home.

Her. I had stopped thinking him, and started thinking her. Make up and good looks go a long way.

We pulled into the drive way and she asked, "What do we do now?"

I sat there for a moment. I knew the alcohol was pushing me a little bit, but it wasn't bad. Besides, I was not just a little warm. I was wet and squooshy. If somebody had slapped my ass my pussy would have squirted.

"Come on," I said.

We walked into the house, through the kitchen, stopped for another drink, and on to the bedroom.

She sat on the bed, I sat at the make up table, and we sipped our drinks and occasionally giggled. I said. "Chuckie, we're going to have to get a better name for you, Chuckie, I need the truth now."

"Nothing but truth with you, babe."

So odd, her saying a 'Chuckism,' but like a girl.

"Have you ever had anything up your ass."

Her face shuttered up like winter was here.

"Come on. Nobody here but us girls. I know you looked at trannies, and you must have wondered…have you ever had anything up your butt?"

Her face as red as a fire engine, she whispered, "Yes."

"What?"

"Butt plug. Made me cum harder."

"Just a butt plug?"

"Well, I tried a regular dildo, I got a strap on, and I tried it, but it was too big, I couldn't take it. I still have it."

"Really? You have a strap on?"

She nodded.

"Show me! Show me!" I actually clapped my hands in excitement.

"Well, I could, but I can't reach it."

"What do you mean?"

I put it on a top shelf in the kitchen. It's too high for you, but I could reach it, and I figured you'd never find it."

"But now you're too short to reach it." I laughed. How deliciously cruel."

She chuckled. "Yeah. I outfoxed myself."

"Well, let's get it down."

So we went to the kitchen, I helped her onto the counter and she managed to pull down a pink box without falling.

Back in the bedroom she pulled out the strap on.

I looked at it. It was most delicious. Six inches, with balls, and the head was round and juicy looking.

I stood up and started putting it on.

"What are you doing?"

"I'm going to fuck you."

"What?"

"And it's not just your asshole, but a real live pussy I'll be diddling. This is going to feel good. Ooh, look!" I showed her how the back of the dildo had nubs Nubs to rub my own pussy.

So there I sat, holding a big, old hefty dick out of my lap, and we finished our drinks. She watched me like a scared, young virgin. I watched her like the predator I was.

Finally, I stood up and stepped in front of her. "Time to learn how to suck cock."

Oh, God, the look in her frightened eyes, the way her red mouth opened up so I could pushed my dick into it.

"Mmm!" she mumbled, and I moved it gently in and out. And I told her how to fondle the balls, how to swirl the tongue around the head, how to poke her tongue into the slit.

It was so hot. I couldn't believe how hot it was. Her sucking me off. Innocent and scared, yet trusting. I understood why men liked virgins then.

I lifted her up, I was hot, but I had to make sure she was. I kissed her, gently, tentatively, and I speared her hole with one finger.

She gasped.

I worked the finger, and I could feel her juices build.

I bent my head and sucked her nipples, and I had her suck mine, and I could feel the heat building.

We fell to the bed, holding each other, chewing on each other's mouths, sucking on tongues and clits and nipples and things.

Then, she was finally ready.

"Up on your hand sand knees," I slapped her ass.

She squealed, actually squealed, and then she was positioned, her ass looking round and beautiful, her slit high and ready and moist. She was hotter than hot, she didn't need any lubrication.

"All right," I muttered, putting my cock head to her pussy. I slipped it between the lips, stared down at it in wonder, then began to push forward.

"Oh!" She groaned loudly. Her pussy withdrew a little, but I held her hips.

"It's okay, it's okay. It'll hurt a little bit, then, if you can relax, it will be the end of the world."

She said something, but I don't know what. I was concentrating on pushing my dick in.

She moaned, half pain, half pleasure, then she arched her back, and I could feel the wonder erupting from her.

"Oh…oh…!"

I struck the hymen, but I was expecting that. I figured a new body would have one. I bounced gently off it, gave her pussy a moment of respite, then began applying the pressure.

"Oh…ow!…Ow!..OH!"

I slid past the ruptured membrane.

Chuck's whole body tensed up and he reveled it the sensations of being penetrated.

"Oh, God!" She blurted, and she began to move back against me.

Soon she was meeting my thrusts with her own, pulling back and feeling the grip of her pussy on my slick cock.

She started crying, good cry, tears of joy cry.

I began pounding into her. I wasn't worried about my own orgasm, but it sure would be nice.

I drove in, wiggled my hips, and felt the nub on the back of the cock tickling my own pussy.

She arched her back, lowered it, wiggling her hips, and fucked me like woman should.

I felt the rub of the nub getting to me. I felt the heat in my groin.

I reached under her and grabbed her breasts. They were too big for my hands, and I pulled on the nipples.

She yelped a happy yelp.

I thrust my hips hard. She grunted and shivered, and then I knew it was happening. She was shuddering, her back shivering, her body shaking. The orgasm swept over her, and I knew her mind was blank, filled only with the white heat of pleasure. And then my own orgasm hit. It was a clit buster of some proportion. It made me ram harder, and then my muscles were locking up. My hips began to spasm.

We cried, we howled, and I collapsed on her.

She lay on the bed, flattened out, under my weight, my dick still in her, but not moving.

She was still crying, but because of the fulfillment, because of the happiness.

"What do you think?" I finally muttered. "Would you like to go back to being a guy?"

She laughed, she rolled, somehow staying under me. she kissed me, hard, and she said, "Not a fucking chance."

END

Sissy Ride: The Book!

A giant saga of feminization!

Check it out at…

https://gropperpress.wordpress.com

Dominated by a Gang of Women!

He was caught and punished!

Published on Kindle,
appeared in 'Tainted Love.'

DOMINATED BY A GANG OF WOMEN!

"Have a great flight, honey." I kissed my wife, Ava, good bye.

She reached out the window and, right in front of God and whatever neighbors happened to be looking out their kitchen windows, grabbed my cock.

"Oh!" I grunted. She had a firm grab. She grinned. "And you'd better have this puppy ready for me. I'm getting a little tired of being denied!"

"I'm sorry!" I wheezed. "I just felt out of sorts the last few days!"

"You've got a two days to get it all sorted, you got that?"

I nodded. She had a death grip on my cock, and my knees were getting weak. My cock was struggling to get hard, and winning because we hadn't done it for five days. Five days is a long time in the life of a horn dog.

Then she let go, laughed, and backed the car out of the driveway.

I waved to her, she waved, and there she went. She was a stewardess and she would take a flight to the Orient and back. Which translated as a full weekend for me to slake my desires.

A full weekend in which my gorgeous wife got to play stewardess, and I got to play…dress up.

Heh heh heh! Rub my hands. Run into the house.

Usually I catch a bit of news while I eat my oatmeal. I catch up on the Trump attacks, find out about the weather, and generally slough off.

But, today, being horny as a dick in a hole factory, I ran right past the TV into the back room. Into the storage closet. Got a chair and stood on it, reached wa-a-ay back on the top shelf, and brought down my stash.

Oh, baby, was I going to have fun!

Now, just for the record, I'm a pretty normal guy. Normal…if you like to dress up as a woman, pretend you're trapped in a dungeon with your manhood all locked up and no place to erect, and, when you have had enough…to pound on the pud, desperately, feverishly, and ejaculate your semen all over the place.

A weekend was just long enough for me to play out a scene.

Let's see, maybe I should do it in the closet. Stuck in a little spot and…no, no. Sometimes it was hard to get comfy.

How about the back yard? God, that would be fun. Trapped in lingerie and chastity tube, struggling to get hard, hearing the neighbors working in their yard just feet away.

Yeah, but what if the weather turned bad? I'd hate to get rained on, or cold.

I guess the best place would just be on the good, old bed. I could be all comfortable while I'm rolling around and getting horny.

I put the box on the bed and opened it.

First, I took out the chastity device. I know, it's weird, some guy locks his junk up. But the frustration factor, the denial, it drove me to heights of horniness not experienced by mere mortals.

I put the ring around my package, then had the usual problem…hard cock.

Fuck.

I ran for the shower and jumped in. Icy cold water. I shivered and cursed and hated it, but my dick went down. I hopped out and, before I could get stiff again, slid my cock into the tube.

Click. All locked up and no place to go. Heh heh! I could already feel my horniness surging.

I dried off, used a hair drier on my package, and back into the bedroom.

A bra with breast forms. I loved this part, the transition from a slender fellow into a stacked woman. Made my cock struggle all the harder. By the time I had my bra on and the breast forms in place I had to remind myself to breath.

A corset. I pulled it up, struggled into it, and, voila, I had a wasp waist. It made my boobs look HUGE. And my butt actually flared out a bit. Wooo!

Then nylons, the good kind that you have to fasten to the straps on the corset. They rolled up smooth, and they should, for I had shaved my legs the night previous. I always did that the night before Ava went on a flight, telling her it was for running.

I took the black dress out of the box and wiggled into it. It was stretchy and clingy, showed more corset than I liked, but, God, was it sexy.

Then I took out the make up kit. I went into the bathroom and made myself up. This was the tricky part, and it had taken me a long time to figure out make up. But, God bless the internet, I finally succeeded in looking like a woman, and not a man in drag.

I cleansed, moisturized, did all the blush and the foundation, and blended everything perfectly. The eyes. I loved doing the eyes. Little shadow caves that made my eyes mysterious and alluring. And, of course, lipstick. Red. I liked my wife to wear this deep red, but she was a little resistant. She said it gave the message of 'fuck me.'

Well…YEAH!

The finishing touch, the long, blonde wig. I attached the clips to my hair, and looked in the mirror. I was a slender babe with world class knockers and…zowie!

I was turned on. My poor dicklet, that's what I call Mr Happy when he's under lock and key, was worming and squirming and pressing on the metal cage, but…heh heh. Sorry, pal. You're in prison.

I slipped on a pair of high heels and sauntered through the house. Out into the garage. In the bottom of the meat freezer I picked up a tub of ice. A string came out of the top of the ice. Inside the ice the string would be attached to the key to my handcuffs. The other end ended in a loop that went around my wrist.

Once, when I was young and foolish, I had knocked the tub over, and the block of ice, which had become water, had spilled on the floor. Desperate, I had destroyed the bed before I managed to fall on the floor and get the key. And that was hard, because I was blindfolded at the time.

That had led to an interesting conversation with my wife. I told her one leg broke and the bed collapsed, and that I had been so mad I had 'beaten' the bed up.

So now, with that in mind, and with the knowledge that I had had to buy a new bed, and Ava had insisted on a more solid one, I kept my key so that it wouldn't inadvertently get 'lost.'

I carried the tub back into the house.

I put a towel on the bed, placed the tub of ice on the towel, then got ready.

First, make sure the string is around my wrist.

Second, attach the cuffs to the bed posts.

Third, a rubber around my caged cock. That was hard to do, but it did catch any drippings. Sometimes I came just from being locked up this way.

Fourth, the blindfold.

Fifth, a little soft music on the computer.

Sixth, a the ball gag shaped like a penis in my mouth.

Seventh, a butt plug inserted into happyland.

Eighth, lock my own wrists to the cuffs.

Wow! I was trapped! And my cock was doing the dance, trying to break out of prison. I began wiggling and writhing on the bed. I was so horny I couldn't believe it.

I bucked and twisted, I tried to get my cock over enough to rub it on the bed, but I was truly trapped.

I stopped struggling and breathed. Oh, God. I loved this.

I began to fantasize. I had been in a caravan, sauntering across the desert. In high heels on the soft sand, heh. Hey, it's my fantasy, so why not?

Then raiders had descended. I imagined big, beautiful, and bountiful, women on horses. I ran, dainty but sexy, across the sands, my flimsy garments fluttering in the wind, my boobs bouncing, but their big horses swooped down and I was caught.

They locked me in chains and carried me off to a castle.

I know, a castle in the desert, but, darn it…it's MY fantasy!

Into the dungeons, and here I was. Struggling, and they felt my tits, with their slender hands. Their red tipped fingers lightly scratched down my body, causing me excitement, causing my dick to…

"AAAIEEE!" I screamed around the penis gag. I had just felt hands on my chest.

I didn't move. I tried not to breath, but I couldn't stop gasping. I was frightened.

Hands touched my chest again. Felt my tits. I couldn't feel the hands, but I could feel the pressure. Yes, somebody was definitely squeezing my forms, pressing them down.

I gasped, "Who's that? Who are you?" But because of the penis gag it came out 'wooohat…woorrooo.'

Not a sound.

Then I heard them walking, over to the computer. The sound of the music went up and I really couldn't hear anything.

"Who's there! Let me loose…" Again, the ball gag made it sound like 'Oooothrr…lelooo'

Snip.

Snip?

I pulled the wrist with the string on it. I should have felt the string tighten up, maybe even the tub of ice rocking. Nothing. Oh, shit!

"I don't know who you are, but you can't do this."

But it just came out a bunch of gobbledegook.

Hands examined me, and now I really struggled. But I had trapped myself too well. The hands were able to lift my dress, I heard what I think was an intake of breath, and then hands examined my chastity tube.

"OoGaa!" I struggled! I tried to pull the cuffs loose, I didn't care if I broke the bed, I had to get loose. But I had bought too well. The bed was like a rock.

The hands lifted the cage, turned it, tugged on it, and I thought I heard a giggle.

Then hands felt my butt plug. They pressed it, and I couldn't help it, I groaned. Here I was terrified, trapped, and still turned on!

Then the hands took my penis gag out.

My mouth was dry, and it was hard speaking, but I managed, "Let me loose!" The gag went right back in.

OhmyGodohmyGodohmyGodohmyGod! I thought.

It wasn't my wife…I had seen her leave.

Could it be a neighbor?

Or, oh, no, could it be a burglar?

But the hands felt soft and feminine. And they didn't rip at my cage, they lifted it gently.

Who could it be?

Then the music was turned off.

Silence. I listened for a sound, a clue, anything!

Nothing.

Then, a sigh. Was the sigh happy? Sad? Something else?

"Uhagaa!" I gabbled around the penis gag.

Then the music came back on, and I sort of heard what sounded like footsteps walking away.

I lay there, trembling, wondering what I was going to do. I was frantic. I was thinking dozens of thoughts a minute, and then something weird happened. I began to fantasize.

I had fantasized while I was in control of myself, and I had made myself hornier, but this was fantasizing out of control.

An Arab chieftain comes to the US and picks my house, out of the millions of houses, to enter. No…no. Not a chieftain, those were female hands on my body.

Okay, a movie star is looking for a house to shoot her next movie in. She chooses my house, and the door swings back when she knocks on it. She walks back to the music and finds me. It gives her ideas. She is out calling screenwriters and I'm going to be offered a part in…no, no. Movie stars have other people go scout locations.

A realtor is looking for a home to sell. She is sexy, wearing a pencil dress that shows off her luscious and well shaped calves and butt. She knocks on the door and it swings back…I must have not closed it all the way, or it didn't latch securely, or whatever…but the realtor, she is blonde with red lipstick, and the bosoms, of course, the tits are large, that's how she sells houses so many and so fast…sex appeal. She walks back to the music and finds me. She is startled at first. Then she realizes that I am trapped. She wonders how I cam to be trapped. Did burglars tie me up…no no. Not in such sexual fashion. Burglars wouldn't have put my cock in a cage or a plug up my butt.

Okay, she knows it's my wife. Yeah. My wife. I always fantasized about my wife doing this to me, and now she has. And she went shopping, yeah, shopping, and left me to get horny. But that leaves her a window to examine me, to let loose her own fantasies. Maybe she went to put on a strap on. Maybe she's going to pull the penis gag out of my mouth and replace it with her own super endowed tits.

Oh my God! That's it! And I began to writhe not so much to escape, but to feel my helplessness, to search for stimulation to my cock. I needed sex. I needed.

"Ahem."

I froze.

God, here I was, totally helpless, and my thoughts had turned to sex. I should have been fantasizing about escape…but the way I was trussed up, the way I had imprisoned myself…I had lost control of my fantasies.

I felt her moving around the bed. Some vibration, maybe a noise on the subconscious level. She took the penis gag out.

"Please," I croaked. "Let me go."

"Beg harder!" I froze at the sound of the voice. It was rough, ragged, almost masculine. But I knew the hands had been feminine! Then I figured it out. She was speaking through some sort of gag. A rag tied around her head, and lowering her voice, and making it all raspy.

"Who are you?" My voice trembled.

"Beg." A deep laugh.

She wants begging? If that's what it takes, then I'm begging. "Please…please let me go. My wife will be home soon. I won't say a word about this. Just put the key in my hand and leave. Please, I—"

The penis gag touched my lips, a precurser to being shoved down my throat.

"Shut up," snarled the woman who sounded like a gagged and muffled man.

I shut. I was shaking, sweating, trembling. I had never been this helpless in my life.

Then I felt the hands at my groin. Unlocking the cock cage. She had seen the keys on the side table and…and suddenly I sprang free.

"Oh!" I groaned as blood rushed in and my rocket tried to blast off. "God!"

Laughter. Raspy, ridiculing laughter.

I tried: "I have money. I'll give you the pin number and my card is in my wallet. You can—"

The touch of penis gag to my lips and I quickly shut up.

She stroked my cock.

"Oh…"

It felt good. It felt fabulous. I was so horny anyway, that in spite of the situation I began to lurch my hips up, and I was almost ready to—

The hand let go. "No!"

"Oh…please!" But was I begging for release of my body? Or for release of my fluids.

Then the hands tried to put my cage back on. That wasn't going to work. I was harder than the icicles on a Polar bear's balls.

The penis gag went back in. I mumbled sounds, but she moved away. Left the room.

I heard sounds in the other part of the house. I heard what I thought was a voice. Voices? Were there more than one? Were there two burglars? Or realtors? Or whatever they were? Or more?

Time dragged. You have no idea how slowly it dragged. My butt plug was feeling a bit itchy, it wanted attention, it wanted to be rocked and rolled, like I usually did when I jacked off after a situation like this.

The penis gag was giving me dry mouth. I tried to work my tongue on it, to create more moisture, and I managed to summon up a bit of saliva. My cock slowly drooped.

I tried to figure out a way out of this mess. Maybe if I moved the cuffs a certain way they would grind on the bedpost and wear a groove and…no. My skin would wear out before the wood did.

Suddenly, I felt the hands on my groin. I bucked, and the voice rasped, "Don't move."

I didn't, and the tube went back on and the lock clicked.

Fuck. This made me horny all over again. I mean, I was horny, but my situation made me soft. But now, the cage trapping my cock I was being denied again, and my cock surged, or at least tried to surge.

The burglar/realtor/whatever left.

I lay there, my dick pounding in captivity. I wasn't cold. It wasn't cold in the house. The music cycled through my computer program. I had thousands of songs in the computer and they were playing randomly.

I lay there, and time passed. A lot of time. I began to fantasize. I couldn't help but fantasize. My throbbing cock made me fantasize.

It wasn't a realtor. It was a female cat burglar. She was wearing skin tight, black leather, and she had awesome boobs. She was casing this house, looking for an easy score, and she had seen my wife leave, and she snuck in to find…me. Tied to the bed. Helpless. Kinky and…and she liked kink.

She had fondled me, and now she was trying to decide what to do. Should she call the gang and ransack the house? Or should she untie me and make wild, passionate love to me?

No, she wasn't going to untie me, but she was going to make mad passionate love to me. She was going to take the penis gag out of my mouth and sit on my face. I could feel her labia sliding on my cheeks, then the inner labia, the lips, I would suck them, and I would insert my tongue. And she would pull her breasts and slap her pussy and realize… she had to have me.

She would rip off my cock cage, stroke my dick, then squat over me. She would slide down, and my dick would feel the luxurious velvet of her love canal. She would move up and down, sliding her slippery innards over my cock.

'Oh! You're too big!' she would scream, but she wouldn't leave, she wouldn't get off. She would keep tilting her hips and moving up and down and then she would orgasm, a mighty, soul shaking thing that left her dazed and wondering what had happened, and that would be enough to set me off. I would buck my hips, I felt like I was going to cum…I was going to squirt, right through the fantasy and the cock cage…I was going to—

"Ha Ha Ha!"

And: "Ha Ha Ha!"

I froze, panicked. I was right. There were two of them. And that meant they weren't realtors…they were burglars!

"He really gets off on this. You see how he was wiggling around?"

The other voice, the second…woman?: "I'll bet he was going to cum. Right through that thing he has on his dick."

Their voices were rough, ragged, all trace of femininity gone.

"What is that thing?"

The second voice again: "It's a chastity device. Men lock up their cocks and it makes them all horny. Sometimes they give the key to a woman to hold for them. The woman is called a keyholder."

"Holding a key like this one?"

"Yep."

They moved around me. I could hear them breathing, hard, almost gasping. Were they getting horny?

Then hands touched me. Two sets of hands. Fondling my balls and my cock cage.

"Oh," I moaned.

"Listen him. He's a kinky bastard."

"How long did it take you to figure out it's a he? That woman get up is pretty good."

"A long minute. But I saw the bulge in the dress and lifted it, and it was obvious."

"Hmm. What do you want to do to him?"

"I don't know. This is a little bit beyond my experience."

"Let's see what he has to say."

"All right. Hey, stupid, if you don't behave yourself I'm going to shove a bigger penis down your throat. You got that?"

I nodded and mumbled a 'yes.'

Hands fumbled at my mouth, then the penis gag was taken out. It was still attached around my head, and the person who took it out just pushed it aside. They didn't have to hold it, and yet it was right there, easy to insert again.

"Hey, stupid. What do you think we ought to do with you?"

"Let me loose. I'll give you money. I'll—Ow!"

A hand had pinched my balls.

"What do you think, do we need his money?"

"What for? We can take anything we want...he's tied up and can't stop us. And if we want his money we just have to abuse him until he gives us the pin for that card I found in his wallet. Doesn't seem like there's much percentage in letting him loose."

"Yeah, he'd probably just call the cops if he got loose."

"I don't know. You think he'd call the cops like that? All dressed up like a woman?"

Giggles, which sounded really weird in the deep, raspy tones.

"Yeah, and with a butt plug up his ass and his penis all locked up."

"Please," I was almost crying. "I'm a married man." I don't know why I brought that up, but I was desperate and willing to try anything.

"Married, eh? What does your wife think about your kink?"

"I'll bet his wife left him like this."

"Say, you think she'll be back?"

"I saw a calendar in the kitchen. There's a line through this weekend, and over the line it says, 'Ava works.'"

"Really? So we got him for a weekend?"

"Yeah. We can take our time."

Then one of the women reached down and fondled my cock cage. God, it felt good. I moaned.

"Horny bastard."

"That he is. Hey, wiggle the butt plug and watch him dance."

Hands gripped the butt plug and suddenly I was groaning and writhing on the bed.

Laughter. "He really likes this shit."

"What a sick fucko."

"Truly sick."

But the hands didn't let up. They kept fondling, and twisting, and pushing and stroking. Soon I was writhing madly, searching desperately for relief.

"Well, we can clean this place out. But not right away."

"Yeah. You bet. We're going to party this weekend."

"I checked the kitchen, there's plenty of booze."

"What about sex toys. They got any of those?"

"I checked the bedroom and didn't see any. That box over there is loaded with them, though."

They let go of my cock and the butt plug and began opening and closing drawers. Finally, "You're right. Only in the box. I'll bet his wife doesn't know anything about his kink.

"What a sucker," snorted the second one.

"Shall we try out that big dildo in the box?"

"Does the Pope shit in the woods? Get your clothes off."

I heard heavy breathing, clothes rustled off bodies, and then I felt a bra tossed across my body.

Giggles. Another bra.

"Hey, watch this."

I felt a big tit pressed on to my face. For a second I couldn't breath, then it lifted. "Suck my nipple, kinky boy." It descended, and the nipple went right into my mouth.

If I had any thoughts that it was my wife, those thoughts were instantly gone. This wasn't my wife's boob. It wasn't my wife's nipple.

The boob lifted, a light slap on my face. "Suck harder, stupid."

The boob descended and I sucked harder. I sucked, and I mouthed the nipple and pulled it with my teeth. I swirled my tongue around it.

The boob lifted. “Hey, he’s pretty good,” In spite of the raspiness I could hear the sex in her voice.

“Fuck him,” dismissively. Then, excitedly: “Fuck me!”

Laughter, and they pressed on my body. They actually climbed over me! I could feel that they were naked, that they had no clothes on, arms and legs flopped over me. I grunted as one put an elbow in my midsection and moved about…they were actually going to fuck on top of me!

“Oh, yeah. Baby. That’s the way I like it!”

I felt breasts on me as one rolled over me. “Let me get this dildo right.”

“Oh, yeah, put your fingers up there.”

The sound of lips pressing, sucking noisily. My poor dick was screaming to stand up, the pressure in my cage was so great I gave a sob.

They paused. “What’s wrong with him?”

“Hey, stupid. what’s wrong?”

“I…I…”

“Come on, spit it out.”

“Can you let my dick loose?”

Laughter.

“The idiot is actually getting turned on by this! Can you believe it? He’s all tied up and yet his dick still wants to get loose!”

“Well, I’m getting turned on by this. Here, let me get…there. Now push that big cock up my pussy.”

I felt the woman on top of me grinding and turning her hips, then I felt the other one kneel between her legs, and she began to move forward.

“Oh…yeah!” And I could feel the movement of her buttocks as the dildo slid into her.

“God! Yes! Move.”

“I’m moving, bitch.” Giggles.

Then they were humping, driving up and down, and I heard the sound of meat slapping on a pussy.

“Oh, you got great tits!”

The sound of sucking.

Their rumps rolled across my groin, squashed my cock in its cage. I felt their flesh slithering on me, the up and down, the in and out, and I kept losing my breath. They would roll this way or that and I would get the breath pressed out of me.

For long minutes they fucked, and I was sort of lost now, just trying to survive through the sexual haze that had enveloped me.

Then: "Oh….yeah. Yes…oh…oh…"

I felt one of the bodies lurch up and freeze, then start to jerk spasmodically.

"Fuck," she finally whispered. "That was fucking good."

"My turn."

"Okay, but give me a minute."

They separated, one on each side of me, and they talked while they played with my dick.

"We should just get a moving van and take everything."

"There's a lot of junk here. I say we just get a small truck and take the good stuff."

"What? You want to get an appraiser to come look at everything?"

Laughter.

"Not a bad idea. Hey, do you think we can sell numb nuts for his organs? I hear you can get 150 K for a good kidney."

"Hell, we can get half a mill for a good liver."

"What about a heart?"

"A mill. Easy. And you don't have to worry about fingerprints."

Laughter.

"Hey," I said, weakly.

"Numbnuts, speaks. Hey, stupid, are all your body parts in working order?"

"Please…"

"What about his dick?" one of the women held up my cage and let it flop."

"You think it's in good working order?"

"I don't know. He locked it up for some reason. Maybe it gets too hard. Hey, stupid…did you lock yourself up? Or did your wife or girlfriend do it?"

I hesitated. "OW!" One of them pinched my nuts.

"I did."

"How come?"

"I don't…it makes me horny."

They laughed. I never felt so humiliated in my life. Threat had gone down to ridicule. Still, to talk about my body on the black market?

"And your wife doesn't know about you?"

"No."

More laughter.

"She must really be stupid."

"Yeah. To marry some numbnuts who does this to himself."

"She's not stupid," I whispered.

A grunt from one, then: "Why don't you tell her?"

I started to pause, felt a pair of fingers getting ready to pinch me, and blurted, "I'm afraid."

"What? She'll laugh at you?"

"She might leave me."

"Huh. Well, if she's so stupid she married you, then she's probably too stupid to leave you."

It sort of made me mad, the way they were talking about Ava, but what could I do?

"Here, give me that."

The sound of the strap on being unbuckled. Exchanged. Buckled. She was right next to me, and I could feel the dildo bouncing on my skin as she adjusted it.

Then they were hugging, kissing, and the whole sex thing started again.

"Get over here…spread."

"Hey! Warm me up a little."

"Mmm. Here's my fingers."

"Oh…yeah!

Then they were twisting over me, rolling their flesh over mine, and I felt tits flop and buttocks squashed me.

"Oh, yeah. Fuck me good."

"Take it, bitch!"

A slurping sort of sound as the dildo penetrated, then the sucking, slithering sound of in and out.

"Oh, this is good."

"I'm going to give up flesh for this."

"Oh…oh…oh!"

The woman ground down on me, squashing my fake tits and cage, as she approached orgasm. Then she began to make quick, jerky movements.

"Fu….fu…"

And it was over.

I laid under their flesh, gasping for breath.

They laid on each side of me again. They played with my cock and balls.

"Heysoos Xristo in a sex store without a credit card! We're going to have to do this again."

"And again and again."

One of them flicked my balls and I jerked. It didn't hurt, but there was no way I couldn't jerk.

They laughed, then took turns flicking my nuts.

"Oh!"

They giggled.

"Ow!"

They chuckled.

"Unh!"

They laughed.

Finally, they tired of the game, and just in time. My nuts were actually starting to hurt.

I mean, they already hurt, from the sexual deprivation. But they were about to hurt from the light tap, tap, tap they were getting.

"Let's eat."

"Hey!"

The penis plug was popped back in my mouth, and they left, giggling.

Shit.

I lay there for a long time. I didn't have much in the way of thought. Oddly, since they had fucked on me, I didn't feel threatened. Even though they had talked about selling my kidneys and stuff.

So what did I feel?

Horny, of course. And, just, sort of…exhausted. I mean, this was stressful. Even the sex on top of me was causing stress. Maybe that was causing a lot of stress. It was certainly causing my dick stress. I mean, just laying there I was so horned up I was having trouble thinking. It was pulsing and throbbing and…and as time passed, I began, once again to fantasize.

In my mind I could hear doors banging and the sounds of struggle. The cops were here, and a terrific fight…then the girls who had abused me were in custody.

A cop came into the room. It was a female cop, and she had a tight uniform. Really stretched out over her massive tits. She sat down on the edge of the bed and took out a notebook.

"Are you all right, sir?"

"Yeah, if you can just release me…"

"In a minute. First, I need a statement. What did these women do to you?"

I stared up at the piglet. She had long blonde hair, and red lips, and she licked her lips as she interviewed me.

"Well, they tied me up and….and they had sex on me.

"Can you undo the cuffs?"

"Not right now. We have to wait for the detectives. They're going to want to take fingerprints." She reached for my cock cage and hefted it, roughly. I jerked as sexual pleasure shot through me. "They might want to get fingerprints off this thing. What's it for, anyway?"

"It's uh…it confines my dick."

"And you like that?"

"Uh…"

"It looks like you like it. The way your dick is wiggling and trying to get hard. Does it make your balls this heavy?"

She held my balls in one hand and gently squeezed. The world went white hot with pleasure.

"Oh…" I moaned.

"Now, these women had sex on you. What else did they do?"

My imagination ran wild. "They took my cock cage off and sucked my dick. They took turns blowing me. One would fondle my balls and the other would put her mouth on me and—"

"Like this?" she squeezed my balls again.

"Oh, God! Yes."

"Go on. They sucked you, and then what?"

"They took turns fucking me."

"And did you cum?"

"I couldn't. They wouldn't let me. They kept saying they needed to keep me hard for them."

"I see. And when did they put you back in this device?"

"After they each took several turns with me. I was exhausted, out of sperm, and my dick was soft for a minute, so they put the tube back on me and locked it."

"I see, and—"

"Oh, my God! You weren't kidding!"

I froze, my fantasy was dashed, and I realized: *A third one!*

"Yeah, ain't he something? All dressed up like a woman?"

"Wow!"

The third woman was also speaking through something, some gag like thing, and her voice was just as rough and unrecognizable as the others.

"What's that thing on his dick?"

"Apparently little Johnny is quite the kink. his wife is out of town, so he dresses up like a woman and butt fucks himself and gets off on having his little weenie locked up.

"Wow. This puppy is one sick fart!"

"You ain't kiddin'.

The third woman sat on the edge of the bed, the other two stood next to the bed. She lifted up my cock cage and scrutinized it. She looked closely, I could feel her breath on my balls, then, "Do you want to take it out?"

"Nah. It gets all big, and then we can't put it back."

The third woman giggled. "This is so weird. Hey, there's a dildo."

"Yeah, we already used it. You want to try it?"

"Not now…maybe later. Right now, I'm thinking…"

"Yeah?"

"Is that his dildo?"

"Yeah. He apparently hides it so his wife can't find it. He's afraid she'll leave him."

"Yeah, I sure would. I mean, what a pervert. But...do you think he uses the dildo on himself?"

Silence.

Then the first woman spoke: "I would guess so. Take the gag out of his mouth.

The third woman pulled the penis gag out of my mouth and giggled. "It's shaped like a penis. You think he goes out and gives blow jobs."

"Maybe. No telling with a sicko like that."

"Please," I stuttered.

"Shut up, numbnuts. Do you use that dildo on yourself?"

"No."

"Why not?"

"It's too big."

"And he wouldn't know it's too big unless he tried to use it."

"An, yes."

"Unh huh."

"Hey, stupid, have you tried to put that up your ass?"

I felt so humiliated. "Yes," I whispered.

"But you couldn't get it up your tight, little fanny."

"No."

"Put the penis back in his mouth."

"Hey, no! I ne—" the penis gag was reinserted mid word.

"Listen up, ladies. Mr. Numbnuts here has a desire. Call it a fetish, call it a dream, but he wants to feel what a woman feels. He's tried, but failed, and I think we should help him."

"Help him put the dildo up his ass?"

There was a moment of silence, pregnant silence, and I could actually feel their thoughts as they cogitated the suggestion.

"Hey! No!" I shook my head and the words came out, 'ay oh.'

"I think he likes the idea."

"OH!" I yelled around the penis gag.

"He's up for anything. We left him alone for a while and he almost got himself off."

"Really?"

"Oh, yeah."

"So butt fucking him with his little dildo is a good idea?"

Silence.

Me protesting in mumbles, then: "Why not? He obviously wants it. Let's do it."

I tried to yell, but they ignored me and all agreed.

"Okay. He's probably a virgin, at least where a dick this size is concerned. We're going to have to grease him up."

"Who goes first?"

"I do." It was the voice of the woman who had discovered me.

"Okay, but I want sloppy seconds."

"And I get thirds. By then he should be pretty big."

"Big enough to drive truck through."

"A train."

"An airplane, with bi-i-ig wings."

They laughed and laughed, then they set out to butt fuck me with my own dildo. How embarrassing!

"How do you want to do this? I mean, we can't very well turn him over on all fours."

"Let's tie his legs to the top of the bed."

"Excellent."

They adjourned to look for rope, and shortly they were clustered around the bed and tying rope to my ankles. Then the first one whispered in my ear. "This is going to happen, and if you try to kick one of us when we move your feet you're going to be very, very sorry. Got that?"

I was terrified, but I nodded.

"Okay, undo that cuff, let's get ready to hoist him up."

I felt the cuff on my right leg open, and then my ankle was being lifted up. My leg stretched out and soon I was contorted, one leg still attached to a bedpost and the other stretched up towards the upper railing of the poster bed.

"Okay, other leg."

The cuff opened and my other leg was pulled up. And there I lay, my legs up in a V, my panties down. My dress up around my waist.

"Nice asshole, slick," said one, running a finger around the rim.

I twitched and she laughed.

One of the girls sat down at the bottom of the bed.

"Okay, I found this in the bathroom." I jerked as a finger pushed a huge glob of lubricant onto my ass. It was spread around my asshole, then the finger started pushing it into me.

"Un huh! Oh!" I struggled and tried to resist, to contort out of the way, but one of the girls simply sat on my midsection. I oofed, and the lubricating continued.

"Boy, he's tight."

She ran her finger around the rim, smoothing lubricant into me. My nerves were on fire and I felt the most delicious sensations running through me.

"Yeah, but he likes it. See how his hips are squirming."

I hate to admit it, but it did feel good. In fact, it felt sensational, but I kept struggling. I will admit that the struggles became less.

"He's getting looser back here. Not long now."

Under my blindfold I was crying. I had never felt so helpless in my life.

"Try two fingers."

"Ahh!" I yelped through the penis gag.

"Yeah, he takes that good. Give it a minute, and we'll go to three. If he can take three fingers then he can certainly take that dildo.

A couple of minutes passed, and my asshole started feeling real good. I was actually moaning, and then the woman slipped three fingers into me. Oh, God, it felt like somebody had just exploded a pleasure bomb in my rectum.

"Told you. He likes it."

For a long minute I felt the fingers smoothing in and out, reaming around and around.

"He's certainly big enough now. Go on, see if it'll fit."

It did. Quickly and easily. I mean, the woman just knelt on the bed and sunk the dildo to the plastic balls.

I grunted, and marveled. I had never felt anything so good in my life.

"Yeah, look at him take it."

The first woman slid in and out, and I was gasping with the pleasure.

"Hey, reach under his titties and rub his nipples."

Two sets of hands pulled my dress down a bit, inserted under the bra and slid under the breast forms.

"Oh…" I moaned.

They pinched and rubbed my nipples. My nips were already pretty erect under the forms, but now they were definitely excited. And that excited my cock.

I felt the big dildo slide up the canal. I could feel the head of it, the plastic balls against my ass, then it slithered out. The woman gave a few twists and turns to her hips and the thing scoured my insides.

"You want me to let his cock loose?"

"Nah. He doesn't want to cum, so we don't want him to cum."

Oh, God! I wanted to cum! Big time!

I felt my sexual urgency rise up higher and higher, and I began to wiggle my ass.

"Man, this guy is a sex hound! Look at him take it!"

There was laughter, but suddenly I didn't care. I just wanted to get off, and this anal fucking seemed to be the best bet.

The dildo slid through me. I gripped it with my rectal muscles and tried to hold it, it made the electric, slithering sensation even greater.

Then into me, a long minute where it felt like a rope was being pulled into my ass.

Then out.

"Will somebody tickle my pussy?" asked the woman who was fucking my ass.

A body shifted, one nipple was ignored, and I felt the weight on the bed as the second woman knelt behind the first woman, put her arms around her and began rubbing her snatch.

"Oh…yes…I'm close.

"Let me help," the third woman stopped rubbing my nipple and I felt more weight shift on the bed.

Damn! I was actually close. If they had kept rubbing my nipples.

"Oh, yeah, your mouth feels good. Can you rub the other one?"

Shit! The third woman had gone from my nipple to the nipple of the woman in my ass! She was getting my action.

"Oh…oh…yes…almost…almost…YES!"

She jerked against my asshole. The dildo went deeper than it ever had, and under the blindfold my eyes opened wide. She froze, pecker deep, then gave a series of violent twitches as her muscles locked up again and again. Then she started to fall forward.

"Whoa…" The other two women caught her and pulled her back.

"Wow! She's almost unconscious."

"She fucked herself stupid. First time I ever saw that."

"Here, honey, put your feet on the floor. We'll just lay you down here. Relax, and I'm going to take the strap on off you."

I heard the mumbles of a woman totally and thoroughly satisfied. Then buckles unbuckled, and rebuckling, and the second woman was climbing on to the bed.

"All right, Mr. Numbnuts. You've had the rest, are you ready for the best?"

I tried to speak, to protest, but my voice was weak and muffled.

Tell the truth, I was so horny I wanted it. I wanted that dildo up my ass. I had been close. I wanted to go all the way.

"A little more lubrication, if you don't mind."

A hand slathered some more grease on my ass, and the second woman pushed forward.

I was broken in. My asshole was ready, and the dick slithered in like a spoon going into a fresh jar of mayonnaise. I grunted, and felt the dick slide all the way in.

I could feel the fake veins. The sides of the shaft rubbed all my nerves. I gasped.

"Oh, yes. Now I know what it feels like to be a man!" the second woman groaned, and she began to pound me. In and out, twisting and turning.

"Here you go, slick," a hand grabbed my nuts and gently twisted and massaged.

"Oh…oh…" I breathed out. I was back in the groove. My hips rose up and my ass gripped the dick, I twisted and turned to get the most traction out of the fake weeny pounding into me.

"Oh, this feels good!"

I could feel her hand, then she was balls deep in me, massaging her pussy.

"You need any help?"

"Nah. I'm going to pop. Watching all this shit…I'm almost there."

She kept driving in, building a rhythm that suited her. I could feel her turning her hips occasionally, and I could feel that her hand was growing more violent on her pussy.

"Oh…yep…her it comes…"

A pause. Then: "YES!" Followed by a series of grunts. I knew her body was locking up by the way she was jerking the cock into my bottom.

Then she was done.

She backed out of me and I felt the fake peter slap against one of my legs. "Man, that is good. Now I know why men like to fuck women."

"Here, give me that dildo."

The sounds of unbuckling and buckling, then the bed was bouncing again as weight knee walked up to my asshole.

"Do you think he needs any more lube?"

"Nah. He's good for the rest of the weekend."

"Excellent. 'Cause I feel like fucking him all weekend long."

With that she pushed into me.

The sexual electrical feeling rose up right where it had left off. I felt the depths of my asshole singing. I started grinding my hips.

"Oh, yeah. Ride 'em, cowboy," the third woman spoke to me. She drove in hard, making me gasp, then pulled out slow.

"Gah!" I said, and I knew a truth. I hadn't had an orgasm, but I had been fucked stupid. Just like the first woman. I was incapable of coherent thought, let alone speech. I just lived for the feeling of that big cock sliding into and out of me.

"That's it, lover. Fuck me back."

She drove into me, and I met her with a will. Our pubics slammed, then she pulled out.

God! Who invented sex! I mean, this was heaven!

And I realized something profound. through all my stupidity and dazement, I knew that I liked being horny. Being horny and frustrated was what kept me going.

Yes, I was a horn dog, and I liked to cum. But I think I liked not cumming even more.

I didn't cum before my wife left on her trips. I didn't cum while I was in lock up. And now I was thrilled by the way I wanted an orgasm… and couldn't get one.

"I got an idea," said the second woman. She let go of my balls and climbed onto the bed. She took the penis gag out of my mouth and sat down.

"UNH!" I almost panicked, it was so sudden, and I was suddenly deprived of oxygen.

The second woman wiggled around a bit, however, and asked, "Can you breath, numbnuts?

I could, and I managed to nod.

"Then get busy."

The third woman rode my asshole, drilled me deep, and the second woman rode my mouth. She ground her hips down and the sweet scent of her hole was thick and musky.

I could feel, as she shifted her weight, that she was leaning forward, towards the woman screwing my ass, and I realized what she was doing. She was kissing the third woman.

I could feel them through my body. I could feel them over the pleasure igniting my asshole. They were kissing, Frenching, swapping spit with darting tongues.

"Oh, yeah. Grab my tits."

The woman on my face grabbed the other woman's breasts. I could imagine her pulling on the nipples.

The woman fucking me said, "Almost there, girls. Gonna be a big one."

She reached forward and grabbed my tits and used them for more leverage. They were fake so she could grip them as hard as she wanted.

"Yes…yes…"

I could feel her breathing quicken, even as it grew more shallow, then I felt the series of preliminary jerks, and she cut loose.

"FUUUUU…" she wailed. It was the loudest cum yet, and the most violent. She jerked and thrashed and drove the penis deeper and deeper into me, and then she collapsed. And I knew she had, like the other one, fucked herself stupid. She was incapable of moving.

As a matter of fact, if the first woman had fucked herself stupid, this one had fucked herself into autism.

The second woman caught her, they leaned on each other, and I felt the big dick leave my asshole.

And I missed it. I wanted it back. I felt like I had a space back there that needed to be filled.

For a few minutes they all sort of laid around, breathing hard, sighing in satisfaction, then I felt them begin to stir.

They slowly rose, got to their feet, and wandered into the other room. I was left alone, my asshole celebrating its christening, my dick trying to get erect, and my body literally burning with sexual desire.

God, did I want to cum. I have never wanted to cum so badly in my life.

No hope.

All I could do was sit there and give an occasional wiggle.

And I started fantasizing!

I heard deep, guttural breathing. Snorting, sniffling, and the shuffling of giant feet.

Oh, no! My wife had left me like this, and there was nothing I could do!

I felt a big shape darken the doorway, then a big monster shuffled in. It was Bigfoot! I had hunted him last summer, and almost shot him… and now he was hunting me…and he was going to shoot me…with a bigger gun!

He slouched across the bedroom and stood over the bed. He was eight feet tall, his head scraping the ceiling, and covered with thick fur. His huge, giant hand was holding his dick and stroking it.

It was a big dick. A foot long. No. Eighteen inches long. A foot and a half of wild beast, filled with white semen, searching for me… searching…searching…and he had found me.

"Hi, Brandon," he growled, his voice twisted by the shape of his mouth.

"Leave me alone!" I pleaded.

But it was no use.

The hairy monster crept to the bottom of the bed and crawled onto the mattress.

"I missed you, Brandon," the beast whispered, his voice like chalk on a black board. Big chalk. Big blackboard.

"Leave me alone!" I sobbed. Yet…back there, in the wee parts of my soul…was I glad to see him? Did I want him…?

"My dick loves you."

"No…no!"

He knelt between my legs and touched my asshole with his monster cock. The head was as big as a tennis ball, but soft and sort of squishy. Still, that was a lot of meat.

Then he pushed it in…slowly, lovingly. That big, long, firehose of a cock slid in and…and it felt like it was in my mouth? But I wasn't giving Bigfoot a blow job! In fact, I wasn't having sex with Bigfoot at all! Bigfoot was male! And I wanted women! That was why—

"Are you awake?"

I opened my eyes…and saw nothing. Oh, yeah. I was still blindfolded.

"Uh…yeah."

"Do you need to pee?"

"Yeah."

"Okay. We're going to put your legs down, and put a catheter in you so you can pee."

"Oh. Is it nighttime?"

"Yes."

I felt the women working on my legs. First one, then the other, they secured my legs to the bed posts. It felt good to let my legs stretch out.

"How long are you going to keep me like this."

"What do you care? You're a pervert, so just enjoy yourself."

Rude sort of a bitch, but what was I going to do? And, truth, there was still a part of me that liked. Hell, loved it.

"His dick looks all swollen and red in there."

"Take it out. We can put him in it tomorrow. It's not like he can jack off, right?"

"You're right."

Then I felt something being pushed into my cock slit. Oh, catheter. Good. I did sort of feel like peeing.

Then they were done. They turned up the music and left.

I lay there in the darkness. I was horny. My dick was erect and pointing upwards, glad to be free. They had not put the butt plug back in, and my asshole felt a little…happy. It liked getting used.

And I wondered what I was going to do.

I was a prisoner. I had wanted sex, and now I was getting it. More than I ever wanted.

And what about my wife? Would they just leave me tied up? For her to come home and discover? How would I explain this to my wife?

The hours passed, and I listened to music. It was sort of pleasant. I fantasized a little, but there was a part of me that was beyond fantasy. What had happened to me this day…that was so far beyond fantasy.

After an hour the door to my room opened and a woman came in.

"How you doing, Mr. Numbnuts?"

"I'm okay."

She sat on the edge of my bed and stroked my cock.

"Catheter working fine?"

"I guess."

"Are you getting enough sex?"

"No."

"No?" I think I surprised her.

"This isn't the way it works. I get horny, I jack off. This is everybody gets horny and gets off…except for me.

"Aw, poor boy." Well, see you in the morning."

"Do I get to eat?"

"Maybe we'll fix you a salad for lunch. girls have to watch their figures, you know."

I didn't say anything. I was horny, and I was hungry, and I was afraid.

She let go of my dick and left the room.

I slept, and was surprised by that fact. My dick was free, and it was hard, and still I went to sleep. And the next morning I awoke to… stroking.

"Good morning, sunshine."

"Uh, yeah. Hi."

"Don't be so glum. Today is going to be a wonderful day."

I didn't say anything. We've two more ladies coming over, and we're all going to take turns sucking you, and fucking you, and we're all going to have so much fun.

And that was what the day was like. Five women, and the woman played with my cock for a while. Two new women tried out my ass, and then they put me back in chastity.

Then they played with me some more, and took me out of chastity and brought me to the edge, and I spent the whole day moaning and groaning, wishing desperately to cum.

But I was denied. Quite emphatically. They really wanted to keep me hard and horny.

The evening came, and I received more and more of the sexual torture. And I loved it, and I was always scared that they were going to do something to me. Harvest my body for body parts? I don't know. I just know that my heart was pounding with fear, and, at the same time, pounding with lust.

And the next day was the same.

They fed me a salad a day, and I was hungry. My dick was purple and dripping, at least that's what they marveled at, and I realized…one more night. They had trapped me, I had been trapped, on Friday. The rest of Friday, then Saturday, and now Sunday. Ava was due home tomorrow morning.

Were they going to let me go? Or leave me for my wife to find?

I didn't know, one more thing to be scared about.

And then I slept. Sunday night. A weekend in fantasy…that had turned into nightmare. And yet was, in a way, so satisfying.

"Hello, Mr. Numbnuts." One of the women entered my room, turned the music off and said, "It's been a wonderful weekend, but all good things must come to an end. Come on out when you get brave enough…" and she put a key in my hand.

Oh my God! The key to my cuffs!

She walked away, and I put the key into the cuffs and turned it.

I unlocked the other three cuffs.

FREE!

I ripped the blindfold off and blinked. It took a moment for my eyes to adjust.

I could hear voices in the other room. They hadn't left? Why not? What was going on?

I was wearing a dress and breast forms. I still had traces of make up on. I might be clean, but I was a mess.

I ran to the bathroom and scrubbed my face, but there were no towels so I had to let my face drip dry.

Then I went to my closet…no clothes!

I opened my dresser drawer…no underwear!

The only thing in the room was my wife's clothes, and I could still hear the women chatting. All friendly and happy and…what was I going to do?

Then a voice called out: "Hey! Numbnuts! Get your butt out here!" And a lot of laughter.

I walked to the door and cracked it. I could see down the hall, but I couldn't see around the corner into the dining room, and it sounded like they were sitting at the dining table.

I tip toed down the hallway. the voices were louder, and they weren't disguised. But they weren't loud enough for me to make out who any of the voices belonged to, if I even knew.

I stood at the corner of the hallway for a long time.

I listened to the voices laughing, joking, and I wanted to cry.

I had been eating salads all weekend. Could I run past them? Make it to the front door?

I had to try. I had to escape. I got ready, and got set, and a woman stepped around the corner. I was face to face with her. She grinned.

"Sally?"

"Hi, Brandon. We've been waiting for you."

She took my hand, and I was so stunned at seeing my wife's friend there that I couldn't resist. she pulled me into the dining room.

"Hi, Brandon!" came the chorus of voices.

I stared in shock.

Sally, Brenda, Joyce and Maggie. All close friends of my wife. And…my wife!

She was sitting at the head of the table, laughing at me.

They were all laughing at me!

Yet it wasn't a cruel laughter, more of a welcoming laughter.

I stood there in shock, in a dress, with my cock in a cage, and my mouth just opened and stayed opened.

Sally pushed me to a chair and made me sit.

The girls all laughed, made remarks, and…and my wife looked at me with the most amused expression.

"How was your weekend, Brandon?"

"Uh…uh…"

"My flight got canceled. Bad weather. I came home an hour later and what did I find…?"

"That…that was you?"

"I find my husband dressed like a woman, enjoying himself. Brandon…I never knew you were so kinky. So, naturally I had to call my friends. We've had a wonderful weekend, Brandon, and we want to thank you."

The girls all murmured their thanks, big grins on their faces.

"You…was that you fucking…somebody on the first day?"

"Me and Sally. I have a confession, Brandon, I'm bi. I haven't been very 'bi' lately, because I was married to what I thought was a pretty strait-laced fellow. The kind who would never do anything kinky. But it turns out you aren't so straight, so I decided to indulge a little."

"And you all…you all…"

"We all fucked your ass. Fucked hell out of it, and it seems that you liked it."

I was blushing now, and starting to come down a little bit from the shock of it all.

"So this whole weekend…it was you and these girls and…"

"We used you, and abused you, and we had so-o-o much fun. Did you have fun?"

I was silent, not sure what to say.

"Brandon? Tell the truth. Did you have fun?"

I nodded.

The girls all laughed and high fived.

"Excellent. Because we enjoyed it so much that…well, we want to do it again."

"Of course, I might not be around, I do have to work, but I'm sure they will manage without me. And, Brandon?"

"Yes?"

"Now I know why you never fucked me much before I went to work. You were saving it for yourself. You selfish, little bastard."

"I…I'm sorry."

"Yes, you are, and you'll be sorrier. You see, I have something that you might want." She touched the gold necklace around her throat. There was a little key on it.

"Is that the key to my…"

"Yes. They key to your happiness. And I will use it sparingly. After all, I don't want one of my friends getting carried away and letting you fuck them. For that matter, I don't think I'll let myself get carried away. Your days of squirting willy nilly all over the place are at an end."

"But…but, honey…"

"And, Brandon, there's one other thing I need to confess…when I travel to the orient I almost always stop in Thailand. You know Thailand? Beautiful women? Men who change into 'Lady Boys?"

"What…?"

"Well, I like to rent a Lady Boy when I'm over there. It turns out that I've been a bad girl. I really like to fuck a man with tits. Do you know any men with tits?"

"Well, no…I…"

"Or maybe we could get you a set of tits. To go with your nice dresses. I've thrown all your male clothes out, by the way."

"Ava, I'm sorry, but…"

"And, last thing on the list…if you want to be abused by my friends anymore you're going to have to pay them."

"Pay them? Like money?"

"No, more like services." She turned to the other girls. "Ladies? I'm starting a maid service. Who would like their house cleaned?"

END

Full Length Books from Gropper Press

Randy catches his wife cheating, but a mysterious woman is about to take him in hand and teach him that when a woman cheats…it is the man's fault.

The Big Tease!

The Feminization of Jackson!

Feminization as a Cure for Sex Addiction?

A 'Silithia' Story.

Published on Kindle.

PART ONE

Jackson Poulter lay naked on the bed. His dick pointed at the ceiling, purple and erect and dripping. His limbs tied to the four posters, he was a horn dog, and he wanted relief.

Funny, he had bought the bed hoping to get his wife to be a little kinkier, but now he was going to be getting something…more than kinky?

The short story was that he had cheated on his wife, then admitted it, then told her he was going to leave her because…well, because she just wasn't wild enough for him.

He wanted SEX! He wanted his cock sucked. He wanted to plumb the depths of a thousand women. He wanted to FUCK!

His wife wanted to hold hands. She felt sex was a sacred thing that could only be indulged in every week or two. He wanted it every day, multiple times a day. He wanted to fuck until his dick dropped off.

So he was honest with her, told her the truth, and he wakes up tied down and not knowing what was going on.

Damn it! He had been honest! Why should she be mad at him?

He struggled against the bonds, but the cords were tight and well knotted. No way he was going to get loose from this mess. And he knew the bed was so sturdy he wouldn't be able to shake it until he broke it. No, he was stuck. Trussed and tied and waiting for…whatever.

Laying there, the curtains drawn, trapped, erect. Heck, he couldn't stop being erect, he was a man, and that's what men did! They got erect.

In fact, though he was tied down, couldn't touch himself, he yet wanted to be able to stroke his cock, to achieve an orgasm, to squirt his delicious seed into the air.

He was just that horny a fellow.

He struggled again, just a little, to enjoy a moment of denial before his wife did whatever she was going to do to him.

He froze, her heard voices. His wife and…it sounded like some other women. The other voice was a little deep, but it was definitely female.

For a second he almost called out, he wanted his wife to fuck him, or untie him. But the other voice, he might not want somebody else seeing him in such straits.

Whatever he wanted, however, was moot, for the bedroom door suddenly swung back.

His wife entered, a short, stacked, little blonde. Blue eyes, built for fucking, but…once a week?

"Let me up," he grunted.

She ignored his words. "I put a sleeping pill in his bourbon, he went out like a light, then I put him here. Like this."

A shape appeared in the doorway and Jackson's eyes opened wide.

The woman was at least 8 feet tall. She had to duck to get into the room. A veritable giant. Actually, a giantess, and what a body!

A normal woman might be 36 by 24 by 36. Like his wife. But only 5 feet tall…like his wife. But this one, amazingly proportionate at 8 feet, was probably 48 by 35 by 48.

Her face was sweet and sexy, the eyes magnetic green, her hair fell off her shoulders in gentle waves.

The two women stood and stared down at him.

"What the fuck!" he murmured, blown away by awesomeness.

His dick suddenly felt harder. Images of a ménage à trois filled his mind. He wanted to fuck his wife…always. But this woman, she had a feeling about her, an ambience, and his dick suddenly felt like it was a foot bigger and ready to spurt. If only…if only…he struggled against the ropes.

"Yes, I see what you mean. He is definitely a horn dog."

His wife nodded. "And he's always like this! I try to keep up with him, we do it three times a week, and I give him blow jobs, but it's not enough, and now I find out he's been cheating." Moisture threatened to spill form his wife's beautiful blues. "I think he's a good man, but he's just got this sex problem."

"Honey, you have to let me loose." He wanted to bone this big woman in the worst way.

Jackson was literally drooling as he behold the giantess. His dick was throbbing, fucking the air hopelessly. Yet in his mind he heard some of what his wife said? What did she mean…three times a week? And… and blow jobs? He felt like he was only getting it once every few weeks!

The woman sat down on the bed, and it creaked ominously. She reached out and put her hand around his cock.

Jackson grunted and thrust his hips upward. He wanted to fuck her hand, to fuck her mouth, to fuck her every orifice.

"Easy, little man," The large woman spoke softly, "There will be time enough for that." She turned to Jane. "So what do you want me to do?"

"I heard…there's rumors…"

"The rumors are true, so what do you want me to do?"

"I want him to be more…normal."

"And what is normal?"

"I like sex, but…maybe just a little less?"

The big woman smiled. The room lit up with her presence. "A little less sex. Hunh. Goes against my grain, but…" she turned to Jackson. "How about you, Jackson? What do you think? Would you like a little less sex?"

"I need more," he managed to groan. Her hand was slithering up and down his pole. Funny, his cock was pretty good sized, 8 inches, but it was small in her hand, but small or not, he had never felt such excruciating pleasure. His balls felt big and red, he was throbbing, but he couldn't…he couldn't get off. He should be able to, her hand was that good, but for some reason he just couldn't manage to get over the edge.

"I'll bet you do."

"So what do you think?"

The woman pursed her lips and considered the naked man twisting and writhing under her ministrations. She leaned over him, and her face became large in his sight. Her breasts were mammoth, and he wanted them so badly.

"Jackson. My name is Silithia. Some people would call me a witch, but I'm not. I am simply a person who has realized her full potential. You, on the other hand, are stuck in low potential. To you the world is a pussy that you are compelled to fill. You are prisoner to your dick, and… would you like to change that?"

"There's nothing wrong with me that a little pussy wouldn't fix!" He grinned meaningfully at her, "Or maybe some big pussy."

Silithia nodded, and turned to Jane.

"To tell the truth, I have never seen a person so low on the, I guess you would call it the 'sexual scale.' He is nothing but a rutting animal. Was he always like this? I can't imagine that you didn't detect this before you married him."

"No. At first he was sort of normal. A little extra horny, but nothing I couldn't handle. Then he was in an accident last year. After that…" she shrugged helplessly.

"Ah, that complicates matters."

"Could you…uh…get me off?" Jackson begged.

"Shush, little man, your betters are talking." She put a finger, a large finger, on his lips, and he suddenly found that he couldn't remember how to speak. He settled on focusing on trying to fuck her fist. He simply had to get off. Thus, though he heard what was said next, he didn't really understand it.

"He's had organic damage. His brain, some switch was clicked on and left on, and it's impossible to tell what is going to happen if I try to fix him."

"But surely there is something…I do love him…I…" Jane did cry then.

Silithia reached out her free hand and curled it under Jane's chin. "It's okay."

And, miraculously, it was. Jane, sniffled, but the tears dried up.

"For me to fix him I'm going to have to have sex with him…"

"Oh, yeah!" groaned Jackson.

"You have to?"

"I do. There must be the most intimate of physical connections to make this work. And, I have to tell you, there is a big chance things will happen that you haven't planned on."

Jane didn't say anything.

"I do want to help him, or at least try to help him, and it's not like his dick hasn't been in some other woman."

"But there's a chance that he'll be…cured?"

"There's a chance. With what I know, a good chance, but there's a good chance that other things will happen."

"Can you fix these other things?"

"Maybe. But I won't know until I know what the 'other things' are."

Jane stood silently for a long while.

Jackson moaned and kept thrusting his hips upward. Silithia watched the woman, held on to Jackson and didn't let him cum.

Jane came to the side of the bed and looked down upon her helpless husband. She contemplated: "We can't go on like this. And maybe we can help him."

She leaned on the bed then, and looked into her husband's eyes. "Jackson…I love you. But we need to do something. We need to help you."

"Oh, yeah, help me, baby!"

She was speaking specifically. He was speaking generally, and thinking of the hand that was driving him wild. She took his words as a plea for her to go ahead and helped him.

She stood back. "Go ahead."

Silithia nodded. She let go of Jackson's dick and stood up. Her face was a mix of resigned and acceptance.

"Well, Jackson Poulter, looks like you get your wish today."

Jackson was drooling as he thrust his penis upwards. He watched Silithia with eyes so hungry they were near rabid.

Silithia unbuttoned her blouse and took it off. She wore no bra. Her boobs were massive, heavy, but her body was at full potential and easily strong enough to hold her breasts up and jutting.

The nipples, especially, were impressive. They were like miniature shot glasses on the peaks of her tits.

"Oh, God!" whispered Jackson.

Silithia unzipped her skirt and slid it down. She was wearing a garter and nylons, and very sexy high heels, but she wasn't wearing underpants. She rather enjoyed the way men would fall into her train, trail her around with noses in the air, sniffing, and not knowing what it was that compelled them after her.

Well, they sort of knew. But Silithia never turned her ambience up enough that men lost control.

She kicked off the high heels as she stepped out of the skirt, and stared down at Jackson. Her face had a musing smile on it.

Jackson grunted and strained and white droplets issued from his slit.

Silithia turned to Jane. "You don't have to watch if you don't want to?"

"I think I'd like to."

Of course. When Silithia made love everybody was awed and wanted to watch.

Silithia reached out and patted Jane's face gently. "Remember, it's just sex. And that's really true in this case."

"Oh. Okay."

"But, I warn you, he's going to become very emotional. He's going to start saying he loves me, and he may even say that he doesn't love you."

Jane gulped. "Okay."

"It won't last long, but he'll occasionally remember this, at least for a few weeks, and he might start talking about me out of the blue."

"Oh."

"But he will be changed, and you may have other things to think about."

"Okay."

"So, it's okay? You can handle this?"

Jane nodded.

Jackson was whining and wriggling on the bed.

Silithia turned to Jackson. "Okay, Jackson. Are you ready?"

"Oh, God! Yes! Yes!"

Silithia climbed onto the bed. It was sturdy, but not built for somebody who weighed as much as she did. And it certainly wasn't designed for what she was about to do.

Jackson stared up at her.

She looked down upon him. A man. A simple, little man, but a man who had to be helped. She lowered herself upon him.

Jackson's mouth and eyes opened as the sensation of her perfect flesh whelmed him. He felt the golden flesh of her pussy slither down over his dick.

He was small compared to her, but her hole was tight, and it gripped him, it almost felt like her pussy was built of a thousand fingers that gripped the sides of his dick and pulled him into her.

"Oh....oh...fuck!"

Silithia rested for a moment. She let him thrust into her. She was very sensitive down there, and she did enjoy a good fuck. Even a mercy fuck like this one.

Jane stood to one side, watching. The look of sublime pleasure in her husband's eyes hurt her. She hated this moment, and, yet, there was a glory to it. It was seeing what a woman at full potential looked like as she administered sex to the helpless.

Silithia reached down and tweaked his nipples. Jackson gave a funny yelp as sexual electricity exploded in his chest.

She leaned down and gently kissed him. Her lips were big and full, super-sized lips, and they dwarfed his. It almost looked like she was swallowing his mouth.

Jackson kissed back, he rose up his hips. He struggled and tried to get free.

"Please," he begged. "Let me cum."

"Nobody's stopping you, little man."

"But...I can't...I..."

"Shush now. The reason you can't cum is because I am perfect and you are not. You know this and you are afraid of soiling me."

"But...I want to...I want..."

"Of course you do. But for you to cum you are going to have to soil me with your seed. You are going to have to make me dirty with your filthy sperm."

Her words were, in a sense, harsh, yet the way she delivered them was like a blessing, and Jackson grunted harder. His eyes bulged with effort, and he tried to let loose.

"That's it, little man. Fuck me."

He did. He fucked, and her ambience began to lift him up.

From being a hopeless horn dog he began to perceive the sublimity of pure and true love.

He began to see a golden light at the end of a long, dark tunnel.

"Do it, Jackson, fuck me. Cum in me. Hurt me. Spoil me." She kissed him, those perfect, red lips sucking at his. Her large tongue sliding between his lips and mouth fucking him.

Jackson tried. He kept humping and groaning, but he couldn't quite get there. He wanted to, he needed to, but she was right…she was too good for him. He started to sob with the effort.

"Jane, undo his ropes."

Jane moved to the ropes, but couldn't undo them. Jackson had pulled on them so hard they had become too tight for her.

"Get a knife. Cut them. He needs to be free."

Jane ran to the kitchen. She came running back through the house with a large and sharp knife. She could feel Jackson's desperation, and even though it was for another woman, she was compelled to help him.

In the bedroom she slid the knife under one rope and sawed. Suddenly it snapped and Jackson's hand was free. He reached up and grabbed Silithia's boobs. He grabbed hard and she groaned. "Yes, hurt me. Be a man!"

Jane cut the rope holding the other hand, and then he was leaning up, doing a sit up to grab her around the body. He was crying and pounding on her back.

"That's it, baby, do me. I can take it. Let it all out."

Jane cut his legs loose, then Jackson was all over Silithia. She rolled, putting him on top, and all the hurt and frustration began to come out.

Jane stood back, holding the knife in her hand. She couldn't believe what she was seeing. Jackson was like a wild man, totally out of control. He was pummeling Silithia, he was fucking her like a mad dog. He was yelling and crying and thrusting.

Silithia merely smiled. She absorbed his blows, she hugged him to protect herself, but she was in no danger. Her perfect body, her full potential body, could take the punishment Jackson was trying to hand out.

"OH…ah! Please! Please!"

He was trying to hurt her, and begging her at the same time, and, finally, he felt it. Deep within, the surge of urge, the throb of white goop flowing up his shaft.

"OH….OH…OH…!" he yelled, pushing his arms straight, holding his body up and his hips down, and his cock began to spew.

"That's it, baby. "Let it out." Silithia crooned.

Jackson lurched and lurched, and throbbed and pulsed, and the liquid kept cumming…and cumming…then, when it felt like there shouldn't have been any more…there was more.

"Wha…wait…"

But now it was Silithia's turn. Her hips drank from his, and he couldn't come loose. He was caught in her, and she kept pulling and pulling, draining him.

He felt like his balls were shrinking, and the world started to get darker…darker…he felt pain…deep pain…everywhere…but in his head…his head…

He fell, spiraling into the darkness and heard a terrible noise.

CRASH! The car tumbled over, and over and over….

He had been driving home, going to see his wife, who he loved, and somebody had T-boned him. Somebody had…

CRASH! The sound kept happening. The moment of impact. The crumple of the door, and his head being jerked sideways, hitting the window…

CRASH! The sound went into his head, crawled through his skull like a snake, and it lodged…it lodged in his brain…it hurt his brain…it…

CRASH! Lived there. Permanently. A little black spot that was nudged up against a light spot, a white spot, a now golden spot…of love.

And that was that pain that had turned the switch in his head and made him….he wanted to fuck…always…he couldn't stop. The golden spot had been turned on by the black spot, and he wanted…he couldn't, if he…

CRASH!

Silithia rose off him.

"Is he okay."

"He's fine," she smiled, and she kissed Jackson's cheek softly. Then she turned to Jane.

"As I thought, the accident pushed something in his head, put something in his head, a bit of pain, and it turned on sex…nothing to do now but wait and hope I got everything…that there are no 'side effects.'

The two women left the room then, and Jackson slumbered. It was his first deep sleep since the accident. A sleep unaffected by insane cravings for sex.

Jackson didn't sleep long. Yes, what he had done had been a struggle, but Silithia's natural recuperative powers were 'catching.'

He awoke, looked around, and one thought struck him: *where is she?*

He stood up, shakily, his body felt like it had been through a cement mixer, and walked out to the living room.

Voices. There were voices there, and maybe…'she' was there.

She was.

Jane and Silithia were sitting at the dining table, drinking coffee and looking out the big picture window.

"I think he'll…oh, hello, Jackson." Silithia smiled.

Jane stared at him. Her face was frightened. She didn't know what to expect.

Jackson went directly to Silithia. His dick began to come erect again. "Please…please…"

"I know, you love me."

Jackson didn't even look at Jane.

Jane bit her lip and felt the tears welling.

"Jackson," Silithia faced him squarely. "I will be leaving now. And if you really love me then you will prove it. You will make Jane happy. You will love her. You will be devoted to her. That is the price of my love."

"Yes," Jackson stood in front of her, leaning slightly forward, as if he would simply fall upon her. He nodded. He couldn't take his eyes off her.

"Excellent." She stood up. "I'll be seeing you," she said to Jane. Jane stood and hugged her. She was like a child hugging a mother.

"And you," she laughed at Jackson, "Prove your love." Then Silithia walked out of the house.

PART TWO

The first two weeks were marvelous. Jackson, as soon as Silithia was out of sight, had eyes only for Jane. It was like before they were married. He was kind and considerate, opened doors for her, asked her advice on everything.

But here was the odd thing: Jane got tired of it.

Not tired tired, but…'old hat' tired.

It was almost as if Jackson had gone too far. He was too kind, too considerate, and there wasn't the odd disagreement which is necessary to a marriage.

She was in charge. She was the earth and he was moon, orbiting her, gravitating only to please her.

Which was cool, but…a bit much.

After all, a man is supposed to have some gumption, not just be a puppet, or a simpering fool.

Still, it was better than when he was a sex addict.

Yet, there were problems there, too.

"Honey, we haven't made love for a week,"

"I'm sorry," Jackson responded quickly. "Would you like to go out and have a date or something? And then I could please you?"

Jane frowned. A couple of weeks of this was too much. She said: "I'd actually like you to drag me in the bedroom, throw me on the bed, and ravage me."

And, in her mind, was a comparison to Silithia. Hurt me like you did her. Break through your frustrations and love me. Totally.

"Yes, dear." He took her hand and led her to the bedroom. Didn't drag her. Didn't use any muscle, just kept looking back, in love, and dedicated only to pleasing. And if he used force…that wouldn't be pleasing. Not in his mind.

He took her clothes off, gently. He folded them neatly.

He lay her on the bed and crawled between her legs.

Oh, it was wonderful, to feel his tongue laving her, slithering up and down her labia, nibbling on the clitoris.

But it was inadequate.

"Are you ready?" he asked, ever considerate.

She sighed.

"What's wrong, my love?" he knelt in front of her.

"I want you to fuck me. Hard. Brutal. Fuck me. Like you did…her."

"Oh, yes, dear."

He took off his clothes then, and she watched, disappointed. He had been so intent on pleasing her he had neglected to even take his clothes off.

The old Jackson, pre-accident, would have laughed and ripped both their clothes off. He would have had his way, tender but rough in a manly way.

The Jackson after the accident, the sex-addict Jackson, would have been in such a hurry he wouldn't have taken clothes off, but his zipper would have been down and he would have been plunging into her, at least roughing her up with his urgency.

But this Jackson, there was no urgency, just a desire to please.

He gently stepped between her legs, a puppy dog with no play in him, and she pushed him away.

"Honey? What's wrong?"

"Nothing," she muttered.

"But what can I do?"

The world can be a perverse place, and what is the world but the people in it, thus Jane surprised herself. "Just stand there."

She reached into a a drawer in the label next to the bed and pulled out a vibrator. A big one. Then she pulled out a small one.

She lay back on the bed and sighed. She needed to be fucked like somebody meant it, and if he wouldn't mean it, then she would have to.

Jackson stood, naked, his dick erect, and watched as Jane spread her legs. His mouth opened as she clicked on the small vibrator and began rubbing it over her clit.

"Oh," he said.

She pushed the large vibrator into her pussy, held for a second, then turned it on.

"Oh...ohhh!"

Pleasure shook her button and exploded through her pussy. She felt the large dildo inside her, and she corkscrewed it so the tip scoured the walls.

"Uh..." Jackson said, and it was obvious what he was thinking. *I should be doing that!*

And if Jane had tossed him the vibrator, invited him in, maybe he would have...come to himself.

But she was frustrated, and dispirited, and she snapped, "Just stand there and shut up!"

She began ramming the big dildo in and out, groaning and moaning as her pussy finally felt a little action. One hand moved hard, the other moved soft. One hand jammed the big fake dick into her, the other hand shivered her burning clitoris.

Jackson stood, eyes gawping, maw open, trying to to understand, to remember what it was like, but he couldn't. For he had been told to stand and shut, and if he was going to prove his love for Silithia then that was what he had to do.

For long minutes Jane hunched over her pussy, driving the dildo in, tilting her hips to get better purchase. Then, easier than she remembered, she began to buck. The golden vibrations swarmed over her and she tilted her head back and groaned loudly.

Oh, after the weeks of deprivation...it was good. Her pussy shivered and lurched. She was so moist she actually sprayed the air with a fine mist of pussy juice, then she fell into the ocean.

"AHHH!" She cried out, her hips breaking out in a series of spasms that seemed to obliterate the world.

Again and again and again.

Then it was over.

She lay back for a minute, one arm over her eyes. God! If it could only be that good all the time. She looked up.

Jackson stood there, staring, numb and dumb and...whatever.

Still perverse, not understanding how she had missed her opportunity, she snapped, "Don't just stand there. Lick me clean."

Jackson dropped to his knees and pushed his head against her snatch. She sighed and laid back.

This was good; this was what he was built for. He was soft and kind and considerate, which was no good before sex, and great after sex.

She felt his soft tongue lap at her, clean up her moisture, her sweat, make her hole clean and tidy.

After a minute, she pushed him away and sat up.

He knelt there, a big, dripping hard on sticking out, and she was struck by how useless it was. Big didn't matter if there was no spirit behind it.

She stood up. "Get me fresh underwear."

Jackson leaped for the dresser. He took out the shelf bra, which she was feeling in the mood for. Some girls feel dirty before sex, she felt dirty after sex, and she liked to let her abused nipples rub against material and stand up and remind her of how good sex could be.

He helped her put on the bra, which surprised her, then he got her a pair of panties…and he even helped her into them!

OMG! She thought. He's like a little maid.

And she wasn't being mean. She was just frustrated and had made a couple of little mistakes.

"Garters," she said, wondering what he would do.

He grabbed a garter belt and some nylons. Lovingly, he put the garter belt around her, then rolled the nylons up her legs. She stared at the top of his head as he worked to get her stockings on.

"The green dress."

Jackson ran to her closet and took out the slinky, green dress. He helped her into it. It hung on her perfectly, and it had deep cleavage. Jackson stared at her cleavage hungrily, but he didn't do anything. He was too kind and considerate to even think of groping her, or to bury his face between her boobs.

"The sling back tan sandals. With the high heels."

Asap, he knelt in front of her, and she placed a hand on his shoulder as he held the shoe for her. Then the other one.

He stood up, staring at her, his penis standing out and a stream of gruel issuing from it.

She stared at him. In heels, she was an inch taller than him…and she liked it.

Him waiting on her hand and foot, him scurrying around to do her bidding…she liked it.

And she liked him shorter than her. It gave her a sense of power. It made her feel…bigger.

Always, she had looked up at him. Not much, an inch, but now, feeling what it was like, to have somebody look up at her with adoration in their eyes, she liked it.

And this 'liking' fed her perversity. She whispered, and couldn't believe she was saying it, "Put on shorts. Only shorts, and go start up the car."

Jackson followed her commands, and while he was warming up the car she called up Lila.

"Lila?"

"Hey, girlfriend!"

"Listen, I called the woman you told me about…that 'Silithia' person."

"Oh," a world of expression in that simple exclamation. Silithia had a reputation, a significant reputation, but she was also an unknown.

A friend of a friend of a friend knows this woman with…power.

But what did that power really do? What did it look like? How did it work?

"You can't believe it…"

"What?"

But Jane didn't know how to describe what Jackson was like, so she said, "Meet me at Chuckie's Grill. Lunch. And you will see something amazing."

The lunch arranged, Jane sat down and put on her make up. She didn't worry about Jackson sitting in the car waiting. He would wait as long as she wanted him to. No complaints, no horn honking…he was too considerate for that.

Ten minutes later she walked out of the house.

Jackson held the door open for her and she slid in showing lots of thigh, watching him.

He drooled, he salivated, but he was more intent on pleasing her than sex.

He closed the door, gently, and ran to the driver's side.

Jane walked through the parking lot like an empress. People actually stared at her sense of confidence and command.

Jackson walked three feet behind her, as commanded, head down.

Head down and wearing only shorts. His hair not even combed, looking…scruffy.

Lila was waiting in the lobby. She and Jane air kissed, then Lila turned to Jackson.

"Hello, Jackson."

Jackson smiled, seemed about to greet her, but Jane interrupted. "Jackson, go wait in the car."

Jackson nodded quickly and trotted out the door.

Lila stared at Jane. "What…what was that?"

"Let's order, and have a drink, and I'll explain."

So they ordered, and had a drink, and ate lunch, and had another drink, then had another drink. And Jane explained everything.

"So he loves another woman, but he has to prove that love by loving you?"

"That's it."

"And you're just…let me call a spade a spade…taking advantage of the situation."

Jane frowned.

"No offense, girlfriend."

"No…no offense. It's just that there is a little bit of guilt. Jackson isn't a bad person. I could easily see myself living my life with him...and then he got in that accident. Now…I don't know. There's a piece of me that loves him, but I don't know that he loves me. And as long as he's willing to be a footstool…" she shrugged.

"I wouldn't worry about the footstool thing. After all, by letting him wait on you hand and foot you're giving him something."

They were silent for a moment after that. They ordered another drink. Then, as if propelled by the same thought, they turned and looked out the window. Across the short outside area and parking lot they could see Jackson. He had a rag and was wiping dirt off the car tires.

Jane sighed.

Lila grinned. "Well, there's one thing you should do…"

"What's that?"

"As long as you've got him…you should see how far you can take it."

Jane turned to her friend. "Is that fair?"

Lila met her gaze. "I think so. Look at him. He's happy. I don't think I've ever seen him so…so satisfied. It's like he's got purpose in life."

"So his purpose in life is to be my footstool."

"Until he gets over this 'Silithia' person."

They sipped their drinks. Maybe if they hadn't been half drunk,… maybe things wouldn't have evolved as they did. But they were drunk, so…

"Come on."

"What?" Jane looked at her friend."

"It's time to go train your maid."

Jane blinked, then she giggled. "What?"

"Come on," and Lila led the way.

Jane and Lila sat in the living room.

Lila had her laptop open and Jane was frowning.

"He looks good."

Jackson stood in front of them. He was wearing a black bodice, a white chiffon skirt with a tiny apron. He had fresh shaven legs and some very tight, black high heels. He didn't complain, he just waited.

"But he looks like a man wearing a dress. He doesn't look like a maid."

"Hmm. Yeah. But…long hair? Boobs? How far we going to take this?"

Lila: "Jackson. Take off your underwear."

Dutifully, Jackson slipped off the panties. He looked around for a place to put them, then just held them.

Jane sighed. "Go put the panties in the laundry."

Jackson walked, awkwardly, high heels weren't his thing, out of the room. A minute later he was back.

They could see his penis, hard and dripping, under the dress, but the dress extended outward so you had to look.

"That's better," murmured Lila. And it was.

"Okay," Jane made up her mind. "We can make him up, but what about boobs? And hair?"

"Amazon," answered Lila.

Jane nodded. "Okay, then we're done for today…"

Lila bent over her laptop. "I'll do overnight, so we can work on him tomorrow."

"What shall we have him do until then?"

Lila snorted. "Whatever you want." Then she looked at Jane. "Will he follow my commands?"

"Maybe. Sure. Once he understands it pleases me."

Lila breathed, "Make him do my bidding."

Jane stared at her friend. They had gone this far, Lila was in it, in for a penny…she turned to Jackson.

"Jackson?"

"Yes, ma'am?" He had been ordered to respond in such a fashion.

"It would please me if you would love Lila the way you love me."

"Of course," and he turned to Lila and smiled.

Lila felt her heart melt. She saw the puppy dog in his eyes. She felt the desire to please her. It was indescribable, and just the way Jane had responded, so did she.

She liked the power. She liked the way he seemed to instantly subservient to her.

"Jackson?"

"Yes, ma'am."

"Would you like to eat my pussy?"

Jane stared at Lila. She held out her palm and forestalled Jackson's answer.

"Well, why not? He eats yours, so what difference does it make?"

"I…well…I…" she turned to Jackson. Her mind flipped through possibilities. She considered that this was the man she had once loved. "Jackson?"

"Yes, ma'am?"

"Are you happy?"

"Oh, yes!"

"And you love me?"

"Oh, yes!"

"And now you love Lila?"

"Yes, ma'am."

Jane mentally shrugged. "Would you like to eat Lila's pussy?"

"Of course?"

At that moment a big drop of pre-cum fell from the tip of his dick.

Lila laughed. "Now there's an answer for you."

Jane: "Then you should do so."

Jackson knelt and gently began removing Lila's shoes. He lifted her skirt and took off her panties.

"Oh, my," whispered Lila. she leaned back and let Jackson spread her legs.

Jackson leaned in and began to kiss her privates. Lila closed her eyes and felt his soft tongue wash her.

"Oh…my…oh…"

Jane took the laptop. Now that it was done there wasn't much to say. "I'll order the boobs and hair. I'll get some make up, too."

Lila just grunted something. Her eyes were closed and she was in heaven.

The next day Jackson wore only shorts as he cut the lawn, trimmed the trees, and washed the cars. He seemed quite happy to be of service.

Inside the house Jane and Lila made a plan. Lila was somewhat of an artist, and she was designing maid outfits. Jane was going through kinkier sites on the web.

"We could have him wear a chastity tube…"

"Why? He won't cum without permission."

"It's just…it's a power thing. If his thingie is locked up it just seems so…powerful."

"Can't argue with that. Here…what do you think of this?"

Jane looked at Lila's sketch. "Oh, that's pretty. Are you going to make it black, though?"

"What else?"

"Pink might be pretty."

"Ooh, I like that," she took out a pink pencil and began shading the latest maid outfit.

Outside, Jackson was waxing the cars, including Lila's. After all, he did love her.

That afternoon the Amazon truck arrived. It dropped off several boxes and went on its merry way.

"Jackson?"

"Yes, ma'am?" Jackson came to the back door. He was supposed to use the back door from here on out, the servant's entrance.

"Come in to the back bedroom."

Jackson followed the girls to the back of the house.

"Okay, no more shaving for you. Here's some Nair."

The girls listened to the shower. Jackson was actually singing. He was happy. He was liking this thing they were doing to him.

"Do you ever want to fuck him again?"

"I'm dying to, but he's…it's like he's not there."

"So? A dick is a dick. What do you care if his mind is on vacation?"

"Well, I'm sort of used to there being a real live human being in my dildos."

They listened and the water shut off. He would be out in a minute.

"What about me?"

"What about you?"

"Would you care if I used him for a, uh…dildo?"

Jane's mind went wandering. She considered everything. Carefully, she answered. "I guess it's okay. But I don't think you want him cumming. He could get you pregnant, you know."

"Can he fuck without cumming?"

"We can find out, but…I think so. But he's going to be a she…isn't that a little too Lesbian for you?"

"A good dicking is not Lesbian," then she turned to her friend, "Is it?"

"I don't know. I mean, it's weird, but it's sort of hot, too."

"Sister, he's been making me horny since I found out about him. I'm so wet now my pussy is spitting."

"Ew!" Jane laughed. "You're gross."

"Sort of 'gross' on you, doesn't it."

"Ooh, bad pun."

At that moment Jackson came out of the shower. His skin was shiny with no hair. The girls stared at him hungrily.

"We need to do his nails."

They sat him down at the make up table and each took a hand. Ten minutes later he not only had red claws, but red toe nails.

"Okay, let's put the tummy shaper on him, then the boobs."

Lila pulled the shaper up, and shortly Jackson was not only skinny, his 'bump' was pushed down.

"Oh," muttered Jackson, trying to adjust himself through the thick material.

"Oh, man up, you sissy," Lila snapped, which caused Jane to giggle.

They glued the breast forms to him and stood back.

"Not bad," Lila was breathing hard. She might not be a Lesbian, but she was definitely horny.

He had a girlish shape. He was thicker than a normal girl, but his waist was thin and his boobs were big. His hips even flared out a bit, a gift of padding in the tummy shaper.

They rolled up his stockings and put some black high heels on him. When he stood up Jane shook her head. "I liked him better when he was shorter.

"Yeah, but he doesn't have to wear high heels all the time."

"He doesn't?" asked Jane, and they both giggled.

"Okay, into the maid outfit."

This was a real maid's outfit, and it was cut to fit. Shortly, Jackson was accoutered like a maid. His chest was massive, and he smiled happily down at it.

Then the wig. There had been much discussion as to color and length. They had finally agreed on a length that reached his shoulders. The color was auburn, very much like his own hair.

And make up.

And he didn't look like a man in drag, not in the slightest. He looked like a slightly heavy woman.

"Oh, wow," whispered Lila.

Jane looked at her friend with a grin. "Did you want to try out that dick before we have him clean the house?"

"Could I?"

"Mi hombre es tu hombre," quipped Jane.

"Oh, baby," Lila took Jackson by the hand and led him back to the bedroom.

Jackson followed Lila into the bedroom.

"Okay, honey. I don't want to mess you up, especially that gorgeous make up, so you just lie back on the bed and I'll do all the work."

Jackson lay down and Lila lifted his skirt and pulled down his tummy shaper. His dick popped up and Lila marveled at it. "Wow, so big and juicy. I love how you're dripping all the time."

"Thank you," said Jackson.

His easy going manner didn't bother Lila, possibly because she hadn't screwed him when he was pre-accident. She took his cock in her hands and began to stroke it. Her hands swirled around, and she could feel the veins. His balls were big and full.

"Now, listen, honey. You're not supposed to cum in me, you got that?"

"No cummey in the yummy," he acknowledged.

Lila giggled. She was a woman who liked men, but it had been a long time since she had gotten laid, and to have Jackson just lay there, dedicated to pleasing her, was just what the doctor ordered. Besides, she didn't want Jackson to take control, like Jane had apparently wanted. She was quite happy being the one in control. She had a feeling that Jane would like it, too, if she ever got over her opinion of sex with Jackson, but, oh, well. If she didn't that just meant more screwing for her.

Jackson started to grunt. Bonehead or not, he liked having his manhood handled.

Lila put her mouth over the head and sucked.

Jackson's eyes opened with pleasure. Jane gave blow jobs, but Lila was better at it.

She squeezed his balls, giving a shot of pain that wasn't quite pain, just a reminder of who was in charge.

"Okay, big boy, you ready for the action?"

"Oh, yes."

Lila climbed on the bed and squatted over Jackson. She looked down at his big tits, she studied his exquisitely made up face. Oh, yes. This was what she needed. She lowered herself.

His penis went into her smooth and slow. It was like sinking into a hot tub of pure desire.

Lila groaned as her hole was stretched out and accommodated his dong.

"Unhhh!" Jackson breathed. Yes, he was in love with Silithia, but she had commanded him to give his love to Jane, who had commanded him to give his love to Lila, so this was good. It was right. He felt her slick warmth engulf him and slide down the shaft. Then she was sitting on him, totally encompassing him. Feeling his blood pulsing through the veins, feeling the throb of his cock as it absorbed the delicious warmth.

"Yeah," whispered Lila, moving her ass in a circle. She could feel Jackson's cock like a stick shift, rammed up in her, going through the gears, swirling and brushing against her walls, exciting her nerves.

"Fuck!" groaned Jackson. He pushed up with his hips, and it felt like he was digging into pure pleasure.

"Oh, yeah," Lila pinched her nipples and pulled. "This is what a good fuck is…"

He reached up and brushed her hands away, grabbed her tits and mauled them. He could feel her nipples hard as pebbles, rolling against his palms.

"Yeah, do me. Do me you bitch!"

Looking down at Jackson, seeing him as a girl, yet feeling him as a man, it was the best of both worlds. It was like fucking a soft, flower of a woman, and yet getting a stiff and manly poke into her very soul.

She squirmed on him, tried to get him deeper into her.

He held her, propped her upright.

She gasped and said, "You ever do anal sex?"

Jackson shook his head. He had wanted to try it, but Jane had always refused.

"Then you're going to love this." She pushed up with her hands, got her legs under her and lifted off his cock.

Jackson gasped. His dick pulsed in the air. He wanted to be back inside her.

She shifted her position, used her hand to fit him to her anus.

"You need lubricant. Pussy juice will do, but don't plan on fucking my pussy after you've been up my asshole."

"Okay," his mouth was slack as he felt her push down on the head of his dick.

It was tight, tighter than her pussy, and there were certain things that were the same, but there was also a different feel. Then she was in and sliding down his shaft with a heartfelt sigh. "Oh, yeah. Fuck me for a while, then I'll have to clean up and go for your dick again. I can cum easy doing it like this."

"Okay," he felt her rising and falling on him.

After a minute she said, "Flip me over and fuck my butt. You'll find it exciting to just sort of bounce off my buns."

Dutifully, but with a deep sense of interest, he flipped her over. She landed flat out, and he was perched on her buns, still deep inside her.

"Ooh!" She grabbed the sheets with her fists. "Fuck me now."

He began to pound her ass, slamming into it, then pulling out. He loved the way it was solider than a pussy, and how it gripped him.

As for Lila, getting fucked in the ass was almost as good as taking it in the pussy. It was a different set of nerves, but the action was the same, the excitement, in a way, was even enhanced.

For a long couple of minutes he bounced off her round buns, then she said, "Get out now…"

He slid out of her. Normally, pre-accident, and especially after accident, he would have been out of control, and nothing could have gotten him out of that tight hole. But he wasn't supposed to cum, and he was feeling very compliant with the women he loved, so he pulled out and waited for her next command.

She rolled off the bed, tottered into the bathroom and came back with a wet rag. She wrapped it around his cock and began stroking him and cleaning him at the same time.

"Don't you cum now, you nasty boy."

"Okay," he mumbled, pushing his hips into her hand, trying desperately to cum, but with a hidden reserve inside that would stop him before he went over the edge.

"What are you doing?" Jane was at the door, leaning against the jamb.

"I took him up the heinie. Now I'm cleaning him. You ever have anal sex with him?"

"No." There was an expression of distaste on her face, but also a play of curiosity. Jane was thinking about it. She never had before, but from watching the way these two bunnies had gone after it, maybe she should try it.

Lila tossed the rag aside and climbed aboard Jackson again. "Come watch his face."

"Why?"

"'Cause he needs to cum, he wants to cum, but he's not going to, right lover?"

"Nu…nu…nu…no."

Jane came to the side of the bed and stared down at her husband's face.

She was struck by how he was a good man, and now this…now he was getting all the sex that he wanted, but never enough. His face was twisted in a pleasurable agony.

"Kiss him," whispered Lila. "Make his day."

Jane leaned down, her face an inch above his. His eyes stared up at her, pure devotion.

She realized: *he loved her. Yes, he loved other women, but she was his first love, and she…she didn't need to do this to him.*

In the eyes of his lust and love she finally perceived how perverse she had been.

"Oh, God," she whispered, and she kissed him. Their lips met, pressed, and she could taste his lipstick. She placed a hand on one of his boobs and wished he had real ones, that he could feel her hand.

She loved him, and she had been abusing him, but…but if she could let go of her perverseness, then it was all right. He was all right with this, so that made it not perverse.

"Honey," she whispered to him.

"Uhh," he groaned at her. Lila's weight was moving him up and down, shaking him. It was requiring some kind of self control not to let his squirtem shoot out.

"Are you happy?"

Balls deep in Lila, his lipstick smeared by his greedy wife, he nodded. "Oh, yeah."

"Do you like this?"

"Un hunh!"

"You like being a woman?"

"I love it."

She nodded, and in that moment perversity disappeared. She saw past his obsession for Silithia and perceived his love for her.

"Ah, God!" Lila came, she clawed her breasts and arched her back and spasms shot through her.

Jane just smiled and kissed her husband.

After a half a minute, exhausted, drained, Lila fell off Jackson. She put out a hand and touched Jane's forearm. Jane looked at her.

"You. Do him. You need to. It's good. Especially…especially with him as a woman."

"As a woman?" Jane mused, taking off her clothes.

"He is and he isn't, but there's this sense of power…especially with him not cumming." Lila rolled to the side of the bed, and there was enough room for Jane to clamber onto the bed and throw a leg over her husband.

Jackson watched her. He was going out of his mind with frustration and love. He wanted to cum in the worst way, but his love for his wife helped him control himself.

Jane slid up and placed her pussy over his cock. She felt the extra slickness left by Lila's juices. She let her self slide down.

Looking at him…as a woman. A sexy woman. But with a giant cock. It was good, and Jane began to understand what Lila had been talking about. She was on top. She was in control. It gave her a sense of power she had never experienced before. It was like he was the bitch… and she was in charge. She owned the moment. She owned him.

He groaned, a wild, drawn out sound of pure lust. He was giving himself to her. He was accepting, becoming the woman, and she was taking charge, taking him, owning him.

"Don't you dare cum," she hissed happily.

"I…won't," he gritted his teeth.

"Do you have a dildo?" asked Lila.

Jane didn't ask, she just said, "Bottom drawer," and pointed at a side table.

Lila got out the dildo and came around to a position to the side and slightly behind Jane.

"Get ready, girlfriend. You're about to have a real ride. The ride of your life."

Jackson was pumping up, fucking her, groaning, and then he froze and his eyes opened. "OH!"

"Keep fucking, Jackson," Lila commanded.

His mouth was open, his eyes were dazed, and he started fucking again, but not so fast, definitely not so hard.

Jane realized what was happening. Lila was pushing the big vibrator into Jackson's rectum.

Jackson began to writhe, to pick up speed, to moan and grunt and move his hips.

Jane had just enough time to lay on him, to grab him, then he was thrashing wildly. Yelping piteously. Out of control.

Now he fucked her with that brutality that she had wanted, and a lot more. Now he was ramming it into her, his arms and legs actually flailing against the bed. His eyes opened and his head moving back and forth. He was out of his mind, taken beyond the breaking point, and yet, still, he hadn't squirted.

"Let him cum," suggested Lila.

Jackson was squirming and worming violently, and Jane held on to him and whispered into his ear. "Squirt, you bitch!"

How he heard her she had no idea, but he did, and the result was instantaneous. His hips rose up further than they had, he cried out, and his cock spurted.

She could feel his gism washing her insides. She could feel him splattering his seed inside her womb.

"Oh, my God!" Jane sat up and watched Jackson keep spasming. His movements were slow now, and she wasn't in danger of being thrown off. He kept squirting and squirting, his balls had to have been really full, and he was giving her everything.

"Now I own him," Jane whispered in awe.

"Lock, stock and whole soul," agreed Lila. she was still moving the dildo in and out of Jackson, but not violently. Just gently milking the last of his manhood out of him.

A minute later and Jackson was done. In one way he was no longer a man. He had been 'cured' of not just sexual addiction, but of the desire to be in charge of a woman. Now he was owned, and he liked it. He felt a profound sense of peace he had never known existed.

A couple of months passed, and life was different for Jackson and Jane.

For one, Lila came and went as she pleased, taking advantage of Jackson as she wished.

Which was fine with Jane.

For another, two more women had been introduced to the taking of Jackson.

Jackson was always dressed as a woman. He was often a maid, and he took care of the ladies' homes. Whenever he cleaned a house the woman of the house would take him, remind him of how men should be treated, and how wonderful it was to experience 'the other side.'

The most important thing that happened, however, came out of the blue.

Jane and Lila were sitting in the kitchen, drinking coffee and chatting. Jackson was vacuuming in the living room.

KNOCK! KNOCK!

"Jackson? Will you get the door?"

The sound of the machine stopped and Jackson's high heels could be heard crossing the foyer. Click. click. click. Then: "OH!" And nothing.

Jane and Lila looked at each other, then leaped to their feet and ran to the front door.

Silithia stood in the foyer, her head almost touching the ceiling. Jackson was on his knees, staring up at the giantess as if in rapture.

Silithia smiled at Jane and Lila. She looked down at Jackson. "Jackson. Go stand in a corner."

Quickly, Jackson ran to the far corner of the living room and stood in a corner. Just standing in a corner was rapture for the poor man.

Silithia entered the living room and sat on the couch, which creaked alarmingly. She motioned to a couple of chairs. Jane and Lila pulled the chairs around and faced the large woman.

"I heard rumors of a man brought to heel, and I wished to see for myself."

Jane and Lila looked at Jackson, then at the floor. They felt guilty.

"Oh, no need for that. In fact, you've done me a service."

"We have?" asked Lila.

"Oh, yes. Men are a problem. It took me many years to figure out how to handle them. And my solution was not common to all. A man should not just be no a problem to me, he should be no problem to any woman. So tell me what you have done."

For the next hour Jane and Lila told of how they had become perverse, but then realized the truth of a man: that he just wants to be used.

Silithia nodded thoughtfully. "Your solution is wonderful, and it encourages me. Tell me, would you two like to come live with me?"

Jane and Lila looked at each other. In truth, they were astonished, and delighted, and almost afraid to show how happy the thought made them. To be allowed to live in the presence of such an ultimate woman….

"What would you have us do?"

"I have been planning a solution for men. All men. I need a few men, men who are devoted to me as if Jackson. But most of all I need loyal women. Men who are enthralled have limited uses, and they are not always what I need. But women who are not slave to their desires, who can still think, who can imagine a future where the parasite known as man is brought under control…I need such far visioned women. what do you think?"

"I think I…" Jane looked at Lila, "I think we would like that. But what about Jackson?"

Silithia smiled. "Jackson."

"Yes, ma'am," Jackson turned and stared at Silithia with fawning love.

"Cum," she snapped her fingers.

Jackson's dick began to shoot out semen. He stared down at his penis, his knees shaking, and groaned.

"Oh, my God!" whispered Lila. "How did you…how did you do that?"

"That's something you will learn, should you come live with me.

But, to answer your question…Jackson will be no problem." To Jackson, "Return to your corner."

Jackson turned and faced the corner again.

Silithia leaned forward. "You will become like me, larger than life. You will have control of the men of the earth. I will teach you such things as you can't imagine."

Lila and Jane stared at the bigger woman raptly.

"Yes," breathed Lila.

"Where is…where do you live?"

"I live in a small valley. Not many men there, and I have a company. Perhaps you have heard of it…'The House of Chimera.'"

"That's a cosmetic, isn't it?"

"Yes…and no. It's cosmetics, but it's heavily involved in making men into women. Only when men understand what a woman is will they be amenable to a new world."

"The House of Chimera," whispered Jane. "Where is this place?"

"It's in a little town called Stepforth."

END

Here is the link if you wish to read the next volume…

The Stepforth Husband

Full Length Books from Gropper Press

Sam thought he was a tough guy. He was cock of the walk, a real, live, do or die Mr. Tough Guy.

Then he made a mistake. He took on the wrong … woman.

This is the story of what happened when Sam finally met his match and learned who the really tough people were.

Too Tough to Feminize

My Husband the Model

He had to wear a bra or…bust!

Published on Kindle,
appeared in 'The Whisper of Flesh.'

PART ONE

"God, that is great! I'm so happy, but…uh oh."

Dorey had just told me she was pregnant, and I had suddenly realized the big problem it was going to create.

"What?" She smiled, she was happy, a bun in the oven, I hated to bust her bubble.

"How am I…we need a model."

"Oh, Rick, that's…uh oh. That is a problem."

"I mean, we're okay for a couple of months, but then…then…"

"Then I'll lose this svelte figure and be a fat, old cow. And then nobody will buy and we'll go broke…and just when things were starting to take off."

We stared at each other, our joy at the news of a child tempered by the dismay of knowing our business was going to fail.

We had opened up a high end fashion and lingerie store the year before. We had struggled and put all our money into it. We only had one worker, and now she might be in danger of losing her job.

"Can't we hire somebody else?"

"Who? And with what? We're barely making enough money to pay Belinda and make our rent. We're still catching up. No way the land lord, or the vendors, are going to give us credit again."

We had fallen behind, worked our tails to the bone, and now this.

We sat in our living room and pondered wearily.

We sold high dresses and lingerie. People came in and expected to be shown. They don't walk down an aisle and pick out cheap stuff from bins, they watch the model and then make a decision. No model, no decision…no decision, no sale…no sale, no money. It was that simple.

Since we had opened Dorey had been the model. It wasn't difficult, I'd put out the cheese and crackers and wine, champagne for the real big spenders, and she'd duck into the back room for a fast change or four, and it all worked out.

But now she was going to be busy making a baby, and I was going to be in charge in the store. No way I could duck into the back and slip into a bra, or negligee, or whatever.

"Of course, there's Belinda."

I looked at Dorey. "Seriously?"

Belinda had a weight problem. She was big and hefty and…and good for just about everything else in the store. But there was no way she was going to slip into leotards and prance around on high heels.

Look, I'm not being mean, that's just the way it was.

So we sat, and talked, and brainstormed, and came up with nothing.

"Well, we can ask Belinda what she thinks tomorrow. After all, it's a couple of months. It'll all work out.

But things were looking grim.

The next day we went to work, and we were not in a good mood. We entered the store without the normal morning cheerfulness, we greeted Belinda dourly, and went right to stocking and returns and dusting and sweeping and…we were gloomy.

"Heysoos, are you guys grumpy. What the heck is wrong?"

It was break, and Dorey and I were sitting in the office, watching our donuts cool and our milk grow warm.

I sighed.

Dorey said, "Have a seat, Bel."

Suddenly looking nervous, Belinda pulled up a chair and settled into it. She stared at both of us for a moment, then blurted, "What?"

Dorey sighed. "I'm pregnant."

Her face lit up like Christmas. "That's great! That's wonderful! You've been…" at our lack of enthusiasm she sobered. "It is great, isn't it? I mean, I thought you wanted a baby."

"We never realized how it would impact the business," I explained.

"Oh, don't get us wrong," Dorey said, "We want this baby. I mean, under the tears and desperation we're leaping and jumping for joy."

"Could have fooled me," Belinda quipped.

I grunted.

That's the thing about Belinda. She's the eternal optimist. You give her a pile of horse shit and she'll look for the pony.

"So…I don't get it."

"In a matter of months I will be losing my figure"

"Well, that's expected, babies and…oh."

I nodded. "Dorey won't be able to model anymore."

Again, "Oh." A little deeper, a little more solemn.

"We might have to let you go."

"Oh…crap!"

Belinda couldn't get by on what we paid her under the table, and she couldn't get by on unemployment. She needed both. And she said something ridiculous. "My cats."

She had two Siamese cats. Love of her life. She called them 'Salt' and, get this, 'More Salt.' I kid you not.

Dorey blinked.

I kept my mouth straight.

Dorey cracked.

I made a muffled sound.

Then we were laughing. Really laughing.

Hey, it wasn't funny, but we had had enough of the gloom and despair. Dorey put her head on the table and pounded on the surface with one fist. I slipped off my chair and started rolling on the rug.

"Well, hey…" Belinda muttered weakly.

"We're sorry, Belinda. It just," I wheezed and tried to sit up. "It just struck us funny."

"Yeah. Real funny. She gets fat. I lose my job. And my cats starve."

Which set Dorey and I off again. Damn it, it wasn't funny, but it just…it made us laugh.

Finally we calmed down and I said, "Dorey, we'll make it. I don't know how, but we'll make it."

Belinda didn't look too happy, however.

Dorey said, "If we have to feed our cats ourselves," and there we went again. I fell back on the floor and Dorey tilted back in the swivel, and the swivel was weak springed and the chair tilted over. Dorey jerked to try to regain her balance, but it was a lost cause. The chair went all the way over and she splatted on her back and lay there, stunned, and then started laughing.

And I laughed, and even Belinda started to laugh.

Cats. Huh.

The day went slowly. Mrs. Jensen came in at ten and Dorey modeled several dresses and we sold one. A thousand bucks. Which, in our posh Beverly Hills location, paid the rent for a couple of days.

John Springfield, the old senator, dropped by with his wife and girlfriend at noon. Hey, it's Beverly Hills, right? He bought them both bathing suits. Ka ching, another couple of days rent. It was the beginning of the month so we were still working on the rent. By the tenth we would have it. Then a few days of working for Belinda. Then a week paying off the IRS, and finally, about the 22th, Dorey and I worked for ourselves. And let me tell you, we hated February. That short month had us eating peanut butter sandwiches for dinner.

But we had made it, month after month, struggling, scraping by and now stats were up and we were actually pulling in good bucks. We were actually starting to pay ourselves before the 20th!

Then…the baby. More expenses, time off for doctors and things, and less money to cover it all. Maybe a lot less. Like close the doors less.

Then Belinda had a bright idea. And, God, did I hate it.

"I've got it!" She had a big grin when she flounced in.

"Herpes?" I asked.

"Shut up, Jason," murmured Dorey.

I looked at her.

"First bit of cheer in a week. Let's take it while we can."

"Oh, yeah. Sorry. What's your idea, Bel?"

"Tell you at first break. We have customers this morning."

And we did. Dorey was kept busy sliding in and out of night gowns, dinner dresses, high heels, bras and shapers.

I watched her moving quickly and lithely as she tried on the various clothes. Heysoos, but she had a good body. Her waist was tight and her boobs were big. Sometimes, when the dress was overly tight, it happened every once in a while, I had to go help her stuff herself into a dress. Actually push on those bazooms with my bare hands and get them pushed down enough so the nipples didn't show. That was a part of the job that I liked. After that I would always be grinning. And horny. And even Belinda would laugh at the silly expression on my easy to please face.

And Dorey was going to sacrifice that killer body.

God. We wanted a baby. There had to be some way…

“Okay. Break time We have two hours before the Johnson kid shows up. Let’s have a seat and brainstorm.”

We sat down in the showing room, it had the plush, comfortable chairs. Dorey sat near the hallway so she could step out of sight if the door opened. She was mid change and clad only in bra and panties.

“Okay,” I said, settling in to the cushions. “What’s this great idea you’ve come up with?”

Belinda grinned a Cheshire grin. “Jason.”

“Yes?” I wrinkled my brow.

“That’s it. Jason is my idea.”

Dorey tilted her head in puzzlement. I blinked. This made no sense.

Belinda, for her part, she sat and smiled at us like the cat who had just eaten the 100 pound mouse.

“Don’t you guys get it?”

“Get what?” I was truly mystified.

She sighed, and held out her sketchbook.

She was a good artist, and she often drew design ideas, or even drew pictures for clients.

I opened the first page and stared. It was me. But under that smiling face was a dress.

“Huh?”

“Turn the pages, silly, and let Dorey see.”

I turned the book so Dorey could see and flipped the pages.

Me. Me. Me. In gowns. In negligees. In dresses. Parts of my body. Hands with long gloves. Feet with high heels.

Me.

“I don’t…”

“Oh, my God!” Dorey breathed out.. “It could work.”

“Like a charm,” announced Belinda happily. “You keep the store, I keep my job, you have the baby, and I have my cats.”

We didn’t laugh this time.

I still don’t under—“

"Jason," Dorey laid it out for me. "You're our new model."

"I'm what…no. This is…" I tossed the sketch book aside.

Dorey turned to Belinda. "He's slender. In two months he can be skinny."

"And we've got corsets if he isn't skinny enough."

"We'd have to work around bathing suits…"

"Hey, wait a minute!" I interjected.

"We don't sell a lot of those, and I don't think most women care about us modeling those."

"Underwear is…what about boobs?"

"Will you guys stop this?" I tried.

They ignored me.

"Falsies will work. We've got lots of breast forms, and we can get different sizes and shapes if we need."

"Cheap enough from Sally."

Sally was one of our bra vendors, and she was a real source for breast forms. Cheap ones. Like big discount, or even free.

"Shoes. He's got to wear high heels."

"You guys have to knock this off."

"Won't take but a day to get some made in his size."

"Hair."

"He wears it long, and then we could always just give him extensions."

"I'm not going to wear all these clothes!"

They both looked at me. Pointed, serious, then they turned back to each other.

"What about his penis."

"He can wear a gaffe."

"Heck, why not a chastity tube? Or even a full belt? That would keep the hamster in the cage."

"I am not going to be the model!" I stood up.

"Honey, sit down," Dorey didn't even looked at me. "There are greater minds than yours at work here."

They chitted and chatted and plotted out my future for the next two hours. And when it came time for lunch Dorey ordered me a…salad. A (choke) salad.

"But I want a sub! With meatballs and cheese and gravy dripping down the front of my shirt!

"Ha!" spouted Bel.

"Nonsense," grinned Dorey. And it was an evil grin. At least I thought it was evil.

"We need to slenderize you, get you ready."

"But I'm not going to do this!"

Dorey finally turned to me. "Oh. Yes. You are." And, man, was she serious. "You are not only going to do it, you are going to like it."

"I am not!"

"Do you ever want sex again?"

"That's not fair!"

Bel actually came to my rescue on that one. "Hey, horn dog needs his relief. Maybe you could just withhold it a bit."

"A lot," Dorey glared at me.

Oh, man. This hurt. I liked my sex. I liked to squeeze her body and lick it all over and suck her nipples and…and most of all I liked to plumb my cock to her depths. In and out, in and out, it was my favorite sport.

Then Dorey softened a bit. "You play this right and you might even get more sex. After all, you know how I appreciate good looking women, and if the woman actually had a dick then I might be willing to turn Lesbian."

"Ooh. That's a wicked thought," Belinda mused, scratching her chin.

"Dress you up in lingerie, maybe a little make up…that's sort of a horny thought."

"It's even got me horny."

Dorey and I turned our heads and looked at her.

Defiantly, "Hey! I have sexual appetites, too, you know?"

All afternoon we argued, and I have to tell you, I was losing.

I mean, I didn't want to, but the girls REALLY wanted me to.

And, that night, Dorey really went after me.

First, she changed into a veddy sexy negligee. Her breasts, proud and pointed, were plain to see. The nipples rubbed against the soft material and became excited. And it didn't help that every once in a while she palmed her breasts and pulled the nipples. And put one hand over her mons and twisted her knees and groaned.

Yeah, I know. I'm a sucker. Right. But what do you expect from a man, huh?

Then she made her face up. Put on the model's make up, shaded her eyes blue and painted her lips red. And flounced around in front of me. Whipping her hair across my face. Rubbing that incredible, voluptuous body against me. Giving me a lap dance right in the middle of (choke) FOX news.

Heck, Trump could have appeared naked on the screen and I wouldn't have noticed.

Okay, maybe that was a bad analogy, but you get the idea.

Then, the knell of doom for me, bed time.

I slipped under the covers. Erect. Dripping. Looking forward to the old in and out.

She took off her clothes, cold creamed her face, and started putting her hair up in curlers.

"Hey!"

"What?"

"I thought we were…you know."

"Oh, I only go to bed with people that turn me on."

"That's not fair."

She turned to me. "Honey, you're going to give in. You're going to do the modeling. Now the only question is how much do you have to suffer before you give in. You can have me every night. All night. Every hole. All made up and hot and eager…or you can have me like this." She turned back to her dressing table and put another curler in her hair.

"That is really not—"

She turned to me, and now she was serious. "Honey. It's only clothes. Heck. You might even like them."

"And make up and…and high heels…and not eating anymore."

She chortled. "Oh, you'll get your salads." More serious again. "But I am fighting for our business, our home, our brand, new baby. What are you fighting for?"

That stopped me. That made me blink, and my mouth to open and close.

Heck, even my dick went down. I turned away from her, rolled over and stared at the wall.

Dorey finished putting curlers in her hair, then slipped into bed.

She didn't touch me. Just laid on her side of the bed and went to sleep. It didn't take long before she was softly snoring.

I didn't sleep.

Just clothes. And make up and stuff.

I knew within a few months, by the time Dorey showed a little baby bump, I would have learned enough. Belinda could help teach me, and Dorey would be able to show me things right up until she went to the hospital.

I had worked in the industry for years. I knew my way around dresses. I knew the tricks for shimmying into a tight pair of jeans, or how to get a bra on, how to plump up the tits so they looked bigger…I knew a lot about make up already. Watching models, and especially Dorey, apply make up over the years…it wouldn't be much trouble.

And we could get special clothes for me. Shoes and gloves and things.

So what was stopping me?

At midnight I said, "I've got a problem."

Dorey woke up, she must have been listening in her sleep, for she said, "What problem?"

"I'm a man."

"Yeah? Really?" then; "Sorry. Sarcasm not appropriate. Me bad."

I said, "I want to stay a man. I don't want…I don't want to be effected by this."

"Isn't that up to you?"

I didn't say anything. Dorey rolled over and grabbed my penis. "I'll tell you this, lover mine. I fell in love with you. Dick came later. Sexy clothes came much later. And, let me tell you the truth, you could be gay and I would still love you. I fell in love with the man, not all his accouterments." She shook my dick, which was pretty damned hard by then, to emphasize.

She rolled over and went back to sleep.

I laid on my back. My dick in the air. Thinking.

A woman. Wearing falsies. Prancing around.

Okay, not prancing around. That is only the transvestite stereotype some people have.

For a baby. And to keep the business afloat. For Belinda and her stupid cats.

Well, actually, they weren't that stupid. They were sort of cute. Dorey and I had been over to Belinda's house and one of the cats, Salt or More Salt, I couldn't tell which was which, had climbed into my lap and purred.

Stupid cats.

I grinned in the dark.

I stopped grinning.

A new baby. What was I willing to sacrifice for a new life? And I knew. Once that kid was born I would be willing to lay down my life for him. Or her. So why couldn't I wear a few clothes?

At three in the morning I made up my mind.

"Okay," I whispered.

I don't know how Dorey did it, but she must have been 'sleep listening' again. She spun over, climbed onto my body and yelled, "Curler sex!"

I started laughing, and she positioned my weenie and slid down.

Oh, God! That felt good!

"Lover. You will never be sorry." She tweaked my nips.

"I will make you the happiest cross dresser in the world." She reached under and grabbed my balls. I gasped with pleasure as she squeezed and played with them.

"You are going to be so sexy that every woman will want you. And the men. but don't worry about the men."

Men?

She felt my thought and laughed. "Hey, you're a Lesbian! You don't care about men, right?"

She was tilting her hips, writhing, squirming, and my penis was starting to throb.

"God, just the thought of screwing you while you're all en femme… it's making me so horny!"

She kissed me then, and the combination, nuts, nips, her chewing on my mouth, it was too much.

"UN!" I grunted.

"Let it come, baby," she whispered into my ear. "Let it come."

I couldn't help it. Not that I wanted to. I jerked and my hips thrust up and I felt the sperm shooting up the shaft. That white hot feeling of pleasure engulfed me, and I came and I came and I came.

"He's in," announced Dorey.

Belinda gav a clap of her hands. "Goodie! When do we start?"

"We already did. He's wearing a bra under his clothes. And a garter and nylons and even panties."

"How cool!"

And, I swear, it looked like Belinda was even getting a little bit turned on.

We worked that day. We didn't have a lot of customers, but we had a lot of alterations to make. And every half hour Dorey had an outfit laid out for me.

"Time!" she would yell.

I would strip off my clothes and put on the new clothes. Dorey would stand there and tap her foot and watch the stop watch on her cell.

"Stop!"

And they would critique me.

"Your bra strap is tangled."

"You didn't get your shoes on fast enough."

"Turn the skirt more to the front. Zipper, baby. You know where the zipper goes.

Chastened, and even a little embarrassed, I would nod and think over my mistakes until the next episode.

"Time!" And I would slip out of one outfit and into another.

And they really mixed the outfits up on me. Sometimes it was a dress. Sometimes it was a corset. Sometimes it was a bathing suit.

I know, we weren't going to do suits, but they wanted me to know everything. They needed me fast and efficient.

Heck, if Dorey could do it, then so could I. Right?"

At the end of the day I was exhausted. "Man," I blurted, sinking back in the passenger seat. "I didn't know it was this much work!"

"You ain't seen nothing, yet. Wait until your boobs come in."

"Oh." I was actually feeling a little dispirited.

Dorey laughed as she turned up our driveway. "Hey, don't worry, lover. We girls have had a lifetime of getting dressed and undressed in sexy clothes. A couple of months and this will all be old hat to you."

I hope so," I yawned.

She stopped the car in the garage and looked at me. "How's the old dickie doo?"

"Oh, God. I never thought I'd be too tired."

"But seeing you all day, your bare flesh slipping into and out of outfits, the bulge in your pants…"

"It was bulging, wasn't it?"

"I think you like this. Think you can fuck me?"

"Oh, God," I whined. But I was grinning.

"Come on, Iron Man. Don't give out on me now."

"But I just came this morning?"

"Hey! You don't have to cum, just provide me with a human dildo for a while."

"Well, if you insist."

She did. We got out of the car and pulled me through the house and into the bedroom.

She threw me on the bed and climbed on to me.

"All aboard!" she bellowed, then laughed.

She began to go up and down, pulling her tits, slapping her mons.

I tried, oh, I tried, but I was exhausted. I actually yawned when she came.

Can you believe that? Yawned?

She sank down on me, lay on my chest and played with my nipple.

My cock was still hard inside her. Pulsing, but not cumming.

"God, that was good."

"Excellent," I yawned again.

"Who ever would have thought that seeing you in drag could be so exciting?"

"I don't know," I whispered.

She kept talking, but her voice became a mumble, a receding mumble, then I was asleep.

And dreaming! I didn't usually dream, but…woman's clothes. I was wearing them. Changing them, putting on shoes and nylons and bras. Slipping into dresses. Modeling in front of a mirror. Changing again, and again, and again. And it was all jerky, like an old movie. And it went on for a long time.

"Oh!" I stretched, and I felt good. The dreams had waned and I must have slid into a deep sleep. I felt quite refreshed.

Except for the boner under the covers. Oh, yeah. That. I hadn't cum.

"Come on, lover babe. Time for work!"

Dorey came in and threw back the drapes. She was fully made up and ready to go.

I sat up, "Did I oversleep?"

"Yup. But alterations until noon. Still, get your lazy ass in gear."

I reached for her, pulled her to me. "First…there's some unfinished business."

She pushed me off and wiggled away. "Tonight. Don't want to mess me up."

I slipped out of bed. "Pretty soon it'll be me saying that."

She blinked, then giggled. "It will, won't it."

I slipped into the underwear she held out to me. Panties and garter. Nylons. Bra and…slip?

"Why a slip?"

"Because you're going to wear a skirt to work."

"Really?"

"Why not? the more girl clothes you wear the sooner you will be expert in them."

"I'm already expert," I complained as I got dressed.

"No. You're a know about, not a real expert. But we'll fix that."

She helped me with make up. And I listened and watched as she cleaned me up, prepared my skin and began applying lotions and powders.

It felt weird.

But it felt sexy, too.

And the sexy was helped by the friendly, little bulge in my skirt.

"Oh, we're going to have to do something about that," Dorey said, giving it a squeeze.

I tried to grab her but she was quick to fend me off. "Not now, horny boy."

"Don't you mean horny girl?"

"Yeah, that's exactly what I mean," she laughed.

Finally, I was ready. Eyes done just right, red lips feeling so strange. And really, really aware of myself. I mean, I felt like I was out of my body. This wasn't just a quick change, this was a lifestyle change.

We drove to work. Well, she drove. I wasn't ready to do much more than fall on my face in my high heels.

But when we walked in, Belinda gushed. "Oh, my God! You look so…so incredible."

I glanced in the mirror. I did look pretty good. My hair was a trifle short, we would have to make it all mussy or something. And my chest was flat, Dorey was already getting me the forms.

"You know, when I got this idea," Belinda walked around me, scrutinized me, "I never imagined…I mean I did…but the reality… you're good looking!"

"Thanks, dahling," I struck a pose.

"Uh oh."

"What's wrong," asked Dorey, stuffing a form down my bra.

"The mouse won't stay in his hole," Belinda pointed at my lap with her chin.

I looked down. I had a big hard on and the skirt was being lifted up.

"Cripes. I just did him yesterday."

I didn't say anything about the hornicizing effect of being ridden to her own cum and the heck with me.

"What do we do?"

"I don't think a gaffe will do."

"Let me look at chastity belts."

"Can't we just tie it down?"

"If it's stiff it will hurt. If he's wearing chastity it won't get hard and we can bend it around."

I cleared my throat and they both looked at me.

"We could just get me off. No offense, Belinda."

"None taken. And if you want to use the bathroom for a minute…"

But I wasn't ready for the big squirt, yet. "Can't we just work around it today?"

"I guess," Belinda stood there, one hand under elbow, one hand under chin, and looked at my crotch.

Hey, she didn't make me horny, ours wasn't that kind of a relationship. She was more like a sister, but it sure made me feel weird. Oh well, I would just have to get over it.

All that day we had me changing. A new set of forms came in and they fit me better, but getting the clothes on over a chestful of tit was… different.

Pulling the cloth over the mounds I had to pull on the dress in different ways, and I actually popped two zippers.

"It's all his man strength. Don't pull so hard," Belinda groused, fixing one of the zippers.

Lunch. A salad. I was starting to actually feel weak. "You keep feeding me this slop and I'll be too weak to break a zipper."

They just laughed at me, and tossed a few extra croutons onto the blue cheese.

All afternoon getting into and out of dresses. In between stocking and altering and answering the phone.

"Time!…Time!"

"Time!…Time!"

"Time!…Time!"

By the time five o'clock came around I was frazzled. I got into the car and went to sleep. Dorey drove me home, woke me up long enough to get me to bed, and I slept.

Heck, I even missed that delicious salad she fixed me for dinner!

But, the next morning I woke up, and even early. I got out of bed, and my stomach felt like somebody had drilled a well into it. And the well had gone dry.

I shuffled into the kitchen and looked at Dorey.

She kissed my cheek and said, "Big treat today! Grape nuts!"

Oh, God. I looked at the glop in my ball. She had sliced a banana into it, and sprinkled a few blue berries, but it was still glop. Unappealing and even disgusting.

Still, it was what women did to keep their figure. I ate it. Every mouth watering bite. Gah!

Off to work.

We had a couple of shows, but that was okay. I worked behind the scenes, helping Dorey into and out of.

"Man," I griped at one point. "You get your own personal dresser."

"But you won't when the babies due."

"Okay," I pushed her tit down.

"Easy, boy."

I looked at her. "Sorry. I'm frustrated."

That afternoon Dorey had to drive down to LA and pick up some fabric. Usually I went with her, but today it was more important that I practice getting into and out of clothes. So Belinda manned the stop watch and I practiced.

"Time!...Time!"

"Time!...Time!"

I slipped in and out. And I was feeling pretty good, and sexy, all the clothes rubbing against me, wearing the filmy underthings, I started getting erect. Like big erect.

Finally, Bel had had enough. She looked down at my crotch and said, "Wait."

I stood there, figuring I had a crooked seam or something, but she reached right down for my lap and pushed my cock down.

"Oh...ow!"

She looked down in disgust. My cock had slipped out the bottom of my panties. "Can't you control yourself?"

"Nope," I didn't actually bad about my condition. Heck, a boner can be a wonderful thing.

"This is why I didn't get married. This is why I like cats more than people."

"Sorry," I murmured, looking down at it.

"Oh, hell." She grabbed my cock.

"Hey!" I squeaked.

"This is going to hurt me more than it does you."

She began to stroke me.

"Don't...you can't..."

But she could.

And I couldn't get away. She had a grip on me. And I was in a corset and couldn't twist away.

"Come on, come on," she manipulated me, reached down with her other hand and palmed the head.

I was horny, I was weak kneed, I couldn't fight back.

"Come on," she was right in front of me, our faces just inches apart, and she worked my cock as we breathed on each other.

"Come on, I don't want to have to suck it. Come on."

That did it. That sucking remark. My knees almost buckled and I shot out my load.

She smiled.

I groaned.

I pumped out semen and filled her hand.

Then she blew my mind. she stepped back and licked the semen out of her palm. "Mmm. I always did like the taste of this stuff."

She turned and walked away, leaving me with my mouth open. She tossed over her shoulder, "Come on, change. We have to practice."

Dully, moving slowly, robbed of my vigor by the shock of my employee's educated hand, I changed.

"I jacked Jason off," Belinda stated, when Dorey returned to the store. We were lifting folds of material out of the back of the SVU.

"Oh," Dorey glanced at her.

"It was getting in the way."

Dorey looked at me, and there was everything in that gaze. Wonder, shock, surprise, and, most of all, inspection. Inspection of me.

We weren't newbies when it came to sex. We played with different holes, she had even fingered my butt a couple times. And we had jerked off for each other Well, I had jacked off, and she had jilled off. Great kinky fun. But to be jerked off by another woman? Had I crossed a line?

I felt small, and embarrassed, and I shriveled up inside.

Dorey watched me. Watched the shame in my eyes. She stood up and came to me and held my face with both hands and stared straight into my eyes.

I blubbered, "I'm…I'm…"

She nodded. "It's okay. If you have to do it again, that's fine. But I can't wait for that chastity belt to arrive.

"But…but…"

Dorey turned to Belinda. "How was he?"

"Lot of sperm. Tasty, too."

"Oh? You like the taste?"

"Love it."

"I thought I was the only woman who got off on eating semen."

"Oh, Lord. I've always loved eating it. I had a boyfriend once, he was a red head, and he tasted like…"

They devolved into a conversation about semen and taste and jerk off methods.

I sagged inside in relief. I wasn't in trouble. At least I didn't think so. Until that night.

"So you got your jollies with another woman."

"I'm sorry!"

I was eating a salad. She was eating a big, juicy hamburger. I could smell it, my mouth was watering, my stomach hurt, then she surprised me.

I said, "I didn't mean to, it's just that…Belinda had a hold of me, and I…I thought you said it was all right?"

"What I say and what I say are two different things," she murmured, staring at me over her delicious hamburger.

"So you don't want her jacking me off again?"

"Oh, I don't care. Especially considering what we're trying to do, and considering the sacrifices you're making. But I would prefer it if you could save it for me. I get hungry, too, you know."

"Oh. Well. I'll try."

We were silent for a second. Then: "Speaking of hungry, is there a chance I could get a bite of that hamburger?"

She grinned. "Mmmm, this is the best burger I ever ate. So juicy. dripping with delicious fat, and the onions are cooked to perfection. Mmm."

She continued to goad me until I felt like crying.

The chastity belt arrived, and it was no lightweight thing. It was stainless steel, fit all the way around, a tube for my cock. My butt exposed just enough for the bathroom. None of those plastic, little tube thingies.

Dorey loved it. It was a tight fit, she had to help me, and we bent and tugged, but when it was on it was snug, and there was no way I was going to get erect. Heck, my front was smoother than a baby's butt.

Dorey inspected me. She ran her hand over the front and smiled.

And, man, did that do something to me. I knew her hand was feeling me, but I couldn't feel a thing. But the idea was there and my cock wanted to get hard.

No chance.

"Oh, this is cute," she grinned and kissed me. I felt my dick trying to surge, but getting nowhere.

"Honey, I don't know if I can handle this."

"Nonsense," she quipped. "If I can wear a tampon then you can wear this."

"Those have nothing to do with each other!"

"There's a similarity of frustration. If you'd ever had a period you'd know."

"No thanks."

I was grumpy all day at work. To make it worse, both Dorey and Belinda took to knocking on my front plate. Rap rap, and I could feel the vibrations inside. My poor cock was so frustrated.

And, to make things even worse, wearing the chastity device made it hard to bend and contort enough to slip into female garments. The panties were easy, and they covered the device. But when I tried to bend over for stockings I had trouble.

"Don't worry about it," observed Belinda. "You don't need to put stockings on much. Once on they're on you only need to worry about dresses."

"And corsets."

"Well, yeah."

So there I was, no more dick showing, and into a new stage of practicing changing clothes.

"Time!...Time!"

"Time!...Time!"

I was getting better, in spite of the chastity device. And I have to admit, the smooth front did make a big difference.

The trouble started a few days after I put on the chastity device. The procedure for the next few days was I put it on in the morning, went to work, and then took it off at night. Dorey checked me, made sure I didn't break out in rashes or start to smell.

All was good.

So we came how from work and I went to take it off and... "Honey? Where's the key?" I was in the bedroom and she was in the kitchen.

"What key?"

As if she didn't know.

"The key to the chastity device."

"Oh, just leave it on," she called to me.

I was into the kitchen like a shot. "What? Wait! What?"

She had just finished mixing me a big drink. Coke and bourbon. My fave. She handed it to me. "Just leave it on. For a few days. I want to make sure you'll be all right over the long term."

"What do you mean...'long term?'

"You know. When I go to the hospital. I won't be there to help you put it on and take it off."

"I can figure it out by myself."

"No. You can't."

I stared at her.

"Now take a big sip."

I took a big sip. Real big. Half the damned glass in one gulp. Burned all the way down.

"Now sit down, dear, and let me explain things to you."

I sat. She had the bottle of bourbon and and a bottle of Coke to keep me refilled.

She down opposite me and smiled.

"How many times has Belinda had to handle you?"

"Uh..."

"How many?"

"Three times."

"Three times in another woman's hands. Three times squirting your seed without me. How do you think that makes me feel?"

"But…you said…"

"And it doesn't bother me. Now."

"Now?"

"Now that we don't have to worry about you needing relief."

"But I need relief! It's been a couple of days since I got off. And…" Blah, blah, blah. I blathered. She smiled sweetly and listened.

When I finally ran down she said, "Are you done?"

"Well…uh…"

"Because I'm tired of listening to you whine and complain. If I had known you would be so whiny I would have married a woman."

My jaw officially dropped. "But…but you're making me into a woman!"

"And maybe when you get there, maybe when you can convince me that you can present yourself as a woman with no mess ups…then maybe I'll unlock you and let you have a little fun."

"But…but…"

She held up her hand. "I have spoken. So let it be written." She mocked the old Moses movie.

"But, honey…"

"And, now that we are on the subject…I want you to be dressed as a woman all the time. Including nightgowns. Including curlers. Cold cream. Immaculate nails. Everything."

"But we're not at work!" But I was getting weaker. I was losing, and I knew it. I tell ya, when a woman holds the key to a man's cock she controls the man. Totally.

"Tut tut. Practice makes perfect. Now, if you want extra croutons on your salad you'd better get cleaned up, wear your underwear and put on a dress, that yellow one would be nice. And don't forget the garters and high heels."

I stared at her. She handed me a fresh drink. "Take. Drink. Come back when you need another one."

Defeated, I turned and walked back into the bedroom. I trudged. And, I swear, I thought I heard her chuckle.

At three months she was starting to feel her belly. And I knew she was going to 'retire' soon. Fortunately, I was ready. Hornier than a brass band, but ready.

I could put my make up on on the fly. Which she made me do. She let me wear Mary Janes to work and put my make up on in the car. While driving. Dangerous, but I did it. And I did it easy.

Then we tried my first show. Mrs. Jenkins came by. She's a bit nearsighted, but whether she could see or not, I was perfect. Of course, it helped that she liked loose clothes. But, still…

"Okay, got some video here. Let's take a look."

"Video?"

"I took a video of your show with Mrs. Jenkins. Belinda, come have a seat. Oh, order some dinner first. Salad for Jason."

Belinda ordered, and she smirked when she ordered me a salad.

Damn it. She was overweight and had to watch what she ate, and it looked like she was getting a perverse delight out of making me follow in her footsteps.

A half hour the food arrived and we ate, and Dorey hooked up the video to the big screen in our office and we watched.

There I was. Long hair, twirling, sashaying, moving my hips as I had been taught.

"Oh, no. Look!"

"What?"

"The way you tossed your hair. You did it like a surfer on drugs. Here, do it like this." Dorey showed me.

I followed her lead, and tossed my hair until my motion was pure girl.

Back to the video.

"Oh, no, you entered the room like a teenager on a skateboard! Don't slide…glide. Watch."

I was treated to a show of how to enter the room so I didn't look like a skateboarder. And I duplicated and practiced.

Back to the video.

"Oh, no! Don't hold your hand like that! Be gentle! Don't rely on strength, rely on grace!"

And…practice, practice, practice.

We drove home late and I was a subdued cookie.

"Don't worry, honey. You did well. We're just polishing the fine points."

"I feel like I totally screwed up."

"Not totally." She laughed.

"Har de har," I mumbled. Then: "Honey, could I get out of the chastity for a while?"

"Why? Whatever for?"

She sounded honestly mystified.

"I haven't squirted for a couple of weeks. I need relief."

"Oh, but honey. I like you this way!"

"What way?" Now I was honestly mystified.

"Helping me around the house. It takes such a load off me when you help with the dishes and vacuuming and everything.

"But…that's…that's not my job!"

"You're my house partner. If I'm your housewife…aren't you my house hubby?"

"Well, yeah, but I'm your business partner!"

"We go half and half at business, why not at home?"

That one sort of stopped me. There was logic there, but I was a man. At least I used to be a man. I needed to do man things!

"Okay, but I need to get my rocks off."

"Oh, nonsense."

I stared at her.

She was at a stoplight, a long one, and she said, "I've noticed that the more you do without sex the better behaved you are."

"Behaved? What does that mean?"

"It means you're more polite, more willing to help out around the house, and…you've got more energy."

"Of course I do, and I need to get rid of some of that energy."

"Now why," she mused, "Would I go back to the way things were? Oh, you weren't bad, but you could be better. People can always be better."

"But you can't hold my dick hostage!"

"Oh, but I can. I've got the key in a safe deposit box," my jaw dropped at her words, "and I'm sure you see the dangers in trying to cut your chastity belt off."

I did. There was no way snips could get between the metal and my skin, and the lock was built in.

"But…but I need to clean it!"

"I'll take care of that."

"What? How?"

"I bought some handcuffs and rope. We'll simply tie you to bed, I can clean your device, maybe play with you a little, and then put it back on. Cleanie weenie."

She sounded so happy talking. I couldn't believe it.

"I want a divorce!" Of course I didn't. But I had to say something. I had to shock the key from her.

"Oh, so sorry. You can pack your clothes when we get home."

"But…I need the key."

"Oh, no. I bought, it belongs to me."

"But you can't do this to me!"

She smiled. She came to another light and stopped. She turned to me. "If you're a good boy, keep the house clean and don't let anybody know you're a man, I'll let you have a cum after the baby is born."

"But…but…but…" I sounded like a motorboat. And she actually giggled.

I turned into myself the next few weeks.

Oh, when we had shows I showed a smile. I am a professional, after all. A professional model…and a professional woman.

But inside I felt like a cake that had been dropped and stepped on.

And I was getting hornier and hornier.

Belinda didn't help. She had a short talk with Dorey, in which she was apprised that my cock was off limits, and why.

Belinda took it with a grin, and began teasing me mercilessly. She patted my front shield. She tweaked my nipples. She cupped my buns.

"You're looking good, girlie," she once whispered to me.

And my only defense was to get hornier. More embarrassed. More desperate.

Dorey's baby bump became more pronounced, and I was working harder than ever.

She was tired a lot, and needed to rest. And I had lots of energy. I had a dickful of energy.

I think back to those times, sometimes, and I realize that if it hadn't been for the chastity device I wouldn't have made it. I would have collapsed.

But all that dick energy surging through me, being so horny I didn't sleep as much, I worked harder and harder.

I took over almost all the household chores. I did all the paperwork into the night. I stepped and twirled and presented dresses to rich people all day long.

In fact, I hate to admit it, but business actually got better.

Look, Dorey is beautiful. I was beautiful, but I could never be as beautiful as Dorey.

But I had something else. There was something about me that intrigued customers.

I can't tell you how many times these people, well to do, successful, came up to me and engaged me in chit chat, and stared at me like…'what's my secret?'

I was a woman, but they knew different. But they didn't really know. So they were fascinated. People began coming to the store more and more, and I reached the point where I was going to have to hire another model. No matter how much energy I had…I couldn't keep up with the franticness of the boom.

Dorey was big now. Real big. And getting bigger. But she still had a month to go.

Big or not, she began interviewing models, and she hired a knock out.

Lissome, big breasted, knew how to walk and talk and everything.

Now I had a true professional to work with, and she helped me, gave me hints and tips, and never made a pass at me.

Of course. To her I was a woman. She had never known me as a man. I would find out later, much later, that Dorey had hired her because she didn't like Lesbians. That should have told me something, but didn't. Of course, I was too busy to think now.

My horniness reached a new high. Dressing sexy, feeling the clothes go on and off. And touching Heidi (the new girl), just in passing, but it was still touching, I began to feel like every part of my body was a dick, a giant turn on.

Belinda would slip a dress over me for alterations, and I would instantly get a charge, a sexual charge, and my dick would struggle in its tube.

Heidi would brush my hair, or help me with my nails, and…boing! Except there was no 'boing.' There was only the electricity running through my body, and frustration.

One day, I was working late. Belinda was there, working on alterations. Dorey waddled in and sank onto the office couch.

"How you doing, dear?"

"Oh, I'm…I'm…" I began to cry. I just put my head down on the desk and began to sob.

"Belinda? A little help?"

Belinda came into the office and looked at me. "What happened?"

"Poor dear. He's having a break down."

I cried for a while. Belinda rubbed my shoulders. Dorey managed to get up and pour me a drink, and I slowly calmed down.

"I'm sorry," I muttered.

"No, dear. It's us who are sorry. We should have known we were driving you too hard."

I saw my opening. "It's…I need some sex to relieve myself."

Maybe if I had been alone with Dorey I could have pulled it off. I mean, my crying jag was real, and she did know what I was going through. But Belinda was there.

"I can handle that," she chirped.

We both looked at her.

"Oh, I don't mean fuck him. Can you imagine fucking Jason? Ha!"

I was hurt by that, but the situation was going to get worse.

"No, what I mean is I can relieve his sexual tension, and without sacrificing my sacred pleasure palace."

Dorey giggled at that. "Sacred pleasure palace?"

Belinda grinned at her. “Sure. We simply use his pussy.”

“What? I don’t have a pussy!”

“Of course you do. A man pussy. It’s right between your buns.”

“My…my asshole? What!”

She turned to Dorey. “I’ll use a strap on. Grease him up. No need for kissing or any of that stuff. They have these special dildos called ‘prostate massagers,’ it will rub his button, his prostate, and he’ll shoot his juice.”

“No!”

Dorey looked at Belinda. She looked at me. She looked at Belinda.

“Yes.”

“No!”

Dorey narrowed her gaze at me. “I want you to do this. I can’t have you having a break down while you’re modeling our clothes.”

“But I don’t want anybody putting anything up my ass!”

“I’ve put a finger there before. You liked that.”

“A dick, or this so called ‘prostate massager’ is a different matter.”

Dorey turned to Bel. “Will it hurt?”

“Nah. It’ll feel good. I’ve popped a lot of cherries, and they always love it. Heck, he’ll want anal sex more than he wants regular sex after I’ve done him a few times.”

Dorey smiled. She turned to me. “It’s settled.”

Well, it wasn’t settled, but eventually it would be. For starters, Dorey wouldn’t let up on me. Everything from buying me chocolates (God, I was starving, and the chocolates…the chocolates…oh, my God!) to slapping me with a belt when I walked by her.

Then I had a second breakdown, and this one was worse. I had just finished a long day. I had changed and changed and changed. People didn’t buy things. Heidi was grumpy. Belinda was in a hurry. I started to sniffle.

Heidi and Belinda looked at me.

And I was bawling.

I was exhausted. I was a fuse that had sputtered to a stop. Even all the sexual energy that I had been accumulating seemed to back up on me.

Heidi reached me first. She put her arm around me and hugged me.

Belinda reached me and soothed me.

Dorey was at home resting.

Heidi said, “There, there. You just need a good orgasm.”

My head jerked up. My eyes opened. Over her shoulder Belinda smiled.

And I broke.

I calmed down, Belinda called Dorey to let her know the good news, and Heidi went home.

I was alone with Belinda in the office. Belinda didn’t even get undressed, she just took a strap on out of a cupboard—“I knew you were close,” she said—and strapped it on. She adjusted the prostate massager into the harness and smiled at me.

“Time to get undressed, slick.”

I was wearing the full get up. I had modeled late, and I was wearing a sexy dress, kinky underwear, and my make up was flawless.

“I…”

“No. Not all the way. Just take your panties down and lift your dress. Bend over the couch.”

So I did.

I lay there and waited.

Belinda moved between my legs and rubbed lubricant into my button. My cock was screaming inside its cage. *This is wrong! This is wrong!*

But I lay there and…it felt sort of good. The lubricant was cool, and her fingers were gentle.

“The trick is to be relaxed. To just let it happen.”

“Okay.” My voice was muffled by a pillow.

Belinda hummed, she pushed lube into me, a lot of lube. “I love doing this, you know.”

“I didn’t.”

“Oh, yes. When you fuck a man it changes him. He becomes more docile. Less of a man, more of a human being.”

“Not a woman?”

“Oh, there’s that. You’ll gain a profound appreciation for sex from the woman’s viewpoint, but…it’s more than that.”

“Oh.”

"You'll find out."

She stepped up and began rubbing my hole with her dildo.

Oddly, it felt good. There was no pressure, and it was a sexy tickle. Made me squirm.

"That's it. Now, remember, relax. Don't fight. Fighting makes pain. Relaxing makes pleasure."

"And that's all there is to it," I asked.

"That's all she wrote," agreed Belinda.

She took her time, a long time, and gently rubbed my buns and my thighs. She stopped every once in a while and patted my ass.

Slowly, slowly, she began to penetrate me. Just a push here, a nudge there, and she began to enter me.

There were moments of pain, but they were quick, and Bel backed off quickly and let me get acclimated.

And, after a half hour of wonder, she said, "I'm all the way in."

I lay there, marveling. My asshole felt…good. It felt alive, and I could feel blood pulsing, and, suddenly, I felt a trickle of sensation. I wiggled.

"Yeah, baby. Let it happen."

I moved, and that's what she was waiting for. She withdrew a couple of inches and my eyes widened.

"Sometimes it's not the push, but the pull. Depends on the guy, of course. Assholes are different."

I wiggled my butt, actually tried to get more sensation.

"Yeah, go for it. Fuck me back."

I couldn't help it. It felt so good, I pushed my butt back and she gripped my hips and wiggled. God, it felt like my insides were being stirred.

"Fuck," I whispered.

"Yep," she chortled. "I love this part."

But I could hardly hear her now. I was becoming enraptured by the sexual electricity stretching my asshole.

I moved back, I wiggled, I pulled forward.

She matched me, harmonized with me, then would give a twitch of her own.

I began to gulp and gasp as she opened me up. The pleasure…the pleasure…I didn't know it could be like this.

After a couple of minutes of feeling my ass slowly go out of control, she said, "It's going to feel like you're peeing. Let it happen."

I was really relaxing now, getting sort of goofy and loose and everything, and, sure enough, it felt like I had to pee.

"Oh," I mumbled.

"That's it, baby. Let it go."

Let it go. I could feel it draining out of my cock slit. But it didn't really feel like pee. It felt thicker, almost clumpy.

Finally, Belinda slapped my ass and withdrew. "There you go, sport."

I lay there for a minute, feeling nice and golden and everything.

Belinda took off the strap on, then came around and stood in front of me. She was holding a little glass, the bottom filled with white…with… my semen?

"Is that…is that me?"

"Yep. Bottoms up." She tilted the glass and drained it. She lowered it and smacked her lips. She glanced at me and laughed. "Sorry, I don't share. Not when it comes to sperm."

She walked out then, left me laying, butt up, on the office sofa. Slowly, I recovered. I got up and used toilet paper to wipe up lube from my ass. I pulled my panties up and let my dress down. I went home.

And I felt too good. Sort of golden, sort of satisfied. It was almost like after an orgasm. But I hadn't had an orgasm. At least, not one that I felt.

The weird thing, however, was that the next day, though my cock wasn't even wiggling in its trap, I felt unbelievably horny.

Well, of course. I had been drained, but my mind didn't know it. My mind thought I still had a full load.

And, the good news, I was relieved. The tensions lessened, the horniness grew, and my emotional break downs stopped. Completely.

A week later Dorey June was born. A beautiful baby girl with Dorey's eyes and my hair. She was beautiful. A delight. A satisfaction of the soul that I had never even imagined could exist.

I was able to be in the operating room, and saw the whole thing, and the miracle unfolded and engulfed me.

I went out of the delivery room for a quick pee break, and Belinda and Heidi were there. They hugged me, and we all cried. Good tears. Great tears.

And, two days later they let Dorey go home.

We stood in the room we had prepared for her and gazed down at our little wonder.

Our arms were around each other.

After a long while we tip toed out to let her sleep.

We adjourned to the kitchen where Dorey had me fix myself a drink.

We sat and looked at each other.

"How's it going?" she asked with a beautiful, tired smile.

"Never better."

"And how's Mr. Happy?"

"Unhappy," I grinned. "Ready to get out."

"Yeah, about that."

"What?" Suddenly I had a sense of foreboding.

"I've grown used to you as a woman."

I blinked.

"I like you better as a woman. And I like that it is so easy to please you. Belinda told me how much you came for her."

"But I didn't have an orgasm!"

"Do you really need one?"

"Well, yeah!"

She smiled and ignored my outburst. "My plan is this: we milk you, and get some artificial insemination. We can milk you regularly. And you stay a woman. I think it would be much healthier for Dorey June to grow up in a household that has nobody but women in it. What do you think?"

I didn't think. I just stared, and knew that I had lost.

Yet…had I?

My life was happier, I was no longer driven by male urges, and I was quite happy to be with women in a non-sexual condition. They were so much more gentle than men, and I liked looking sexy. And I even liked cleaning the house.

"So I would never get to cum again?"

"Why would you want to?"
I sat back and sipped my drink.
She watched me.
And I said the only thing I could.
"Wow."

END

Full Length Books from Gropper Press

Jim Camden was a manly man, until the day he crossed his wife. Now he's in for a battle of the sexes, and if he loses...he has to dress like a woman for a week. But what he doesn't know is the depths of manipulation his wife will go to. Lois Camden, you see, is a woman about to break free, and if she has to step on her husband to do it...so be it. And Jim is about to learn that a woman unleashed is a man consumed.

The Feminization Games

Being a Woman!

A role remakes an actor

Published on Kindle,
appeared in 'The Shivering Bone.'

PART ONE

"Honey, I got you the perfect job. It pays well, no heavy lifting, and…well, you're going to love it."

"Really?" I looked at Stella with interest. I had been out of work for four months, it was getting harder and harder to pay our rent, and I needed something.

I mean, Stella had a fun job, had her own catering business, but it wasn't steady.

But I had worked in the movie business and somebody said I was a Republican. Which I'm not. I vote for the issue, not the politician, and especially not the party.

But in the 'Woke' movie business that was it for me.

Heck, I was right on the edge of success, had been tapped for a supporting role in a sit com, and we had shot a half a dozen episodes and it looked like I was stealing the scenes. Success, baby, then…failure.

But that's Hollywood.

I mean, I'm good looking, a studly stud type, but there are a lot of studly stud types, and, well, that was it for me.

"What kind of job? I mean, who would hire me?"

"I met n old friend, we talked, she knows you and loves you, and she shoots films."

"Really? I can be an actor?"

"Absolutely."

I felt it then, the little grey area behind the answer. The evasion. The, 'oh, he doesn't need to know about that.'

"Okay, drop the other shoe."

"What other shoe?" Good, she was good. But I'm an actor. I can tell when somebody is playing the part.

"The shoe that you know something that you're not yelling me."

"Oh, that shoe!" She grinned.

I nodded.

"Okay, maybe there is something. Make me a spritzer and I'll tell you, outside. On the patio."

"You can't tell me now?"

"I've got a quick something to do in the bedroom."

I leered, "Yeah. Me, too."

We were in the kitchen. I was in a bathrobe and she was in work out garb. I reached for her.

Man, Stella is better looking than any actress I've ever seen. Better boobs, flawless face, make up and hair and all that, and…she just turns me on.

But I guess that's the way a good marriage should be.

"Ease up, Rick," she laughed and pushed my chest. "I just need to take a quick shower. Now make me a drink, and make yourself one. It's party time, you know?"

She trotted through the house, we live in a small bungalow in Hollywood Hills, and I turned to the duty of mixology.

I had worked as a bartender, and I put together her wine spritzer quick snap. Then I made myself a delicious bourbon and Coke. I know, it was early in the morning. But I had a job! At last! And it was going to be a good one!

I sat on the patio and sipped my bourbon. Stella took a while and I enjoyed the vines and flowers creeping through the wood trellis. Through a 'window' in the shrubbery I could see a valley filled with square houses and people with small dreams.

I had big dreams. I was better looking than Brad Pitt at his best, and I wanted to cash in. I wanted to be an actor, a twenty foot tall man on a silver screen that people had to bend their heads back to see.

Yeah, baby.

I caught a glimpse of Stella passing the picture window.

"Hey! I got your drink out here!"

"I know," she yelled back. "I'll be right there."

A minute later she stepped through the sliding doors and my heart stopped. She had cleaned up all right. She had scrubbed herself rosy, then put on a thong and bra. Her breasts overflowed the shelf and her face was perfectly made up. She had smokey grey eyes, sparkling with glints and secrets. Her lips were full and red and ripe. Like ripe for kissing.

"Oh, baby," I started to stand up, pushing the wrought iron chair back with a scraping sound.

"Not yet, lover," she avoided me with a twist and a sidestep. I had a full view of her charms through the see through peignoir.

She placed another Coke and bourbon in front of me.

"Wow! We really are celebrating."

I sat back in my chair. She pulled hers around so we were closer. She sat down and placed her feet in my lap, and she looked at me.

Looked at me with those bedroom eyes. BOING!

"Rub my tootsies while I tell you about this dream job."

Her feet were resting on my hard cock, and she knew it, and had that knowing, smirky smile. I'm so easy.

I put my hands around her feet and began rubbing. The red toe nails turned me on. But, then, everything about Stella turns me on. I pulled her toes and squeezed her feet, and she sat back and sipped and sighed.

"Okay," I said.

"Okay. The job. I ran into an old friend, you remember Becky?"

I blinked. "Now there's a blast from the past."

Becky had had a thing for me, but I had refused, I had met Stella, which didn't go over big with Becky. She's a babe, but a hard charger. She didn't like it when people said no to her.

"Yeah, you remember she was a little miffed with me? Me going with you?"

"Oh, that's old history. Anyway, Becky has a production company."

"Really?"

"Really. She got involved with a guy, he wanted to retire and go live in Costa Rica, and she took over the business."

"Wow."

"Now, they do ads. Lots of ads."

"That can be good work. That can open the door to an acting gig."

"No, hon, I told you, it is an acting gig. They're doing well and they're branching out. They're going to do a string of shorts for a Youtube channel, and when she described what she needed I suggested you. She didn't even blink. She said, and I quote, 'That hunk is just what we need.'

"See, it's about the business, no personalities. She wants you, the actor."

"Man, this sounds better and better. What's the name of the Youtube channel?"

"Chimera."

I put her feet down and put my own feet on the ground. "That's a gay channel."

"Not any more," she fired back. "The ads are straight."

"And this string of shorts…what's it about?"

"It's about, uh…" and she said something quickly.

"What? Did you really do that?"

I was referring to Ash in one of those Evil Dead movies. He has to say the name of a mystical book or something and he has to say the word perfectly. He can't remember it and he flubs it so he pretends he's coughing to obscure the fact that…well, you get the idea.

"No, look, it's legit. And you'll be acting again."

I stared at her. "And what is this string of shorts? What are they going to have me do?"

"Well, uh," her voice lowered again. "Crossdressing."

I blinked. I opened my mouth and started to speak, then stopped myself. My midwest values weren't going to mess with my opportunity.

"I can do that."

"You can?" she almost squealed in excitement.

"Hey. I'm an actor. I wear funky clothes and make up. I shave my body in all the weird places…I can do a little cross dressing."

"Oh, baby!"

She launched herself out of her chair and onto my lap. She placed her hands on the sides of my face and began kissing me.

I laughed. "Hey, were you really worried?"

"Well, I know you're sort of a homophobe…"

"I'm not. I know gay guys, and cross dressing isn't gay, anyway. I know lots of people that crossdress."

"Really?" She looked at me.

"Really. In fact, you know Josh?"

Her eyes opened. "He's a crossdresser?"

"Tried and true."

"But he never says anything!"

"Why should he?"

She kissed me some more, and she worked her hands between the folds of my robe and I gasped.

"Ooh, Mr. Happy is happy."

"Mr. Happy is ecstatic," I grunted as she worked her hands over me.

She stood up, and she lifted my balls.

"Oh!" I blurted, standing up quickly.

"You're going to be the best crossdresser in the world," she murmured, stroking me and clasping one bun with the other hand and kissing the hell out of my mouth.

Then she moved back a bit, but, fortunately, did not relinquish her hold on my shaft. "I need to talk to Josh."

"What for?"

"I'm going to help you prepare. I want to ask him questions."

"Oh." This was new. Usually Stella would help me read scenes, but this was a whole new level of involvement. She sounded so happy and excited.

"Well, I guess you could…"

"Oh, goodie! Is he on your cell?" sadly, she let go of me and ran into the house for my phone.

"Under 'J' for Josh."

I sat back down, picked up my drink, and smiled. A job. Work. In front of the cameras. And so what if it was with Becky. If she really had gotten over our parting…heck, we had had good times together, before I met Stella. Hopefully she was just remembering the good times.

I heard Stella talking, presumably to Josh. Josh was a great guy, and you could have knocked me over with a feather when I found out he was a transvestite. But I was younger then, and since then I had found out how sordid Hollywood could be. Heck, a crossdresser was mild in these climes.

I finished my drink, wandered back into the house, and Stella was still on the phone. She was talking seriously, in a low voice, and looked almost like she was an interrogator. But she was happy. Real happy. And I was glad. These last few months had been rough.

Finally, an hour later, she put down the phone and came into the TV room. I was watching an old fifties noir. 'The Maltese Falcon.' 'I love you, baby, but I'm not going to be the sap for you.' Ah, Bogey was my man.

"Okay, I have it all figured out."

"All what?"

"We need to train you."

"Train me?" I sat up.

"Crossdressers don't just throw on a dress, they study the movements, they learn about their character, right? You know what I'm talking about?"

"Of course I do. That's what actors do."

"Excellent. So let's get started now."

I grabbed her and pulled her down to the couch. I kissed her delicious mouth and ran my hand down to her crotch.

"Ah ah. No." She pushed away.

"Hey! I thought we were going to celebrate?"

"And we will. We will have the biggest and best celebration in the history of Tinsel Town, but first we have to prepare you."

"I'm prepared!"

"Honey, these last few months…they haven't been kind to us. Now I need you to do what I say. I need you to take direction, and I'm going to help you. There is no way you're going to lose this job."

That was a low blow, but, I guess I deserved it. After all, if I hadn't said I was okay with Republicans then…then maybe I'd still be in that series, raking in the big bucks.

"Okay, Ms DeMille, I'm ready for my close up," I mocked Gloria Swanson in Sunset Boulevard.

She giggled, then she grew serious. "And there's one thing."

"What?"

"And it's a big thing."

"So tell me."

"You're not going to want to do it."

"How about telling me and letting me make up my own mind?"

She paused, then said, "Josh says the reason people cross dress is to get horny. He says he can always recognize a transvestite by the horny gleam in their eyes. You're going to need that gleam."

I laughed. "Is that all? Hell. I can put that gleam in my eye easy," and I reached for her.

She came, she smooched me, she stroked me, then she backed off. "Uh…"

I sighed. "Okay, make your point."

"You need to be horny."

"I am horny."

"For when you're on set. You need to be so horny we have to tie your dick down."

"I'll wear a gaff," I laughed, then I started to get it. "Wait a minute," I looked at her suspiciously.

"You have to be horny." A mix of request, and demand, and shyness, and…

"Are you saying…we're not going to…"

"Not until you've got the part locked down."

"But…we're married!"

"I married a crossdresser, and he gets off on being excited with his little, dirty secret."

"Wait a minute."

Then she was kissing me. "Rick, please. For me. Do this for me." She kissed me, she pulled my nipples, she lowered her head to my lap and began sucking me.

"Oh," I said. "Oh…"

She jerked her head up. "Oh, I shouldn't be doing this! You can't cum!"

"Baby, I need to! One last time before…before…"

I begged and pleaded. I wheedled and whined. And finally, she gave in. Sort of.

"Okay, I'll tell you what. I'm going to edge you to…one drop."

"What?"

"Then you'll be horny…and yet you'll have cum."

"I don't…"

"Rick? For me!"

The way she begged me, and held my cock. The way she pleaded, and stroked me. The way she…you get the idea.

"Okay," I finally gave in. One drop, the idea was intriguing, and the way she had been kissing me, and playing with me this morning, I was getting a little desperate Even one drop sounded good. "But it better be a big drop."

She giggled. She held up her thumb and forefinger, close together. "It's going to be so teeny tiny."

"Hey, come on!" But I was laughing, and we were having fun.

"If I let you in me…will you promise not to cum? Until I can jack you to a drop?"

"Uh…I guess so."

"Oh, goodie. Because this is making me so hot…I need to cum."

"Now just one minute!"

"You said…you promised…one drop!" Then she was hugging me, stroking me yet again. "Oh, Rick, this is going to be so good. I just know you're on the edge of stardom."

A bit role in a crossdressing show on Youtube. Right. But it was a start, and no actor turns down a role in the beginning. No actor.

Foreplay over, sort of, she pulled me by the cock, that seemed to be her favorite handle, and led me to the bedroom.

"Oh, this is going to be fun," Stella said, depositing me on the bed. Then she went to her closet.

"Hey? Where you going?"

She looked out, leered at me, then dove back in.

Puzzled, I sat back and just sort of enjoyed the throbbing in my dick. So I was going to be horny for. awhile. Hopefully not too long a while. But that was okay. I have to admit, there is something delicious about being horny. About being a little out of your mind with desire. About always being hard and, if I got too horny, dripping.

I was smiling when she came out of the closet.

"What's so funny?"

"Oh, this whole thing. I'm going to have to wear a dress. Kinky. You know?"

"Josh likes it. Maybe you will, too. Here." She tossed a bundle at me.

"What's…oh, no!"

"What?"

I held up a slip and a bra. “Not now!”

“If not now…when?”

“Honey…”

She sat next to me and took my penis in her hand again.

“Honey, yourself. This is making me horny. And if I’m horny…”

“If you’re horny you get off…and I don’t.”

“Oh, come on. You like being horny. You’ve told me so.”

“Yeah, but…but this is weird.”

“Hey, it’s acting. It’s what you do. Now put your legs up here.”

She didn’t bother taking off the bathrobe off me, just slid the slip up my legs. She pulled me off the bed and adjusted it, then she took the bathrobe off. “Now this.”

I grinned as she fastened the bra on me. “Looks a little loose in the cup department.”

“I can fix that.” She went back into the closet.

I looked at myself in the mirror. I had a slender runner’s body. Nothing in the chest. Nothing in the butt. I knew they could pad me and all that, but…staring at myself, I could actually see the potential. Arrange the lights just right, I had long enough hair, or they could wig me…it could work.

“Here,” Stella came out of the closet. She was holding two breast forms.

“Where the heck…”

“Remember Barbara? Had the mastectomy?”

“Oh.”

“Yeah. We had a lot of talks, a lot of tears, but when she had her reconstruction she came over and gave these to me. They were sort of a weird thank you for standing by her. She said, and I quote, ‘I hope you never use these,’ end quote.”

I hefted the two globes. They were perfectly shaped boobs. Even had nipples that stood up.

“Heysoos,” I muttered.

“Here,” she took one and slid it into a cup, then the other one.

I looked in the mirror, and damned, that made a huge difference. I didn’t have curves down below, but the curves on the chest were magnificent.

"She was a hefty woman," I observed.

"And now so are you. We'll take these with you when we go to work."

I looked at her. "You're coming to the shoot?"

"I've got a couple of days off, and I could have Danny run the business if I need more. Believe me, lover," she pinched one of my boobs, "I wouldn't miss this for the world."

I stared at the mirror, then I turned to her.

"Ooh, somebody likes a little kinky underwear," she grabbed my cock yet again.

"I was hard from earlier."

"Yeah, right," she laughed. "I know you. You're a horn dog. Doesn't take anything to get you going."

"Speaking of which," I kissed her, "You owe me something."

"Ha," she said, and she pushed me back on the bed.

I scooted around and laid there, my boner tenting my slip, my new tits thrusting upwards.

Stella was grinning so hard I thought her mouth would bust. She climbed over and sat on me. She slid right over, which was a testament to her wetness.

"Oh, yeah," she wiggled and settled, then she leaned forward and placed her hands on my chest. "Remember, no cum. And when I'm done I'll extract a drop from you."

"A single drop," I whispered, already feeling the need to romp and thrust. "Heysoos."

She worked me then, slipping and sliding and moaning, and she watched me with a hawk eye.

"Oh, God!" I said.

She got off me. Waited, slid back on.

"Oh…Oh!"

She got off me and frowned. "This isn't going to work. You're going to pop."

"So let me pop."

"Would you rather be a famous actor…or pop?"

"Right now you don't want to ask me that."

She laughed. She went to the side table and took out her vibrator.

"Hey! I thought you got rid of that! We agreed no more beating off!"

"You did," she quipped, climbing on me.

"We did."

"Okay. I cheated. But I needed to."

"Why?"

"Because, lover, I hate to break the news, but you're a little too quick on the trigger.

It was true. I was a premature ejaculator. I often shot my load, and then had to finish her off with my fingers. Or, when she was real insistent, my mouth.

So what's a little cum between meals, right?

"That's why I was jacking off," I responded.

She looked at me, ready to sink down on my shaft again. "I know, you were jacking off for me." She sounded so droll.

"Well, I was! I figured if I was empty before we screwed then I could last longer."

"But you didn't, so…" she slid down my shaft, heaven, wet, moist innards gripping me.

"Now, hold on. Try not to do anything," she was breathless as she fitted the vibrator down to her pussy."

"Heysoos," I said, wanting to cum, but absolutely fascinated by what she was doing.

HMMMMM! The vibrator started up and her eyes went big.

"You better hurry!"

She nodded, her eyes were glazed, then she began cumming.

"Uh…oh….yeah!" I felt her muscles contracting, and it was pushing me closer and closer to the edge.

"You'd better hurry!" I gritted my teeth.

Then she was done, and she popped off me. Her eyes were gleaming with victory. "God! That was hot! Fucking you and you…you just sat there like a dildo!"

"Yeah, it was great, honey." My turn to sound a wee bit droll.

She lay back for a moment, breathing hard, then she turned to me. "Okay, slick, let's get that drop out of you."

I grinned. "How do you expect me to stop at one drop? You know that once I start spewing…I spew."

"I've got a plan," she said. She moved around and sat on my face.

"Hey!" came out sort of garbled.

She lifted slightly. "Sorry, babe, but it's the best position."

She began tuning my fork then, stroking the shaft and licking the head. She spent a lot of time playing with my balls.

My balls were full, we hadn't done it for a week, and very sensitive. I groaned and jerked and she gave them a little slap.

"Fuck!" I yelped.

I felt it then. That slap to the balls did it. I felt the trigger click, and the semen started to boil.

"I'm going to go!" I shouted. In a way I didn't want to. I wanted to hold it back. One, for Stella, two because it was kinky, and three…I wanted to last, and undo my rep as a premature ejaculator.

But I couldn't hold it back. I felt the semen start to rise, then Stella grabbed the base of my cock and squeezed.

"Ow! Oh! What!"

I thrashed around and tried to dislodge her, but she had a death grip on me. The semen couldn't go up the tube, so…no orgasm.

And, when she got off me, I could see one, little drop half emerged from the slit of my cock.

"Oh…that wasn't…"

"I did it, lover, and that makes me hot all over again. God, what power I have!"

I felt robbed, cheated, and was even hornier. My dick was red. My balls were throbbing. But it was over.

One, little drop.

PART TWO

Stella awoke, and instantly was perky and excited. "Oh, boy! You're going to be a star!"

She had had a full night's sleep. An orgasm induced sleep that was deep and refreshing.

I hadn't slept much. I was too horny. I felt like my balls were steaming, and I had that electrical sexual tension keeping me wired. I groaned, "I feel like…tired."

"No time for tired! Come on!" And, once again, she grabbed me by the handle and pulled me out of bed.

Which woke me right up. My cock was hard, it wanted, I wanted, and her hand felt so good I started thrusting my hips into her fist.

"No, no. You naughty boy." She threw me into the shower.

"Oh, fuck," mumbled. Yet the steamy water helped me. I began to wake up. It was daylight, and I was the male hunter, conditioned to go out and slay beasts while the sun shined. Shone. Whatever.

"Use this!" Stella handed me a razor. "And shave everything."

Yawning, but coming alive, I twisted this way and that, contorted, and shaved everything. Face real good. Legs and chest, okay. I didn't have a lot of hair there anyway. Then the groin area.

Lord, it's scary working a blade right next to your best friend. But I did it, and I jumped out of the shower. "Ta da!"

Stella laughed. "You missed a spot!"

"Where?" I looked under my arms.

She took the razor and said, "Bend over."

"Oh, no. Not really!"

"I don't mean to be indelicate, but you have crack hairs. Very untidy, if you know what I mean.

I had never had anybody shave me that close before, but I bent, and held, and she quickly divested me of the real short and curlies.

"Okay, let's put a little of this on you," she slathered a bit of cream on my body.

"Hey! That smells."

"Smells good, too. You are going to be the best smelling transvestite in Hollywood."

"You realize this is just a role?"

"Oh, I know that. But it's fun. So let me have a little bit of fun with it. Okay? Mr. Grouch?"

"Okay," I gave in. After all, she was just helping me.

"Now then, let me work on your hair. I think we can do without a wig, but the final say will be up to them."

She sat me down at her make up table and bushed out my hair. Then she picked up a pair of scissors.

"Hey!"

"It's okay. I'll just tidy it up."

So I sat and she snipped here and there, and brushed, and snipped some more, and it was obvious that she wasn't taking it off, but simply 'arranging' it.

"Oh, yeah. This is going to be good. She fluffed my hair, then sprayed it with hair spray. I looked in the mirror and my jaw dropped.

She had given me a layered cut that curled around my face. It was very feminine, and suddenly I had a very much more feminized face. I was still male, but I was topped with female.

"Your outfit is on the bed. Put it on and I'll get your make up ready."

No slip now, but tight panties, and the bra with the forms. There was also a tummy shaper, open at the bottom and with garter straps, and nylons.

She arranged things on her make up table and turned to me. "Don't put the nylons on, yet. We have to paint your toes."

"Really?"

"Absolutely."

So I got dressed, and felt pretty well stuffed into a pencil skirt, and my tits looked huge, but real, in a translucent blouse. Then I sat on the edge of the bed and Stella painted my to nails.

"This is weird."

"This is bad. We need a professional mani/pedi for you. What have you been doing with these poor tootsies?"

Not much I could say to that.

After my toes were done she helped me unroll the nylons up my legs. Man, that felt sexy. I felt slithery, like a snake about to shed skin.

"Ooh. That's good looking!"

She led me over to the table and began doing her real magic. Clean, moisturize, eyes, lips. When she was done she led me over to the full length mirror.

I almost took my own breath away. I was slender, but stacked, and the face was feminine. I didn't look like a guy in drag…I looked like a woman.

"Wow."

"Uh oh," she said. "Houston, we've got a problem."

I looked down to where she was looking. I had a sizable bulge in my pencil skirt.

"Should have got me off last night," I gloated.

"Not a chance. Sit on the bed."

I sat on the bed, then she had me get on all fours, and she pulled my dick down and taped it to my thigh. Then she wrapped more tape around my leg, and I knew that this puppy was in for the duration. Mr. Happy was not happy.

"Try and stand up."

I backed off the bed and stood, and I was hunched and pooched over.

"Straighten your shoulders."

I did, and it helped, and I could feel my dick getting a bit of wiggle room. It wasn't standing up, but I was able to. But I was still pooched, and my butt stuck out a little.

"Oh, this is perfect," Stella clapped her hands.

I looked in the mirror. I now had an ass. Baby got back.

"Heysoos," I groaned. "This is…painful."

"Hey, sacrifice for your art, okay? Now, come on. Let's get your jewelry on and hit the road."

We drove downtown. Well, she drove. I was wearing heels and didn't trust my foot on the pedals.

To the Chimera building. Heck, I didn't even know Chimera had their own building. That was a good sign.

We walked into the building and there was no lobby to speak of. Just a guy with a clipboard.

"Hi, ladies," he chirped. "You here for the shoot?"

"Yep," Stella acknowledged, and she nudged me. Yes, the guy thought I was a woman. I reminded myself to speak in a high voice.

"Down the hall to the back steps. Up the steps and follow the signs."

Stella thanked him and we sauntered on down the hallway.

"How you doing?" Stella asked.

"I'm trying to stay upright, and thank goodness you let me wear the short heels."

"Don't get too happy. Becky will probably want real heels."

"Great."

We walked past a couple of racks of clothes and into a large room. Two cameras were being trundled into place and Becky was by a drinking fountain talking to a script writer.

"Hey!" She noticed us and walked over to us. She air kissed Stella, then checked me out and whistled. "Wow! I knew you'd be good for the part."

"Thanks."

"Now, you look good, but let's get make up over here and double do you. I've got a dress all picked out."

Shortly I was sitting in a folding chair and a girl named Shelley was fussing over me.

"Mm, yeah. Good job. But we need long eyelashes, and…your shave will probably last for a while. Do some Nair for tomorrow. Okay?"

I opened my mouth to agree and Stella cut in. "No problem."

Shelley did a few more things to my hair and make up, then repainted my lips, a deeper, shinier red, and smiled. "Okay. Let's see if you pass muster.

I did, and Becky explained the scene.

"I know you're a pro, and we're going to give you lines, maybe a lot, but today we just want to take some fillers. Shots of you walking, sitting. We want you to get used to the camera, and the camera to get used to you.

"Can I watch the dailies?"

"I don't mind, but all film gets sent to the production offices at five o'clock. So if you want to see them, you'll have to go there."

I frowned. That meant extra long day, driving after a long day under hot lights, and I didn't think—"

"Sure," said Stella. Man, she was really getting into this.

We began shooting.

We walked through the halls, through doorways. We walked up and down stairs. Then we took it outside. A small crowd gathered to watch as we shot our scenes.

Stella was right by my side. As soon as Becky yelled 'Cut' she was all over me.

"How you doing? Need water? You've got a smudge, where's Shelley?"

I smiled. I liked it. I was horny and being fussed over. I was the center of attention, and that is something every actor desires.

We ate lunch. It was a warm day, and the crew was fun, and then 'he' showed up.

"Hey! Tommy!" Everybody, including me, turned towards the door, and a big hunk entered.

Tommy James. He was almost as good looking as me, and a famous porn star.

When that six foot frame, bulging with muscles, unleashed the snake audiences cheered.

And, he was a nice guy!

Most people in Hollywood are nice. If they aren't they don't last long. Nobody wants to work with an asshole. But a lot of that is surface nice. Tommy was nice all the way through.

Tommy shook a few hands, waved to people, then he caught sight of me.

"Hey, Rick! I haven't seen you since…what was it…acting school?"

I got up and he hugged me.

God, it felt weird. He was a giant of a man, and I was a. slip of a girl, and when he hugged me he hugged me like he was hugging a girl.

"I'm glad you got the part, man. You always were the pro. This your wife?"

I introduced Tommy to Stella. Stella shook his hand. No hug for her, and I wondered why?

But she was looking at him with a slight tilt to her head. Hunh?

"Okay, people, time to shoot the meeting!"

The meeting. Tommy and I bump into each other. I fall down and he catches me, and we…meet.

So we walked through the scene a couple of times, Tommy and I talked, and he said, "Can I bump you hard enough to make you fall? Make it look real?"

"Sure. Just make sure you catch me."

He laughed, showing white teeth. "No problemo. I been working out." He flexed and we laughed.

"Action!"

I came down some steps, Tommy came through a door, bump, and I fell on my ass. My legs were up, he had missed the catch.

"Jeez! I'm sorry, man. I didn't expect you to fall so quick."

"It's the high heels," I explained, rubbing my ass. Thank goodness I had a tiny bit of padding on my rump.

"Okay! Let's do it again!"

Down the steps, Tommy through the door, bump! And it went perfect. I fell almost down, and then he had me, his big arm around my waist, and his face was close to mine. We stared at each other, and the cameraman zoomed in for the close up.

I stared at him, I felt his strength, and I felt…weak. I was a man, but…I suddenly felt weak and fragile. I wanted to move back, assert myself, but the scene didn't call for it. It called for me to just look at Tommy in the eyes and…look.

He said, "Baby!"

And that was it.

"Perfect. Let's shoot it again."

That's the thing about Hollywood. They always say perfect, then they take the shot again. And again and again. Well, if it was perfect, why do you have to do it again?

But I knew. They would be adjusting lines, lighting, make up, everything. When they were finally done they would have a large base of film to select their final cut from.

Stella came to me. "You all right? That fall didn't hurt?"

"Just my pride."

I looked over at Tommy. He glanced at me ruefully, then gave a thumbs up.

I thumbed him up back, and grinned. But I couldn't get over how weak I felt when he had caught me.

After shooting we drove over to the production offices for the dailies. Dailies are the raw film, presented to the producers and directors and whoever else. Some actors like them, some don't. I didn't care, except…sometimes they were useful for honing your craft. An actor could tell when a slight adjustment in his motion should have been made, or maybe a better delivery for a line.

We sat in the small screening room and watched scene after scene of me walking, climbing stairs, sitting in chairs.

I could see when I looked like a woman, and I could see when I didn't. I made mental notes, and I knew that Stella was doing the same. Finally, the lights went on. There were two old guys in the room, money men, and Becky and one of the cameramen.

Becky and the cameraman traded notes, the two old guys stood up, and they were smiling. One of them turned to me, "You're good. You're perfect."

That made me happy, and thrilled Stella. We were about to leave when Becky broke from the cameraman and came to us. She had a lopsided, pleased grin.

"I love it when I'm right. You make a good woman. Your eyes are sparkly, they have that horny look that a cross dresser always has."

Stella smiled victoriously. Being horny had worked.

"Thanks, dear," I projected a modest femininity and she laughed. "Okay. We're going to shoot some a real scene tomorrow. You up for it?"

"He's ready," said Stella.

"I'm ready."

"Okay, and, by the way?"

"Yes?"

"I don't have to tell you, but stay in character. All the time."

I nodded. Crap. I wanted to get out of this dress. It was tight and the shoes hurt, and my poor dick wanted to fly.

"See you tomorrow."

And the day was done.

At home I sank into a seat and sprawled, and every muscle in my body felt…tight.

"Wow, that was a long day."

"Yes, it was. Want a drink?"

"I do, but you sit, I'll get."

I sat, and my poor peeny throbbed. And the dress was tight and the bra straps were cutting into my shoulders.

I was almost asleep when Stella put a drink in my hand. "Don't go to sleep yet, lover."

"Oh, I need to."

"Yes, but you have lines tomorrow. And we have to practice."

"Oh, heysoos."

She smiled and placed a hand on my lap. "Tell you what. I'll untie Mr. Happy, and you can take that skirt off, and we can loosen the bra a little."

I smiled, and sipped, and she began helping me.

"How do you stay so energized?" I asked.

"For one, I'm not the one under the hot lights. For two…"

"Yes? Two?"

"You as a woman…it's…exciting."

"Exciting?"

"Okay. Horny. But exciting."

"So that's what I have to do to get you in bed? Dress up like a woman?"

"Oh, baby," she untaped my dick at that moment and it sprang upwards. It was red and it actually flung a few drops of pre-cum around.

"Uh oh. We're going to have to wear an absorbent pad."

"Cripes. Well, okay."

She brought out the scripts and we began reading, and it wasn't long before I had everything down.

She went to fix dinner, and when she got back I was snoring.

"Up and at 'em!" Stella opened the blinds and the sun poked me in the eyeball.

"Unh…" I threw a forearm over my eyes. Then, blinking, I looked around. "Did I sleep out here?"

"You were out like a light and I didn't want to wake you."

"Thanks, I think."

"Okay, let's get you out of yesterday's duds and into today's."

I struggled out of the recliner and staggered, then got my balance. I wasn't totally awake, but I was functional. Sort of.

I used the Nair, then hit the shower. I didn't have much visible hair, but little specks swirled down the drain, and now I really felt naked. Electric naked. Baby butt naked.

Stella creamed me, checked my nails, and began putting make up on me. Then, into a dress. A slinky dress, and we really had to tape Mr. Happy down.

God, was I horny. I felt electric all the time, surging, and like my blood was actually boiling.

"Oh, your eyes are snapping," laughed Stella.

"I'm so fucking horny."

"And it works. Baby, if this works then I'm never letting you cum again."

"Oh!" I groaned. "Even that made me pulse."

Finally, we were on our way.

"I'm hungry," I groused, as we walked into the Chimera building.

"You had a piece of toast for breakfast, what's the problem?"

"I need a steak."

"Not if you're going to keep your figure…oh, Hi Becky."

"Hey, kids, are you ready?"

"Yep."

I went to make up, wardrobe checked me out, found me palatable, and then on to the lights, camera, action!

The scene was later in the script. Tommy and I were on a bus, and he whispers something naughty to me. I didn't mind naughty.

We didn't use a real bus, didn't have the bucks for that, but the set was pretty good.

We ran through the scene a couple of times, then got down to business.

"Action!"

I entered the bus and tottered down the aisle. There were no seats, and then I saw one. Next to Tommy.

The script had me not liking him at that point, but…a seat on a downtown bus? I would sit.

So he pulled his legs back, I faced him and slid by, and the cameramen all shifted here and there, and the bus hit a jump and I fell forward. He caught me. And kissed me.

My eyes went open! I pushed back, I was mortified…and didn't know what to do!

He had kissed me! Planted his sexy lips on mine. He was supposed to whisper something to me, but he didn't. He just…kissed me!

"Cut!" Perfect.

Tommy smiled at me. He wasn't a real smart fellow and didn't read me right.

I stood trembling, and people were all shifting around, getting ready for the reshoot.

Reshoot? Of him kissing me?

"Becky?" I turned and called.

She was right there. So was Stella. "Yeah?"

"Can I talk to you?"

"Sure. Let's find a corner."

"We found one, and I blurted, "He kissed me."

Stella: "What?"

"He kissed me. Not just our lips meeting by accident, but…he put his lips on mine and actually kissed me."

"Really?" Stella stared at me. Then she turned to Becky.

Becky looked at me, and she looked at Stella, and she said, "I rewrote the script."

"With me kissing a man?"

"I wanted to get honest surprise."

"You got that."

"Look. I'm sorry. But when you see the dailies, when you see the surprise on your face, the shock. It is priceless, it is good movie making."

"Kissing a man was not in the contract."

"Rick, I'm sorry. This was an artistic decision, and I made it. I'm sorry, but it didn't hurt you, and…it's done."

And it was. Spilt milk.

"Is there going to be any more kissing?"

Becky hemmed and hawed, then finally admitted. "There might be."

"No!" I said.

"We want more money," said Stella.

"What?" I looked at Stella.

We all looked at each other. Then Stella said, "If I can have a moment alone?"

Becky nodded and was glad to take off.

I stared at her. "More money?"

"Rick, we stretched thin. More money won't hurt."

"But I'm kissing a man!"

"You're kissing a pair of lips. Like mine."

"No. Not like yours."

She moved closer to me, our tits were touching. "Rick, we need this. If you do this…if you can get over your silliness and examine the situation…I'll do anything for you."

I wasn't satisfied.

"And if you don't…then I won't."

"What does that mean?" I was starting to get angry.

She shifted her position so nobody could see. She pressed a hand against my groin. "It means, lover, that if you don't kiss a man, and make us LOTS of money, then it's going to be a cold day in hell before you get me to lay down and spread for you."

"What?" But I wasn't loud.

"Rick. think of that kiss. Flesh meeting, without the passion, just like…two hands shaking. You can do that all day long. That's acting. No passion, but show the passion. You can do it."

"I…I…" But she had me. And she knew it. We needed the money, her argument was sound, and…and I hate to admit this…but I was thinking of the way Tommy's lips were warm, and soft. I mean, he splatted me, but he was gentle. Was it really that different from kissing a woman?

"Now let's fix your make up and get ready for the reshoot."

"Action!"

I entered the bus, down the aisle, the look between Tommy and I, and I slid almost past his legs.

Bump! I fell, he caught…he kissed me.

I wasn't as surprised, and sensations registered. His lips were moist, they felt…sexy. And I felt helpless, getting kissed. Man, I reacted by ad libbing. I slapped him.

Rick looked surprised, everybody was surprised. I stood up and straightened my dress and glared at him.

"Cut! Oh, my God! Perfect! Rick! Perfect! The surprise on Tommy's face! My God!"

People stirred around me, I felt a hand on my shoulders. Patting me. A couple of people murmured things like 'Well done. Nice.'

Even the crew gave a hand clap.

I stepped back, red in the face, but somehow pleased. And thinking about the way he had kissed me, and how it felt. I felt my dick, down under the tape, struggle to get free. Mr. Happy liked it.

We took a short break then, and Stella came to me, led me to a chair and gave me a cup of water.

"Fucking brilliant," her eyes flashed at me. "That's the Rick I know."

I had kissed a man. But…

Then Stella said, "God, I don't know when I've been so horny."

I looked at her.

"Me kissing a man?"

"It's magic, Rick. It effects everybody. You saw the crew clapping.

We sat, and I thought. And I realized, though I didn't want to… kissing a man is easy.

But it was gay.

"Honey. I don't want a man."

She laughed. I kiss my mother, and I don't want her. I kiss my father and…and you can kiss Tommy all night and it doesn't mean you want him. That's acting."

Yes. It was. And it worried me. It worried me that my dick was pulsing under my dress.

The next few shoots were easy. Just drama, dialogue, set ups for later scenes. I did them well, and I was quite convincing as a woman. But on Wednesday trouble reared its ugly head.

Becky came into the studio late, and she looked like had eaten a box of nails and had indigestion.

I knew better than to mess with her then, but she came directly to me. No chance for me to escape the gun.

"Rick? Stella? We have to talk."

We didn't just go into a corner, we went into an office, and she closed the door.

"Sit."

We sat.

She rounded the desk and sat in the swivel.

"Rick…" she stopped and just stared at the ceiling.

"Becky? What's going on?"

I was sort of stunned. I had seen Becky be a bitch, but this was ten times over.

She looked at me. "In a way, it's your fault."

"My fault? But I've seen the dailies, George and Henry (the producers) are ecstatic. What have I done?"

"You're too good."

I blinked. Stella sat back and was dazed.

"So I'm good and you're mad. Who gets to be good and mad?"

"Maybe you."

"Why?"

George and Henry want a scene.

"So we give them a scene.

"Without clothes."

"What?"

She sighed. "George and Henry…look, let me start from the beginning. Okay?"

"Okay."

"This is a movie and the crossdresser is a second banana, a throw away. Not important. We could rewrite this movie ten ways from go without you."

That had me worried.

"Then you show up, and you take over. Shiela was supposed to be Tommy's love interest, but have you noticed we've been stalling her scenes?"

"Yeah."

"And Tommy, bless his heart, is getting more scenes. I mean, he's not the brightest, but he's perfect, and the tension between you two is overwhelming. It's like you hate him…but love him. It's magic!"

"So about taking the clothes off?"

"They want to shift the focus of the movie. You get to be a main character. Instead of being shuffled off by a girl, you occupy Tommy's interest."

"Wait a minute."

"Your salary is going to skyrocket, and there's even talk of more bucks for our budget."

"Wait."

"But you will have to act naked with Tommy."

"With no boobs?" What a weird thing for me to say. Why didn't I object to the nakedness, instead I found fault with...my boobs.

"We can put prosthetics on you. Hell we could give you real boobs if you want, but the point is that we can make it look like you are a real tranny, with a real cock and real tits."

I stared at her.

she stared at me, and she knew she was losing. I had come here to make a movie, but to be…revealed…as a transgender person…it was…it was—

"How much money?"

I turned to Stella.

"I'm not doing it!"

The shoot was delayed while Stella and I went home and mulled it. Which meant she would try to convince me of something I definitely didn't want to do.

"I think you should."

"I'm not a gay actor!"

"No, but you're an actor."

We were in the kitchen. She poured two drinks. A wine spritzer for herself and a stiff bourbon and Coke for me. She handed me the drink, hesitated, then made another one. She turned and handed it to me.

I blinked, and stared at her. I had a drink in each hand.

"What's this for?"

"So you can't stop me when I punch you."

She punched me. Right in the gut. I bent a little bit, but I was wearing a corset, and I have tight belly, and I grunted. "Ow!"

She straightened me up, moved one of the glasses to my mouth. "Drink this, you idiot."

I drank, and sputtered, "Why am I the idiot? I don't want to do a porno and you call me an idiot!"

"It's not a porno. It's soft porn, and there is a market for it."

"So I'm supposed to become rich and famous being a transgender actor in soft porn?"

"Porn is bigger than mainstream, goofball."

"But it's not acting!"

"Bullshit!"

We stood there, glaring at each other. She moved one of the glasses to my lips again and I drank. Not a sip, but a gulp.

Then, while I was savoring the burn, she undid my dress and started pulling me out of it.

"What…what?"

"Shut up."

I shut, drank some more, and she raised the slip and undid the tape. My poor, struggling cock went up like a flag on the top of Mt. Everest.

"Fuck!" I blurted. At that moment I hated my wife…and I was horny for her.

She grabbed my cock and held it. "You get horny from wearing women's clothes. Don't lie."

"But I'm not gay."

"What is gay? Who cares about gay? Do you know how much money Becky offered us? Do you know that soft porn is just a stepping stone? When people can see that you act…"

"When they look past my dick," I said bitterly.

"Then they'll know you can act."

"Bullshit."

"Ask Sylvester Stallone."

I stared at her.

"Hell, ask Traci Lords."

"Yeah, but…" I was running out of steam. First, Stella was madder than me. Second, she was tweaking my dick like there was no tomorrow.

"Look at this cock!"

I looked down. It was dripping.

"That's not fair," I accused.

"I'm making you richer than shit! Anything is fair!"

"So when do I get to cum?"

Funny, I had gone from being upset and righteous to wondering about my dick.

"When I say so," she snarled.

"That could be months."

It will be months. It will be until Hiatus, and there might not even be a hiatus this year! And I'm going to play with you every single day. Do you know what milking is?"

"No."

"Well, you're going to get milked. And you will be relieved, but you won't lose that horny spark in your eyes. In fact, it will be worse."

"How worse?" What was I doing? Who was talking for me? Why wasn't I defending my position.

"I'm going to show you, right now."

She pulled me by the dick into the bedroom. She threw me on the bed.

"Lay down, on your face."

I did. I felt incredibly vulnerable, laying there in a slip and stockings, my tits mashed under my chest.

"What are you doing?"

She grabbed a bunch of scarves and began tying my wrists to the posts.

"Shut up!"

I did, and I stared at her, and I was shocked into immobility. I didn't move. I just let her tie me to the bed.

"I don't understand."

"Good," she was mad. She had me tied up and was talking about milking and…and me not cumming for months, and… "What are you doing?"

She reached into her drawer and pulled out her vibrator. It wasn't a big thing, but it was shaped like a penis, and she turned it on.

HMMMM!

She turned it off.

"Rick, this is for your own good. You're going to be rich and famous, and that's that. Do you understand?"

"I don't understand anything!" I started to feel a worm of fear in my chest.

"Well, you will."

She went into the bathroom and brought back a big tube of lube. She sat on the bed and spread my cheeks. For all her anger, she was soft, and she slathered lube onto my crack and pushed it into my asshole.

"Hey! What are you doing?"

"Making you grow up." She began running her finger around the rim of my asshole.

I began to struggle, at last moved to action, but it was too late. She tied good knots, and she kept reaming me and reaming me, and…it started to feel good.

"Stop!" I begged.

"Not until you grow up and be a man."

"A man with a dress? Getting fucked in the ass by a woman?"

"I'm not fucking you in the ass. I'm draining you."

She pushed her vibrator into me. I grunted and arched. She held it still for a long moment.

"Inside the ass is the prostate. Rub the prostate enough, just the right way, and it pushes your semen out of your dick. It drains your balls. That's milking."

"I don't want to be milked."

"No. You want to be poor. Well, I'm not having any of that."

She turned the vibrator on, and I spasmed.

It was electrical. I felt sensations rush through my whole body. I was suddenly and unbelievably turned on.

She worked it gently, pushing it in as far as it would go, wiggling it, then pulling back.

"Oh, fuck…fuck!"

I gritted my teeth, I wanted it to stop…but I wanted it to continue.

"Stop fucking me!"

"I told you. I'm not fucking you. I'm draining you. And if you'd relax a little you'd notice how good it feels."

I was noticing. I was struggling, but half of my struggles were to show that I wasn't enjoying this.

"Come on, Rick. Give it up." Her voice was soft now. She could feel me breaking down. "You know I'm right."

Was she? One part of me didn't think so. Another part of me started thinking about kisses, and lips, and how it didn't matter if there was no passion.

But this was…nakedness. Exposing myself.

So what? I'd get paid big bucks just for taking off my clothes. It's not like people don't do that.

I groaned, and suddenly I was aware that I was pushing back.

"That's it, baby. Give it up. It's going to feel so good. All you have to do is relax and let me do my magic.

She moved the vibrator, I could feel the shivers running through my groin, and, suddenly, I started to feel loosey goosey.

"Excellent. Here it comes. Just let it come."

"It feels like I'm peeing."

"It's supposed to. Come on, baby."

For another minute she moved the vibrator in and out, and at first I pumped back, tried to fuck it with my butt, then I just sort of went limp. I had the funny feeling that it was all over, and she pulled the vibrator out of my rectum.

"Good boy." She slapped my ass and untied me.

"I don't get it?" But I was feeling good. Satisfied.

"Look on the bed."

I did, and I saw a big patch of cum.

"What is that?"

"You, lover. You came your brains out."

"But I didn't feel anything!"

"You will tomorrow," she kissed me in passing as she cleaned up. "Tomorrow you are going to be superhorny, and erect, and feeling like you want to fuck the moon. But there won't be any gism in you. We drained you, but your mind doesn't know that. It's still going to be horny…you will feel more horny than you ever have in your life." She laughed. "Oh, the magic in your eyes."

Her arguments won. At least, I didn't have any male machismo driving me and making me stand up to her. Instead, I was loosey goosey, easy going, compliant, and didn't even care that I had to take my clothes off.

It's only clothes, and it's only bodies, and…what the hell? Right?"

I woke up suddenly, my dick trying to drive a hole through the blankets.

"Fuck!" I muttered. I suddenly had the desire to throw my wife over and fuck her. Fuck her pussy. Fuck her mouth. Fuck her ass.

"How you doing, lover?" she was on elbow on her side, watching me. She was laughing.

"Heysoos. I need some relief."

"You only think you need some relief. Now, come on. We have to get you ready."

I leaped from the bed. I was like a wire, electricity shooting through me.

Stella just hummed and did my hair and make up and checked my nails. I got dressed, and. I didn't need much help. I was moving fast.

"Slow down, baby," Stella giggled. "You're moving wa-a-ay too fast."

"I can't help it! I have so much energy?"

"You're going to have to slow down for your scenes today."

"Okay." And man, it really was okay. Everything was okay

As we drove to the studio I turned to Stella. "Baby? Honey?"

"Yes?"

"That thing you did to me last night?"

"Yeah?"

"I really like it."

"I know you do."

We entered the studios, and everything was different. There was less crew, and everybody was sort of pre-occupied.

That's the way it always is when an actor gets naked.

"Okay, people…ready to go?"

Nods and murmurs.

Becky came to me. "Ready?"

"Yeah," I said, showing a lot of confidence.

"That's my man," she patted my cheek and moved on.

"Action!"

Tommy spun me around and yelled, "You can't treat me like that!"

"Shut up, you pussy!" I screamed back at him.

The crew stared, rapt, we were making real magic. This was looking really real.

I turned around, and slipped, and Tommy caught me. He was supposed to kiss me. Plant his lips on me.

That was okay. I didn't love Tommy, but…but my heart was pounding. Passion, baby. I thought I was acting.

But he didn't catch me right. He caught me while I was facing down, and then he lifted me up, and…and his dick pressed against my ass.

I froze. He froze. My dick was straight out in front. His dick was straight…pointing into…my ass.

I had been lubed up the night before, and I was still slick back there.

He slid right into me.

Shock. The shock of being kissed was nothing compared to this.

Everybody in the room froze.

"Oh!" I exclaimed. But it wasn't an angry exclamation. It was a surprised one. It felt good. His dick felt good. Warm, strong, pulsing.

I couldn't help myself. I pooched my butt back.

Tommy was blinking, he didn't understand, but he understood a good feeling. He pushed forward.

We fucked.

I fucked a man. And I was the fuckee.

In and out. Slithering flesh. Pulsing, throbbing.

"Unh!" grunted Tommy.

"Oh!" I repeated.

"Unh…unh…"

We sawed back and forth. The cameraman came to himself and moved around, caught our action, focused on the entry, and the way that big cock was sliding in and out, opening my aperture and having its way.

"Fuck!" I whispered, and the camera caught it. It caught the look of amazement on my face. It caught how my face twitched with pleasure.

"Oh, yeah!" exclaimed Tommy.

He began to cum. His dick was big, and he wasn't drained, probably had had any for a month. I mean, he just kept spewing and filling me up. Cum started to drip out of my asshole and the cameraman knelt down and caught it all.

Finally, Tommy was done. He let me go and I stood up, shaky on my legs, a look of surprise on my face.

"God!" I leaped at Tommy and kissed him.

And he kissed me.

"Cut!"

"You're up for another award."

"Excellent." I cut my steak and chewed.

"The studio has offered you more money for a sequel."

"Get as much as you can." I sipped some Coke and bourbon.

We were living higher in the hills now. We had sold our little bungalow and had a gated mansion.

"You're going to have to stop gorging yourself."

"I know. One more steak, tomorrow, and we'll put me on my diet."

Stella leaned back. She was done, and she smiled as I pushed my plate away.

"How do you feel, Mr. Big Shot Rich and Famous Actor?"

"Like I want to take advantage of Hiatus."

She frowned. "Rick? Does it bother you to take it up the ass?"

"Nope. Feels good."

She nodded. "Because the public is demanding it. They want to see your ass take it big."

"Can't argue with that. Now, can we go to bed? I need to lose a drop."

"I can take a drop, but just one." She giggled, and we stood up and went to bed.

END

Full Length Books from Gropper Press

Tom Dickson was a happy camper. He lived a good life, had a beautiful wife, then he started to grow breasts, his hair grew long, and his body reshaped. Now Tom is on the way to being a woman, and he doesn't know why.

My Husband's Funny Breasts

I Changed My Nephew into a Girl!

Published on Kindle,
appeared in 'Stories to Pump Your Heart.'

PART ONE

Lana is an idiot.

Lana is my sister, and we have never gotten along, and I couldn't believe it when she called me up out of the blue.

"I'm going to Europe, but I need to find a summer home for Chuckie."

Oh, great. My least favorite sister is going to saddle me with my least favorite nephew, and…and then I got an idea.

"Lana, is Charles still cross dressing?"

"What? Oh, I don't know."

"Don't avoid the issue. Does Charles Cross dress?"

Silence. then: "Well, maybe a little. Just every once in a while."

Huh. He probably wore gowns on the golf course. I said: "Well, I always liked his softer self, so I'll tell you what I'll do. I will let Chuckie stay here for the summer as long as he does exactly what I say."

"Well, of course he will. He's a good boy and…" blah blah blah.

"No, Lana, you don't understand. I said 'anything.' Like what you did for Charles twenty years ago.

Blah bla—what? I could hear her mind shrieking. "You want to what?"

"I want to do what you did to Charles 20 years ago."

"But I don't…no. You can't—"

"Good bye." I hung up. And I grinned, and I chortled, and I poured myself a glass of sherry. I gave her 24 hours and she would come begging.

She didn't have a lot of friends, her nephew, as I recalled from seeing him some 13 years previous, was a brat, and there was no way she was going to find a home for him for a summer.

To add to that, she wasn't fond of the male of the species.

She met Charles, found out he was rich, and told him to marry her.

When he wouldn't, she spent a summer converting him into femininity. I hadn't seen him for years, but I could still see him in my mind, prancing about in high heels and a bra, lipstick and red nails. His penis flopping about like it was big. Have I used the word 'sheesh?' Well, here it is again. Shee-eee-eesh.

The rest of the day I spent thinking over my plans. I wrote scenarios, I checked out the price of girly things in a male size, I imagined fixing up the bedroom, and the dungeon.

Ah, the dungeon. I hadn't used it lately. But all my toys were still down there. A little dusting, a little polish, and Chuckie would have a fine place to play. Heh heh.

And, feeling a little horny, all that planning and thinking about what I was going to do to Chuckie, I ran upstairs to polish my dildo. And I think you know what I mean.

Then I swam in the pool, went for a run, and called Martha, my BFF. I just had to share the news

"Hello Daphne, you bitch."

"Hello Martha, you cunt."

Then we giggled. We always started our conversations out like this. For over two decades we had been bosom buddies. Emphasis on the word bosom. We were both stacked, the boys chased us, and we found we were particular suited to each other.

"Guess who's coming to dinner?"

"You mean 'cuming?'"

"Get your head out of the gutter, sister…"

"I'd rather keep it in the gutter, with you."

"Hardy har har, now guess."

"Jeffry Epstein?"

"Oh, you silly…my nephew!"

"Your nephew? I didn't even know you had one."

"My sister's son!"

"Your sister? I didn't even know you had one."

"Argh! That did it! Get that stupendously fat rhino ass of yours over here right now!"

"Ooh, goodie, I'll bring some refreshments."

A half hour later the doorbell dinged and I strode to the door. Click. Click. Click. "Who's there?"

"A handsome stud with a really big dick!"

"Oh, goodie!" I swung the door open.

"Oops, I lied," Martha entered, air kissed and hugged me. Her big tits pressed against mine. She was carrying a bottle of champagne.

"Champagne?"

"They were out of Vodka."

We giggled. We walked into the kitchen where I took out two flutes. Expertly, she popped her cork—not that way, at least not yet—and poured us a pair.

We leaned our butts against the island and sipped the ambrosia of the Gods.

"Champagne in the morning," I chortled. "How evil."

"It's what the doctor ordered."

"An evil doctor."

We hugged each other again, then stood back and looked at each other. Then I turned us towards the side wall, which was a big mirror.

In body we could have been twins. We had started out with big boobs, and they had just gotten bigger.

We had the same shade lipstick, a metallic red. Her eyes were smoky grey, mine light blue. She had brunette locks that poured over her white skin. I had blonde curls that waved halfway down my back.

She sighed.

"What?"

"Look at us. Divorced, horny, and turning into fat cows."

"Speak for yourself, Miss Double Ds."

"I'm bigger than that."

"No!" I looked at her.

"And you probably are, too."

I checked myself out again. I still had a good waist, not a 23, like in college, but probably not over 28. "We're going to have to measure."

"So what's this stuff about a nephew."

"Chuckie. My sister is going to Europe for a few months, she's trying to palm the boy off on me."

"Oh, goodie. A slave boy!"

We giggled.

"You're reading my mind, sister."

"So what does he look like?"

"I don't know."

"What?"

"Oh, they send me family pictures every Christmas, but I just throw them in a drawer."

"Well, where's the drawer?"

"Upstairs."

In my bedroom Martha opened a drawer, pawed through scissors and papers, a tape measure, a dildo—she held it up and winked at me—and a stack of Xmas cards. Quickly we looked through the cards.

Pictures through the years. Lana looking like a bubble brained blonde. Charles, looking so manly. "He's a cross dresser," I explained, "and an idiot. I told Lana that if she palmed her idiot son off on me I would make him into a cross dresser."

"And she's okay with that?"

"She's okay with anything that diddles her pussy and makes her money. I'm sure her nephew doesn't diddle, and he's probably a lazy snowflake. So she won't care."

"Ah, this generation…" Martha commiserated, then she found last year's card and held it up.

They stood in front of a tree weighted down with lights and tinsel. A tomountain of packages surrounding their feet.

Lana on the left, holding a glass of cheer and looking a little wasted. Charles on the right, holding a flute up with one hand, and tipping Chuckie's Santa hat down over his eyes. Chuckie didn't look too happy, and Martha and I weren't too happy. Sort of ruined the picture. A guy in garish PJs, a stupid hat on in his head, squeezed between two drunks. Hmm.

"Doesn't look promising."

"Well, at least he's not fat."

"No." I turned to Martha. "I'm going to make him a cross dresser."

She stared me and waited.

"I have been wanting to get back at Lana for 20 years."

"For what."

"Charles was my boyfriend."

"Aha," she nodded. "I thought I detected an extra bit of vitriol."

If I can send him back to her a prancing fop it will serve her right.

Daphne stared at me. Hard.

I slumped. "I know."

"He's an innocent."

"So what do we do? We use him for a slave boy, let him jack off a lot, and that's it?"

"Well, it is cruel to hurt somebody else to get back at another person."

"Oh, damn. You rain on my parade."

She sat down on the side of my bed and sipped. She watched me.

I straightened up. "Okay. Slave boy only."

"And I get to help?"

"Yes."

We clinked glasses, and, at that moment, the phone rang.

I grinned. "She broke. It didn't take more than a couple of hours."

"Well answer the phone, girl friend."

I picked up my cell, put it on speaker, and spoke in my haughtiest voice, "Yes…who is this?"

Martha laughed silently.

"I don't want you to abuse Chuck."

Daphne nodded. She was right.

I sighed. "Well, I don't know why I'm so kind, but I'll tell you what. I won't do anything he doesn't want. Any abuse that occurs will be self abuse."

"Don't try to be funny about this."

"I'm saddled with your bonehead offspring for a summer. Yeah, I guess it isn't funny."

She was silent at that, but only for a moment. Then: "We just put him on a plane. And listen, I warned him about you."

"Warned him what?"

"I told him you were strange and that he should be very careful around you."

I soughed. "Well, okay, sister mine. Text me the data and I'll pick him up at the airport."

"No need. He'll Uber."

"Excellent. Have a great Europe."

"I will."

Click.

No thank you. Just…click. I turned to Daphne. "On his way."

"Goodie. Let's measure your boobs, then have a swim."

We measured, and that was fun.

"Take off your blouse."

"You just want to get your hands on my boobers."

"Accurate measurements in the name of science," she reprimanded me.

She held up the tape measure and circled my chest. I felt the cold material slide across my flesh and it gave me a shiver.

"Getting horny?"

"Be serious." I was.

"Okay, 58 Z."

I laughed. "Now you be serious."

"Okay. 40 EE. You cow!"

"You're just jealous."

She put the Xmas cards back into the drawer and took out the dildo. She said. "Lay down and I'll get you off." Her voice was throaty.

Now, we weren't Lesbians. We were just efficient. We didn't want to kiss, we just wanted a quick bang, relieve the pressure, get on with life.

I lay back, pulled up my skirt and lifted my legs.

She pulled my panties down with one hand, then began massaging my cooch.

"Oh, that feels good."

"It'll feel better in a minute. You have any lube?"

"I'm wet enough."

"Oh, she likes it rough."

"In the bathroom."

She went for the lube, brought back a jar and placed it on the night table. She coated the dildo, then put a finger glob onto my snatch.

"Ooh," I gasped.

She smiled and pushed the dildo into me, and I really gasped.

"Geez Louise! You ever hear of foreplay."

"We don't need no stinkin' foreplay," she giggled, and she began ramming it back and forth.

"Oh…oh!" my hips responded with jerks.

"I think she likes it," she quipped.

Being penetrated in such hard fashion, it was so caveman, it just woke up the survival senses. The only way to survive was to fight back, and fighting back with a pussy is always fun.

"You bitch!" I moaned, trying to hold her wrist with my hands.

She swiped my hands away and kept jamming into me. "Take it like a cunt, you cunt!" She laughed.

Within a minute I was spasming, twitching, my pussy muscles gripping frantically and losing to the lube.

"Ha," she said, as I went over the edge.

"AHHH!" My back arched like I was getting electrocuted. My mouth opened wide and I felt the white heat consume me, lift me up, and deposit me on the sheets, a puddle of sweat and happiness.

"Ah, God," I said, after a minute. "You really got me."

"Well," she said, licking the dildo, "You could always return the favor."

"Grrr," I said. I reached up and pulled her arm. She fell to the bed as I stood up. I took the dildo and stood over her. "Vee haf Vays of deallink vith cunts!"

"Oh, mine fuhrer!" she threw a hand across her big chest in a mockery of fear. "Please…not the cock!"

I held up the dildo. "You are takiink it all!"

"Noooo!" she wailed, as she pulled up her skirt.

I pulled her panties down and spread lubricant over her hot, little honeypot.

"Oh, that does feel good."

"How about this?" I growled, and I jammed…my little finger into her.

"Oh, come on!"

"What's the matter, is it too big?"

"Use the dildo!"

"I am, it's just that…you've grown."

She tried to sit up but I pushed her back.

"This big, giant dildo, I remember when it could at least touch the walls. But now…what have you…been fucking elephants?"

She finally managed to reach a hand down and grabbed my wrist. So I pulled out my finger and stuck the dildo in. Hard.

"Gah!" And she let go of my wrist and sank back on the bed.

"You want turn about? Here you go!" I used both hands and began jackhammering the thing into her slit.

"Fu…fu…fu…!" she writhed on the bed. It looked like she was trying to escape, but I knew the truth, she wanted more. I gave it to her.

I pushed her back on the bed using nothing but the dildo and my well toned muscles. I shoved that dildo as far as I could, and she humped back in little half inches, trying to get traction, but she couldn't.

"Oh…oh…!"

Her eyes were glazing and her boobs were shivering with the impact of my fucking.

Finally, I tired, my arm muscles gave out, so I used one hand to push on her mons, which included squashing her poor, little clit, and circled the dildo in her.

I fucked her, I scooped her innards, I excavated her lust.

"AHHHH!" she almost screamed when she came. I have never seen a body lock up so hard. And it lasted long. For a full 30 seconds she was locked in spasm, and I knew she was having a REALLY good cum. I kept worming the dildo into her, making it last longer.

She finally broke, and collapsed. For a long minute she just lay there, trying to regain her breath.

I grinned as I cleaned the dildo off and placed it in the drawer.

"Come on down to the pool when you recover. Don't forget to make us a couple of drinks. Make mine bourbon and Coke."

The last thing I heard, as I walked out of the bedroom, was her wheezing, "Oh, you fucking bitch."

I laughed all the way downstairs.

I swam laps in the nude. I always swim in the nude. If God had wanted me to wear a bathing suit I would have been born with one. Right?

Finally, I got out, walked around the pool and lay on a lounger. At that moment Daphne came out of the house with a couple of frosty ones. She handed me one and sprawled on the lounger next to me.

We sighed. The sun warmed us, we were fucked out, but feeling that delightful tingle of having just cum.

"What a life," murmured Daphne.

"I'll drink to that."

We sipped our drinks, chatted, and before we knew it, we were ready for our second. And then our third.

"It looks like a lost weekend for us," commented Daphne.

"Just in time," I answered.

DING DONG!

We looked at each other.

"That can't be…"

"Not yet!"

I looked at my cell phone. Only a couple of hours had passed.

"Well, whoever it is, you have to answer it."

"We have to answer it." Giggling, I grabbed her wrist and pulled her to her feet. I dragged her through the house. She protested, but she was drunk and laughing.

Tell the truth, it was something that only a drunk would do, and we were drunk, so we did it.

We stood in front of the door and I swung it open.

On retrospect, I wondered what we were doing. What if it had been an UPS delivery. Or a pizza driver with the wrong address?"

But it wasn't. It was Chuckie.

His mouth opened, his jaw dropped, his eyes were as wide as pies. He dropped his suitcases and stared at us.

Two buxom, naked, drunks. Our tits flopping in the wind, our cheer exuding out the front door and into the great, wide world.

"Come on in!" I was slurring my words slightly.

"Yeah, put up or shut up!" drawled Daphne.

He blinked, but then, as we stood back and held the door for him, he picked up his suitcases and entered the house.

He was not a tall boy. He was actually a couple of inches shorter than me, and he had long, brown hair. It was in a pony tail, and I had the urge to pull it as he passed us.

He stopped in the foyer. He just stood there, looking at us.

We giggled and held each other up.

"You're my Aunt Martha?"

"Ooh, you're an Aunt," Daphne laughed and poked me in the ribs.

"And you're my nephew Chunkie. Chuckie. Whoever. Put your bags upstairs, last room on the left. Then come down and go swimming."

"And don't wear no stinkin' clothes."

"Clothes? Why would he wear clothes?"

"That's what I'm saying!"

"Clothes?"

"Bathing suit," Daphne figure it out and corrected herself.

We laughed and staggered back to the pool area. We laid down on our lounges and kept laughing and giggling.

A short while later Chuckie came down.

In the light he was slender, soft, sort of like a miniature of Charles. Except that Charles was studly, and Chunkie wasn't. Chuckie.

He had soft brown eyes, full lips, his skin was beautiful, slightly olive with no blemishes.

The interesting thing was that he had little mounds for pecs. Not like muscle, but like actual tits, but small. That made me wonder.

"Ooh, he's bootiful," slurred Daphne. "Take off that stupid swim suit, Chunkie."

She was having the same trouble I was with his name.

Blushing, Chuckie slid his trunks down over his thighs and stepped out of them. He had, of course, a boner.

For a skinny, little fart he was fairly well endowed. From perverted research I knew that average American men were 6.5 inches. Chuckie was at least 8. An inch and a half over average. Lucky boy.

"Go get a drink, Chunkie. Chuckie."

Chuckie walked back into the house. Both Daphne and I, though drunk, were obsessed with staring at his ass. It was not big. But if his waist was a little skinnier…hmmm. Then I shook myself. I had told Lana

I wouldn't mess with him. Too much.

He returned with a drink.

"Wush that?" We stared at his drink.

"It's called a Beggar's Banquet. It's got maple syrup and lemon and a splat of beer in it."

Daphne and I stared at each other. Then I asked, "Can you make me one?"

"No."

"What?"

"You're too drunk. It would be wasted on you."

"You can't tell us what wasted is!" protested Daphne.

He smiled, a polite, little good boy smile. "Mother told me not to serve people too drunk to drive."

"Mother?"

"Lana?"

"Mother insisted that I learn how to make and serve proper alcohol. She also warned me not to endanger drunks."

"Drunks? Did he call me a drunk?"

"Listen, buster," I started, and I stood up.

I wavered, he reached out to steady me, and we fell in the pool. Well, I actually fell, and I grabbed on to him and pulled him in with me.

I spluttered and gasped and then I felt his hand grip my biceps and lift me up. My head appeared above water and I gasped for air.

"WEE!" and Daphne cannonballed us.

Then Daphne and I were laughing, laughing so hard that Chunkie… Chuckie…started smiling.

"Thash it, sweet cheeks," burbled Daphne. "Throw all hope aside."

"You ladies are really…something else."

We splashed for a while, then we climbed out of the pool. Chuckie put us in our loungers and we stared at the sun. We were at the end of our drunk, dazed, feeling great, and wondering what was next. The world was circling a bit, and I looked at Chuckie.

"So, it's your summer. What you want to do?"

Chuck then said something which totally blew me out of the water. Even drunk I was gobsmacked by what he said.

"Mother said you're going to feminize me."

I blinked, and blinked, quite owlish, and Daphne was laughing and laughing, and that's the last thing I remember.

"Unh…oohh…what happened?"

I was laying in my bed. Fortunately it was a wide bed, because Daphne was groaning on the other side.

"Martha? Is that you?"

"No. Leave me alone."

We slept again, and when we woke up it was about ten in the morning, and it was a beautiful morning. The sun was creeping through the window, the air was fresh, there were even a bunch of stupid birds singing in the trees outside.

Slowly, I swung my legs out to the floor, then I held my head. Surprisingly, it didn't hurt. Oh, it was a fog, but I must have slept through the major part of the hangover. I looked at the clock.

10. An ungodly hour in my condition, but it was what I had.

"Hey," I shook the bed. "Get up."

Daphne groaned, then stretched. "I need a drink."

"Hair of the dog," I agreed. I reached over and pushed her and she fell off the bed.

"Ow! Hey!" Then she stood up, rose up like a muddy Frankenstein. "I'll get you back for that."

"Later. Let's go swimming."

We walked down the stairs, a little staggery, then out to the pool area.

Chuckie was reading a book, the cover said, 'We Made Him Our Fem- Boy: Three women, one, boy, one summer.' It was by some idiot named Grace.

He put it down and lifted his sunglasses and inspected us.

"Oh," I said. "I remember you." Then I fell into the pool. When I came up he was walking into the house. Oh, well.

Daphne and I swam our stupor off and began to brighten up. The world started to make sense, and we swam laps slowly, but appreciated the water sluicing off our outer bodies, and smoothing out our inner thoughts.

Finally, we climbed out of the shallow end. The sun threatened to dry us off, so we just stood there and faced it. Then I heard a sound. We turned around. Chuck was carrying two plates, one on each arm, and two glasses, one in each hand.

"Breakfast, ladies."

We looked at each other in delight, then hurried over to the little wrought iron table with the glass top. We sat down and he placed drinks in front of us, and then. our plates. He was a good juggler.

"These are Palomas, they will hold off any alcohol hangover, and the citrus will replace nutrients. I didn't know how you liked your eggs, so I made simple omelettes. A bit of onion, peppers, seasoning, and, of course, cackleberries."

"Cackleberries," I laughed and then sipped. God, it felt good, and I felt what muzziness remaining in my skull dissipate. "You've been talking to my sister."

"Occasionally," he agreed.

We ate then, Daphne and I, and we soon were refreshed and strong and ready to go. And Daphne suddenly blurted, "My God, I remember you. You were drinking this crazy drink, and you said something... something important..."

She tried to remember, but I remembered first. "You said... you said your mother said...we are supposed to feminize you?"

He smiled. He was cute when he smiled. He looked so young.

"That's right."

Daphne and I looked at each other. I remembered talking with her about that, and deciding not to. And here it was again, being offered on a silver platter. I looked around.

"What?" he asked.

"My cell phone."

"I put inside. Last night. Would you like...of course you would like me to get it. Or you wouldn't be looking for it. One moment."

He trotted into the house. Trotted, like in hurried, and in hurried to do my bidding. My mind was starting to get boggled by his perfection.

"Can you believe him?" whispered Daphne.

Then he was back and handed me my phone.

I hit Lana's number. Ring, ring, ring. No answer.

"Try a text. She's probably talking with somebody, she's always talking with somebody, but she'll check her texts no matter."

So I texted.

Lana, are you serious?

I put the phone down, expecting an answer in an hour, when she finally got off the phone and checked her messages, but I had an answer within ten seconds. That girl might be a twit, but she was quick.

Of course. We've discussed. Ask him. Now go away.

Bitch.

I turned to Chuckie. "I'm supposed to feminize you."

"Yes, ma'am. If you would."

"And you want this?"

I've talked it over with mother. A lot. And I really want to experience this. I'm afraid of permanent, I want to see what it's like."

"Why?"

"I've watched my father for years. He is the happiest man I know. I love my father, and I want to be like him."

I looked at Daphne. She put her hands up and shrugged and gave me a WTF look.

And I knew that my sweet, loving sister, the bitch, had managed to put one over on me. Grrr.

"Okay. Have you tried any cross dressing or anything?"

"When I was young. But when mother found out she made me stop."

"She did? How come?"

"She said I wasn't old enough. She said I had to mature a bit before I made such decisions."

Hmm. Maybe Lana wasn't so stupid after all. Well, she was, but at least she had done one right thing in her life.

Daphne blurted, "So let's get this straight. You will turn yourself over to us for the summer. You will do anything, absolutely anything, we ask, and in return we just have to gussy you up. Make you soft and sweet. Tenderize you."

"Like a girl," he nodded.

"Oh, my God."

We had a few more questions, but he was quite serious, and finally Daphne dropped a bomb.

"Okay, look. I'm with this, but I've got a problem."

"Yes?" he arched his eyebrows, and I noticed that it looked like he had done a little pre-plucking. And it looked good.

"Well, I don't know how to say this, so let me just blurt it out."

"Okay."

"I need sex."

His eyes opened a little, but he didn't say anything.

"I like young men, they are a gas, and the idea of fucking a girly girl…that sort of makes me wet. So, do you think…could you…"

He smiled. "Of course."

"And you don't mind that I'm a bit older than you?"

He knelt then, the darling boy knelt, and he looked her right in the eyes. "When I first saw you yesterday I was afraid. I didn't know which of you was my aunt. But I got an instant boner, and," he looked at me, "no offense here, Auntie," he called me auntie, the dear boy, and he looked back to Daphne, "I didn't want you to be my aunt."

"Oh," I could feel Daphne's heart do a flip, then lay down and give up. "You dear boy."

"In fact," he stood up, "I don't mean to be forward, but mother always said you," he looked at me, "were sexually adventurous. I wanted to learn about that. But I am so afraid."

"Of what?" I asked.

"You're my aunt, and because we shouldn't have sexual relations, I was afraid that you wouldn't…show me how to be sexually adventurous."

We were silent for a long moment after that. We kept exchanging glances, grokking things, trying to absorb certain things, feeling our way through this strange, new relationship.

"Well," I said. "I know we're related by blood, and that we shouldn't…shall I say,'do the deed?"…but we can certainly play with each other. It's just that I'll get the short end of the stuck, which in this case is no stick at all."

"That's okay," murmured Daphne. She was now staring at Chunkie hungrily, like she wanted to take him into the bedroom, cook him on one side, turn him over, and cook him on the other.

I looked at her. "Okay for you, bitch."

She giggled. "There are those who are pure as the driven snow, they get their wishes. Then there are the ugly hags who get nothing."

"Did you just call me an ugly hag?"

"If the shoe fits…" she reached out and felt his trunks. "Lose the trunks, bozo."

Quickly, Chuckie shimmied out of them. That delightful cock sprang up and I felt my heart sink. I wanted it so-o-o much.

Daphne grabbed his cock and pulled it.

Chuckie grunted and began to move his hips. For a few seconds they explored the hand job, then I cleared my throat.

"What?" asked Daphne, feigning irritation.

"There are times and places."

"And this is the time and—"

I held up a hand, "hold it, don't say it, because it's not."

"It's not?" now she was curious.

I turned to Chuckie and smiled sweetly. "Tell me, dear boy. Have you ever seen a dungeon?"

Daphne yelped a chortle, stood up and walked away. Chuckie's dick being in her hand, he was compelled to follow. I didn't think he minded.

And I ran for the computer room.

I am not a loose woman, but I have appetites, and every once in a while I meet a man I'd like to sample. So I set up the playroom, my dungeon, and one of the little tricks about it was that there was a video feed that led directly to my computer. When there were no men around, and I got a little horny, I had a complete set of videos to get myself wet and wild.

I was about to get another one.

PART TWO

I powered up the computer, pulled up the security system, tapped on line 4, and, voila, I was looking at the dungeon. Full color, full sound, full lights.

Daphne and Chuckie enter. Daphne tried to turn the lights down, but they wouldn't go. Of course not. I was controlling them, and I wanted to see.

So she showed Chuckie the dungeon.

Against one wall were whips and boas, handcuffs and feather, dildos and butt plugs. In short, everything a young man, or woman, would need to titillate themselves or others.

At various places around the room were pieces of furniture.

In one corner was a pillory. I loved to be locked in it, my butt projecting to the rear, defenseless and ready.

In another corner was a Sybian. Oh, the hours I had spent letting that thing take me to the stars.

In yet another corner was a simple poster bed. With leather circlets at the four corners.

In the center of the room was the piece de resistance, a specially made table. You could tie a person to it, and his arms and legs to moveable arms, and then you could arrange him, or her, as you wanted.

You could move it upright into a St. Andrew's cross. You could move it horizontal open open the legs, for a suck from down under or a fuck from up above.

I tall ya, that table was a masterpiece.

In the basement: "Tell me, dear boy," Daphne held his arm and snuggled her boobs against him. "Have you ever had anything up your butt?"

"Oh, yes."

"And what have you had up your butt?"

"Well, when I was younger I tried to sit on a coke bottle…"

"Things do go better with Coke," Daphne laughed.

"…but I didn't understand about lube so it just sort of hurt. But then, a few years ago, I discovered butt plugs. I use them all the time. I even have some in my suitcase."

"Okay, pick a plug, any plug," she indicated the wall.

"Chuckie walked to the wall, a focused look on his face He examined my collection. He chose a good-sized one, a glass one. One of my favorites.

"I always wanted to try out glass plugs."

"There'a a bottle of lubricant on that shelf over there."

Chuckie got the lube and began slathering it over the bulbous object.

I chose that moment to turn on some music.

Nights in white satin
Never reaching the end

Moody Blues. Great stuff. The four speakers in the dungeon would be caressing their ear drums delightfully.

On the screen Daphne suddenly looked up at the camera. She smiled. She knew I was watching them.

"Here, let me help." Daphne went to Chuckie.

Chuckie gave her the plug.

"Spread your legs," and she grabbed his cock and stroked it.

"Oh," I could hear his groan.

Daphne put the tip to his rectum and pushed it in. It went easily, which showed that Chuckie was experienced in the art of butt pluggery.

He straightened up slowly, feeling his way through the barrage of sensations exploding in his asshole.

"I don't usually use ones this big," he admitted.

"Does it hurt?"

"Oh…oh, no. I t doesn't hurt." I could feel the awe in his voice.

"Excellent," she reached behind him and grabbed the base of the plug. She began to rock it in his asshole.

"Oh!" his face lit up and his pelvis rocked back and forth, "Oh, my."

Daphne played with him then. One hand on his cock, holding him in place, squeezing hard so he couldn't cum, she pushed and pulled on the plug. She corkscrewed it and wiggled it, and Chuckie moved this way and that. His knees buckled, and he put one hand out and grabbed the counter.

Daphne let go of his cock then. She reached around and pulled his head around and down to her. She pressed her lips to his.

He was groaning, moaning, making guttural sounds that sounded like they should have been made in a cave a million years ago.

Her hand went back to his cock. They continued kissing as she fucked him with her hand, squeezing so he couldn't cum, and working the plug against his prostate.

I tell ya, that girl is a pro!

Finally, she backed off. He was holding to the counter with one hand, and the other arm was around her shoulder. He was so weak she was holding him up.

She whispered into his ear. "I can't wait to get you into the pillory, or maybe on to the Sybian, but right now, I have hunger."

He moaned as she screwed his butt a particularly good one.

"What…what do you…"

"I want you to fuck me. I want you to put that big dick in me and stir my pussy. I want you to suckle my breasts, and stick your fingers up my asshole. In short, I want you to do me as good as I'm doing you.

She went to the poster bed and sat down.

He stood for a moment, breathing hard, trying to collect his thoughts, then, good boy, he walked over to Daphne. He walked a little gingerly, he did have a full asshole, but that was good. It was driving him over the edge. I could see the long string of pre-cum issuing from his cock.

He laid her down then, and he began to kiss her. He kissed his way up her legs, sliding his tongue and lips over her flesh. He dove into her cunt with his tongue, and I could tell he had a long one. He groped her breasts, yet delicately, feeling for what she wanted and trying to give it to her.

Finally, he set his cock to her pussy and began to tease her. He ran the rod up her lab, flicked her clit with his head, then back down. Over and over. Inserting an inch, then drawing back and continuing.

She began to lurch up at him, tried to ensnare his manhood with her pussy.

He moved back, pulling away so she couldn't quite engulf him.

She groaned in frustration, and he stirred the outside of her slit with his dick again. And again and again. It was one of the most educated teases I had ever seen.

"Don't worry," he said. "I'm not going to cum until you do. I won't even cum then, if you don't want me to."

Oh, my God, what a dream. He could make drinks and omelettes. He was polite. And he could hold himself back until the woman was actually satisfied.

At that moment I wanted him more than anything. But I knew the rules. No fucky fuck between blood. All I needed was to get pregnant by my own kin and spit out an idiot.

On the screen Daphne was thrashing back and forth, desperate for a cum, but he kept it just out of her reach. A true master, he tantalized and titillated and brought her along. And, finally, her begging and crying and even pounding on him with her fists, he pushed her over the edge.

She groaned loudly, so loudly that I could actually hear it in the computer room. She closed her eyes and squeezed her body, and the orgasm hit. It overwhelmed her, blew her away, and she was obviously out of her mind.

God, what a cum. I was so jealous.

Then I got an idea. Giggling, I ran to my purse and took out a lipstick, then I ran for the stairs.

They were still just laying there, him on top of her, and I ran across the cement floor.

He looked confused, "What?"

She just looked, and I realized that he had actually fucked her stupid. What a man!

I squatted next to the bed, and I colored his lips.

His eyes went wide, were sort of shocked.

I kept pressing the tube, rolling on the color, and, suddenly, he groaned and arched his back.

"OHHHH!"

He was still in her, and her eyes opened. She could feel him squirting his batter deep into her.

I ran back across the room, laughing. The dear boy had actually cum just from having lipstick put on him. He really was ready to be a girl.

"I'm sorry I came in you," Chuckie said to Daphne.

"Oh, I never mind a little sperm up the coosh. She leaned forward and looked intently into his eyes. "But tell me, how did you ever learn to…be so good?"

He actually blushed a little.

"Well, I'm not supposed to tell anybody, but you are family, after all."

We were sitting on the patio having the first of our afternoon drinks. The dear boy had fixed us some Smoked and Salteds. Here's his recipe…

2 oz Bourbon

.25 oz maple syrup

5 dashes bitters

Stir with ice and strain into a glass with a large ice cube. A slice of orange on top.

And they were de-fucking-licious!

They were made even more delicious when we insisted that he stir them with his beautiful, iron hard cock.

"Out with it," I muttered as he hesitated.

"Well, I showed an interest in sex right away, and mother finally realized that she might just well give in. We never fucked, mind you, but when father was away and she was horny she would have me get her off manually or orally. But I was never allowed to put it in her. She liked lengthy sessions, and she taught me quite a lot. But," he looked at me, "she always said that you were the expert when it came to sex."

"Well," I agreed modestly, "I have been known to take a man to heaven a time to two.

"Oh, I can't wait!"

Daphne laughed.

I said, "Maybe later."

He looked disappointed, so I patted his cock and said, "You just came."

"So no cuming until I recharge."

"Don't worry. you're young. It won't be long. But we may need to put you on a diet at some point."

"Oh." That didn't sit well.

"But the more you get into loose lips over there, without cuming, the better."

"What? Did you just refer to a part of my anatomy as—"

"If the shoe fits," I waved a hand airily. To Chuckie: "But that doesn't mean we can't get started. Go get a pillow to kneel on and we can start your lessons right now."

Chuckie actually clapped his hands in glee. He rushed into the house.

Daphne leaned towards me. "Why does your sister think you're better at sex?"

"We used to have contests, who could make each other cum the best. I always won."

She giggled and Chuckie returned. Quickly, he was on his knees, tongue deep in my pussy, and learning the fine art of getting a woman off.

The rest of the day Chuckie practiced what he learned on Daphne. The poor girl actually had two screaming Os. Then he fixed us a sumptuous repast: he barbecued ribs and served those viands with cheese dipped potato skins. The boy could cook, and I wondered if maybe I was going to have to revise my opinion of my sister. She had done a marvelous job with Chuckie.

Then we drank for a while, Chuckie screwed Daphne some more, and I went upstairs to diddle myself. God, I was getting horny.

The next day we took Chuckie to the make up table.

"Now then," I asked as I brushed out his hair. "I noticed you have a couple of bumps. Have you been taking hormones?"

"I have," he admitted. "But I've been careful. I want a big set of boobs, but I want my penis to still work."

I nodded, brushed his hair this way and that, analyzed what style would suit him best. The dear boy did have luscious hair.

"Well, until you get large enough, there are tricks."

I showed him how to wear a bra. He had his own shelf bra, and it was perfectly sized. It showed his nips. His nips were larger than normal, the hormones were doing their job.

"Now, we tape under the pecs, the mini boobs in your case, like this." I squeezed his little titties together and it gave him better cleavage instantly.

"Oh," he said.

"Daphne?"

I held his hair back and Daphne applied a streak of make up, a shadow to create a valley, and suddenly his eyes went real big. "Oh, my God!"

Daphne and I grinned. In the mirror it suddenly looked like he was a C cup.

He turned a bit and the effect lessened. "Oh," a slight disappointment.

"Don't worry," I touched his shoulder. Yours're coming, and until they do, don't turn sideways."

"Huh."

"And choose your lighting," Daphne instructed. "Learn when lighting will accentuate the shadows, or expose them. A little dim lighting and you are going to look a D cup."

"Oh, my," he breathed, absolutely thrilled.

"Now then, let's talk make up."

For the next two hours we had a wonderful, girly time. We laid on the concealer and the blush and the foundation and all that. We curled his eyelashes—is it my imagination or do boys really have better lashes than girls?—and shadowed his eyes until they were mysterious vales. In the vales his eyes sparkled with secrets.

Then, my favorite, lips.

"This is plumper. You already have good lips, but we want you to have great lips."

"An Angelina mouth," he whispered. He knew what he wanted.

Then we stained his lips.

"Why not lipstick?"

"This is longer lasting. Then you don't have to put on as much lipstick. It will make clean up easier, too."

We chose a shade of red that was not exactly shiny, but metallic. He smacked his lips several times and admired the look.

"Okay, now the clothes. Any thing in particular that you would like to wear for your first foray into true feminism?"

"Sorry, I only have two suitcases and I didn't have enough room to pack anything."

"Oh, I have lots of closets. I've been collecting clothes for years and I never throw anything away."

We crossed the hall and entered one of the rooms I use for storage. In the room were racks and racks of expensive dresses, shoes, skirts, blouses, lingerie, everything.

He was like a scamp in heaven, going from one rack to another, holding up articles of clothing and asking our opinion. Daphne and I sipped our drinks and thoroughly enjoyed his childish joy. It was so good to be young. Daphne had told him she preferred younger men, and I did, too. There is just something so refreshing about having a large and dripping and always hard cock at your disposal. Young men never get tired, are never jaded, and are more than willing to live dangerously.

In fact, I recommend, if you older gals want a true fountain of youth, that you take on younger lovers as often and as many as you can.

Anyway, Chuckie finally decided on a slinky black dress. Classic. It had a slit up the side for showing off the stems, and a low neck that would just work with his new boobs.

We put him in garters, nylons, slipped the dress on him, then gave him high heels.

Now he was our height, or so close it didn't matter. And, you know? It is a better world when everybody is the same size. No looking up or looking down.

"Okay, girlfriend, you are almost complete. Shall we adorn your loveliness with jewels and gems?"

"Oh, please!"

We took him back to the make up table and I brought out my dazzlers. I've managed to accumulate a pretty good collection of jewelry over the years, and he stared in awe at the necklaces and earring and bracelets and rings.

He looked at me. Or, perhaps I should say 'she' looked at me. "Are you sure? These must be so expensive!"

"Jewelry doesn't usually wear out. Besides, the joy they get from being worn by someone so lovely as yourself makes them feel younger."

He looked at me and giggled.

I smiled, "At least it makes me younger to see them so appreciated."

We went diamonds then. Daphne picked out some string earrings that really caught the light. I selected a necklace that would make the eyes glitter and sparkle and reveal his chestal charms. Then we bangle-ized him with shiny silver, and he picked out a selection of rings.

Then we stood in front of the big mirror in the hallway downstairs. We oohed and awed, turned this way and that, showed a bit of thigh, a flash of titty, and posed and posed and posed.

Two full breasted women with the cheer of years and moist vaginas. One slender girl with rather amazing boobs, who looked like a diamond in the night.

And took lots and lots of cell pictures.

The end of this summer," I told Chuckie, "We're going to get you a professional photo shoot. Guaranteed this is a summer you will remember."

"I'm already remembering it!" his eyes filled up. "I've never felt this way before. It's…it's everything I've ever dreamed of."

Quickly we group hugged and hushed his tears. "Don't mess your make up, dear."

Finally, we all sat down in the living room and sampled some more of Chuckie's awesome mixology talents.

We were sipping 'A Place in the Suns,' the recipe being,

1 oz fresh lemon
1 oz fresh orange juice
2 oz Rye
Shaken, not stirred, thank you James,
and a slice of orange.

It wasn't an expensive concoction, but it was a true sip of what those nasty old Gods liked to imbibe.

And I said, "Are you ready for a little fun?"

Chuckie looked at me. "Really?" The dear boy was almost drooling. Then, a little dismay, "But I just got dressed like this," he inspected himself winsomely.

"Tut tut," I waved away his objection. "Why do you think girls get all prettied up?"

He looked at me.

I grabbed his cock and squeezed. "So they can be ravaged a bit."

He giggled.

"Come along," I took his hand, "Let Auntie show you what that dungeon is really for."

We descended to my sacred sanctum and I turned on a mix of my favorites, things like:

I don't Know (McCartney)

Still the Rain (Karen Lovely)

Bad Romance (Ariana Savalas)

And so on.

The dungeon filled with soft but savage music, guaranteed to thrill the soul.

I took him on a tour of butt plugs and dildos. The dear boy had a liking for tall hose holy hole fillers, and I felt he should know the ins and the outs of them. Sorry about that pun, but I just couldn't resist.

"This is delicious, but it needs a slight curve. There is a brand that is heat shapable, you can put the curve in it, but I don't have one right now. I broke it."

"You broke a butt plug?" asked Daphne.

"I have an ass that works, unlike some of us," I sniffed.

She pinched mine and giggled.

"Now this one is so much fun," I held up a plug with a horse's tail on it. "Don't try to run with it, though. You may feel like a gorgeous, prancing horse, but you can trip if you don't force yourself to plod lightly."

Daphne and Chuckie giggled.

After I had finished my spiel I turned to Chuckie. "Now then, dear boy, choose a toy."

For right now?

"Nope," I answered mysteriously.

Curious, he examined my wall and chose a beautiful pink and bulbous prostate massager with a slight curve.

"Oh, you're in for it now."

"Why?" he asked me.

"You'll find out. Daphne, since you're the baggage, I must insist you perform layman duties." I held out my empty glass.

"I'll put arsenic in yours," she retorted. she ran up the stairs, ran across the house, we could hear her feet padding along, and returned just as quickly. She was getting somewhat of an education and she didn't want to miss a thing.

"Now then,"I opened a drawer. "Here is the Sybian equivalent of what you picked out."

I took out an attachment that was shaped very similar to the butt plug Chuckie had selected.

"A real Sybian? Oh, my gosh," Chuckie's eyes lit up. "I always wanted to…mother has one…but I heard they aren't good for men. They just make the asshole numb."

"That's only if the man tries to use it like a woman. A Sybian is designed for a woman, and it fits her anatomy, and it is particular designed to rub that clit and find the G-spot.

"A man simply must turn the setting way down and choose a shape that is more suited to his anatomy, which, I might add, you have done." I held the attachment up. "This little fellow is going to acquaint you with your prostate, which is the equivalent of a woman's G-spot. It is called a P-spot."

We all sipped our drinks, and I led them over to the poster bed. I picked up a remote and pressed a button. A motor lurched into life, and the sound drew their attention upward.

A Sybian descended from the gloom above the bed. It was on four ropes and sank until it touched the bed. I put the attachment on and stood back.,

"Now then, when you seat yourself you should wrap your wrists around the ropes to help you stay upright. Let's grease you up. This is going to be a hell of a ride and I don't want you hurting yourself."

Daphne and I applied lube, a lot of lube, to his asshole, then slathered it all over the Sybian attachment. “Okay,” I said. “Upsy daisy.”

Carefully, Chuckie got onto the bed and positioned himself above the Sybian. He wiggled his dress up his thighs and his hips and spread his legs and I helped him fit the massager to his brown button, then he sank slowly but determinedly down.

“Oh,” he whispered, his eyes wide.

Daphne grinned and gave his cock a few strokes.

“Feel it in there?” I asked.

“Oh, yes.” he was already gasping for breath.

“Good. Here’s the first and only setting.” I clicked the remote.

We heard the sound of the Sybian motor, a very low hum, and Chuckie instinctively arched his back at the unfamiliar vibrations that ran through his rectum.

“Oh…oh…”

“Now, wrap your hands in the cords and relax.”

Daphne and I sat on the bed and sipped our drinks. We began chatting like he wasn’t even there.

“He really is a dear boy, isn’t he.”

“The best,” I agreed.

“How did you learn this stuff?”

“Well, there were the contests with my sister, and then there was a long assortment of lovers, sometimes shabby sometimes a wonder. And, of course, I am a well read woman.”

“You are?”

“Oh, yes. Have I ever showed you my library?”

“Why, no! I didn’t even know you had one.”

“Chuckie, dear? We’re going to go upstairs for a half hour. You be a good boy, and don’t cum.” I walked to a drawer and took out a cock ring. I returned and put it around Chuckie’s red and drooling member. “Now, don’t take this off. Store up your juices and when I get back I’ll show you how to expel them. Okey dokey?”

“Uh…uh…yeah.” he was red faced, eyes closed, lost in the wondrous vibrations of the Sybian Goddess.

Daphne and I went upstairs, to my attic.

"I fixed this room special. No moths or bugs, proper atmosphere, no mold."

I turned on the light and she stared around in wonder. "Oh, My. God!"

The walls of the room were lined with shelves, and the shelves were packed with books.

There was a reading chair in the center of the room, and a table with an assortment of dildos on it.

We went to the shelves, and Daphne picked out books at random and leafed through them.

`A Defense of Masochism,' by Anita Phillips.

'A Woman's Guide To a Female Led Relationship,' by Victoria West.

'Erotic Power: An Exploration of Dominance and Submission,' by Gini Scott.

A complete collection of Anne Michelle's works.

Then we came to a glass fronted section, and Daphne asked, "What are these?"

"My pride and Joy. A collection of works by Grace Mansfield, and this shelf is her friend, Alyce Thorndyke."

Daphne picked up a Thorndyke book and examined it.

"That one, Alyce Thorndyke, she has an incredible background. She was actually kidnapped by drug dealers. Now, how do you think she survived months of being used and abused?

"How?" she looked at me raptly.

"Like the Arabian nights, keep them enthralled with incredible stories. Except, in her case, she used her imagination and thought up new ways of sex and kept the drug dealers too horny to kill her."

"Are you kidding?"

"Cross my heart." I ran a finger over my chest twice.

Daphne handed me the book and I returned it to its proper place.

"I'd love to get that girl in my dungeon. I'll bet she could teach me a few tricks."

"I doubt that," Daphne said wryly.

I giggled and cupped her breast.

Shall we get back to Chuckie? It's probably time to turn him over and cook the other side.

Laughing, arm in arm, we left my library. And let me say only one other thing. People who are serious about sex, who aren't just dilettantes, or youngsters who think they know something but don't, should have a library. A real live library. Proof against computer crashes and energy black outs. There is absolutely nothing in the world like a little alone time with the masters, hearing the rain patter on the roof while you explore your inner self with a king-sized plastic lover.

In the basement dungeon Chuckie was just right.

His cock was purple and dripping, pulsing, trying to get past the cock ring, and failing.

He was lurching on the Sybian, his eyes closed, his hands wrapped in the cords so he wouldn't collapse and fall off the beast.

And he…she…was so beautiful. The way his breasts bulged with him gasping for breath, the way his face was flushed and covered with light perspiration, the delicate set of his desperate features, the way his bangles jangled as he lurched. He was ready.

"Okay, Chuckie. It's time to take you to heaven."

"It…it…is…is?"

He could hardly speak.

"Daphne, I want you to suck on his cock. Not too much, and be careful of the area under the head."

Daphne crawled up on the bed and took his cock in her mouth.

Funny thing about a man getting butt fucked, they don't always remain hard. They just start focusing on prostate pleasure and forget about their cock. It opens up a whole new erogenous world to them. But a little oral stimulation and that cock gets harder than it ever did before.

Daphne was on all fours, her boobs hanging down to the bed, her neck bent back a little, and she looked like a dog sniffed an ass. But her mouth was doing its job. Chuckie was groaning and lurching, and it was plain to see that he was totally ready.

"Now, then, my little Chuckles," I took his nipples in both hands and squeezed them. His whole body spasmed. "I want you to forget about cuming." I laughed.

Daphne actually tried to laugh, with a mouthful of cock.

I went to my workbench and brought back a tens unit. I had Daphne draw back, and I attached one of the leads to his cock ring.

"Back to work, girl," I advised Daphne. "But don't touch the cock ring."

I then attached the other lead to a slim probe. I put that probe underneath Chuckie, slid it up the underside of the massager and into his ass. I could feel it when it touched the bulge of his prostate inside.

I stood back and held the tens unit. "Okay, Chuckles, are you ready for the orgasm of your life?"

"Uh…uh…" He nodded. He was drooling. I knew his cock was drooling into Daphne's mouth.

"Three, two, one…" I flipped the switch on the tens unit and current went through his sexual organs, his balls felt like they exploded, his asshole muscles began to contract spasmodically. His chest arched.

In front of him I saw Daphne's eyes go wide. His cock was bulging and purple, and I knew he was forcing the sperm up the tube and into her mouth. Cock ring be damned, he was having the orgasm of his life.

His mouth opened and his eyes stared into some wonderful Neverland.

For a long twenty seconds he hung there, his hands now clenched because of the electricity coursing through his sex organs, holding the ropes and he wasn't able to fall.

I turned the tens unit off.

Still he jerked. Sperm was leaking out of Daphne's mouth. She couldn't swallow it all.

He was like a marionette, lurching and dancing under the strings of electrical sex.

I placed a hand on his face and said, "It's okay. It's okay. Let yourself relax."

Still, he couldn't. Not for a whole minute. He had no semen left in him, his body was jerking, and he was totally helpless.

Then, finally, the spasms became less. His shoulders started to slump, and his hands relaxed.

Like syrup pouring out of a frozen can, he collapsed. He fell forward.

I gently tugged Daphne and she moved back and made way for him.

He lay there, breathing, wondering what he was doing on earth. Helpless and unable to move.

"Come on, Daphne. Let's leave this poor soul to recover.

Daphne and I went up the stairs, poured some drinks and went swimming.

It was a full hour before Chuckie finally came out to the patio. At that, his legs were shaking and he needed to hold on to things with his hands.

He managed to make it to a lounge and sat down.

Of the girl, there were still traces.

His make up was smeared, his dress was ripped. His hair looked, well, electrified.

He wasn't smiling, he was just alive. More alive than he had ever been in his life. We handed him a drink and he sipped it, and we laughed.

That was a glorious summer. The games we played, the sex was grand. I even got off a lot of times, though not by dick, and boy did I want that.

But I will always remember that moment when Chuckie was sitting, drained of his semen, scoured down to a nub, and what he said to us.

He didn't even look at us. He just asked, and in tones that indicated he was asking the whole universe… "What 's next?"

Daphne and I, of course, rolled with laughter.

END

Full Length Books from Gropper Press

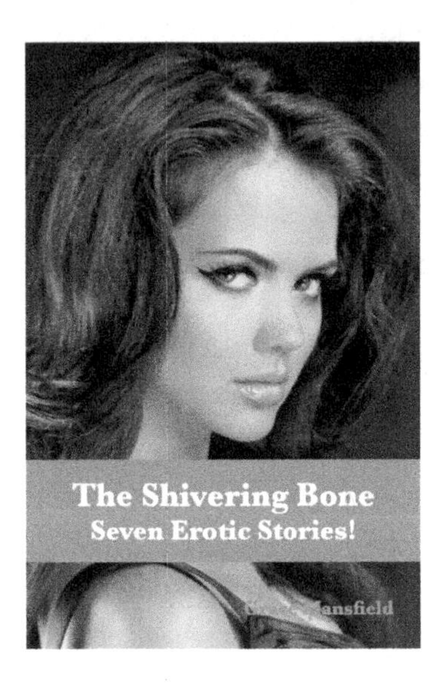

Save money! Get more stories or your buck!

Feminized by a sorority…an actor has to get feminized for a role… escaping the United States through sex…He thought he was born a man…and more…more…more!

The Shivering Bone

The Great Gender Revolt

Published on Kindle,

appeared in 'The Secret is Out.'

PART ONE

"I'm sorry, Mrs. Hardy, but there's nothing we can do."

I stared at the ring of doctors standing in the waiting room. "But…I don't…what is happening?"

The doctors hemmed and hawed, and finally a nurse shooed them out. All of them, and they were glad to go, which should have told me something right there. What doctor gives up his position to a nurse? Unless it is really something so bad the doctor can't confront it?

"Mrs. Hardy, sit here. I'll go over what has happened."

Dully, somewhat in shock, I sat down. Ten days ago I had brought my husband in. Joe had COVID. Corona Virus 19. I knew he had had a rough time, but I had waited outside, talked to him on the phone, and prayed to God.

Then the doctors called me in, and they were going to tell me something, but that something had fallen to the nurse.

"Your husband didn't have COVID 19."

"What? But why did you keep him here?"

"As you know the virus has been mutating, and Joe presents what we think may be the final phase of the mutation."

I shook my head, not understanding.

"The doctors have labeled it COVID SC, and it is quite a bit more virulent than the normal COVID."

By this time I was ashen and even trembling. My wonderful husband had…had…

"What COVID SC does is attack the Y chromosomes in a man's body."

"Wait a minute. A woman doesn't have Y chromosomes…does this thing only attack men?"

"Yes, Mrs. Hardy."

For a long moment I grappled with the concept, attacking Y chromosomes? Why? And what did it do?

"So is he going to be all right?"

"He's ready to go home right now."

That was too easy, and I stared at her suspiciously. "What aren't you telling me?"

I had visions of Joe being a basket case, of him laying in bed for the rest of his life and myself having to wait on him hand and foot.

"Joe has turned into a woman."

"What?" I felt like somebody else was asking her the question. I felt like I was outside my body.

"That's right. All the Y characteristics have been deleted from his body. The COVID SC made him into a woman."

"Okay. Enough. Tell me the truth. I want to see my husband!"

I was pretty frantic, my hands were shaking. Heck, my whole body was shaking, and the nurse placed her hands on mine and tried to calm me down.

"We can go see him whenever you'd like. In fact, we don't have to go see him, I'll have him brought down. But I need to know you're calm enough to handle it."

I did deep breathing, under her advice, for a minute, then I managed to frame a decent question. "You're not a nurse, are you?"

"No. I'm a doctor who…let's just say my specialty is helping people undergoing transition."

"Transition?"

"Sex change. People are born male and want to be a female, or the other way around. I counsel them and—"

"I know…I know." I wanted her voice to stop.

She waited a while, she was willing to wait for me to come to grips with my new situation. Finally, I nodded. "Can you bring him down now?"

She hit a contact on her cell phone and spoke into it. To me she said, "He'll be right down."

I sat on that uncomfortable chair in the waiting room for five minutes, and the things that went through my mind.

Bruce Jenner. Transitioning. Having the testicles and manhood cut off. What had happened? The doctors said they didn't do anything, but Joe was now a woman? How could that be.

The elevator dinged at the end of the waiting room, the doors slid back, and my husband was pushed out.

Joe had been six feet tall, 200 pounds, lots of muscles, short hair. He owned a construction company, and he looked like it. He even watched football and smoked big cigars.

Now he was five foot six, maybe 120 pounds, and his face was a delicate oval. His hair was longer, much longer, and his lips were plump.

But he was still recognizable. He was Joe, but he was a she.

I fainted.

I drove home, and Joe cried all the way.

I had never seen Joe cry before in my life.

"What am I going to do?" he kept asking.

So, by the time we were home, I said, "First off, you're going to suck it up. Being a woman isn't the end of the world. You might even like it."

Tough love, eh? Well, he needed it! Heck, I've been a woman for 30 years, and I have enjoyed the heck out of it. Men opening doors for me, pulling out chairs, whistling when I show a little leg…it's all good.

Of course, I have had to learn to bite my tongue, people who are physically weaker don't deliberately provoke people who are physically stronger. But that's sort of universal, you know?

We pulled into the driveway and got out of the car, and first thing idiot Bob comes over.

I call him 'Idiot' Bob because he's sort of a goof. Always making stupid remarks, acting all manly, and looking down on women. He even treats his wife, Joanna, like she's a lame brain. Now that's an idiot if ever there was one.

"Hey! Joe…you're not Joe."

Joe was on the other side of the car, head down and hair hanging in front of his face.

"That's Joe."

"What?"

He went around the car before I could stop him, bent down and looked up into Joe's face.

"Holy fu—what the hell happened? This isn't Joe!"

Denial, in the face of proof. I told you he was an idiot.

"Joe caught a new strain of COVID."

"And it changed him into a woman?"

Suddenly Bob backed up. "Whoa, man. Don't come close to

me! I don't want to catch that shit!"

What we didn't know was that it was already too late. The doctors had said Joe wasn't contagious, but they were working off old COVID 19 data, not new COVID SC data.

"Go home, Bob."

Bob went.

We entered the house and I threw all the medicines that had been given to me for Joe into the trash. The damage was done, no medicine was going to help Joe now.

Joe went into the living room and sat down in front of the TV. He didn't turn it on, he just sat and stared at the floor.

And I knew I had to do something. The gloom was thicker than Joe's farts after chili. It was the kind of gloom that, if left alone, would swelter and finally flare up into suicide.

Heck, just because he was a girl didn't mean I didn't love him. In fact, I liked how cute he was. His big honker had turned into a cute button. His hair was really thick and luscious, though it needed a combing. And his face was…I blinked.

Joe was sitting there sad as Jesses James after he got shot. And what do women do when they are sad?

I turned Pandora to a classics station and turned it up so it filled the house. The neighbors might think I was nuts, celebrating after my husband had been in the hospital for ten days, but half the neighbors were. like Idiot Bob, and the other half were like me, sexy women who needed no excuse to party.

"What are you doing?" asked Bob.

I took his…her…hand and lifted her up. I led her to the kitchen table and sat her down.

"What?"

I poured her a big, old whiskey and Coke. I didn't know, maybe she would like wine spritzers, but she used to love Coke and bourbon, so…

I went to the bedroom and grabbed my make up kit and brought it back to the table.

"What's that?"

"It's good looks in a bottle," I cracked. "Now drink some more."

So he sipped, and protested and said he didn't want to put on make up.

I held up my hand mirror. "You see this?" He stared at himself. "That is an ugly woman. Do you want to stay an ugly woman?"

"Uh…I don't want make up."

"Why?"

"It's…it's all gooey stuff and things."

"Gooey stuff and things? Are you kidding me? That's not what your dick says when I wear make up."

"That's different."

"Why?"

"You're a woman."

"And I'm a beautiful woman," I smiled, flipped my chestnut hair, and puckered a kiss at him. He stared at my red lips. "You, on the other hand, are an ugly woman. Now shut up and drink and let me do my magic."

So he sipped, a lot, and I worked him over. Eyebrows, pluck those babies, leave nice, little arches. Moisturize his face, foundation, base, all that stuff, even a little rouge. Then, my real fun, I worked on his eyes. Oooh, sweet charcoal on the lids to accentuate his grey eyes. Lengthen those lashes. Mmmm. And, finally—by now he was fascinated—I painted his lips.

And showed him the hand mirror.

His eyes went wide. He was no longer an ugly woman. He was beautiful. Pardon me, I keep slipping, SHE was beautiful.

"Oh my God. Is that me?"

"We should have done your hair first, but I'll just comb it out. We can style it later." I combed her lush locks out, and it was gorgeous. I trimmed them and brushed his hair with a wet brush and managed to get it to curl around his face. Mmm. Good looking bitch, if I do say so. In fact, I think I was a little jealous.

DING DONG!

Joe panicked. "Oh, no!"

"Just sit here," I commanded, and I went to the front door.

"Hi Jesse. Bob told me that Joe is…changed. I'm sorry, please forgive me, but I had to see for myself."

I brought my neighbor into the kitchen.

Joe was frozen. He was totally frazzled. His face was bright red under the make up.

"Joe? Oh. My. God! you are…" she turned to me, "She's beautiful!"

"The magic of cosmetics. Want to help?"

"Absolutely. What's next?"

"Nails."

"Long and stylish?"

"The longest. And the reddest. We have to make sure that Joe never forgets how beautiful she is. You can imagine how messed up the poor dear is. She doesn't even want to be a woman. Can you imagine that?"

"Oh, Lord," Joanne breathed. "Why not? Especially if you look like that?"

So we spread Joe's hands out and put on inch long stilettos, and we painted them blood red. Mmmm.

Then we took pictures.

"You know, she's still in that stupid hospital gown."

Joe looked down at her gown. She looked up, and her eyes were just so doe-like and cute and trusting.

"I've got a dress that might be perfect, but her feet…I don't have any shoes."

"I've got some heels that will work. You get the dress."

Joanne rushed back to her house, and maybe that was when Idiot Bob got infected, though I tended to think that it happened what he got close to Joe earlier.

I got a blue dress, very metallic and shimmery, and I helped her put it on, and that was when it finally hit me. I was sitting there, staring at her, and Joanne re-entered the kitchen and stopped.

"What's wrong?"

I couldn't speak plainly, I was so shook by what I had just realized, that my speech was sort of…burbly, if you get what I mean. But I managed to say, "He…she…has no dick."

And it was plain to see. The dress hugged her mid section and presented her crotch, and there was no familiar man bump. There was no peeny lump, no hill where a cock might have been. Instead, it was just smooth.

"You're right," Joanne said, standing next to me and staring at Joe.

Joe was drunk now. I had been refilling her as needed. And she looked down at her crotch, and she looked up at us and in her sweet voice she said. "I have a cunt." And he began to cry. And not just little sniffling sobs, but a full blown make up shattering hysterical cry.

Joann and I rushed to her. "Don't, honey. You'll make your mascara run."

"It's okay, Joe. It's okay."

And: "A cunt is a lot better than a cock, anyway."

Her tears slowed down and she looked up at us. "It is?"

"Absolutely. If you get a boner, as a man, then everybody can see it. It's almost embarrassing the way guys are always walking around trying to hide the bump in their pants."

I added, "When you have a pussy it's easy to hide. you can be horny as all get out, and the only sign is going to be if somebody sees your panties are wet.

Joe giggled. Then she sobered. Then she said, "Instead of hard ons I'll get wet?"

"That's the skinny, Minnie," I reassured her.

"Have another drink, Joe," suggested Joanne. To me: "Do you have nylons?"

I did. And a garter belt. I got them and we lifted up Jo's dress and helped her put on garters and showed her how to roll nylons on.

Finally, we were done, and it wasn't a bad job. Her face was pretty, and her form was good, and I suddenly noticed something. "Her boobs are bigger."

"Really?"

"When I picked her up at the hospital she had little mounds. Now they're big."

"Well, she is stacked."

And Joe said, "I've got boobs." But, fortunately, he didn't break out in tears again. Of course, he was getting drunker, and that might have helped.

"Wait here," blurted Joanne suddenly.

While she was gone I had Joe walk across the room, and I gave her pointers on how to walk in heels. "Toes in line, keep those knees pointed inward. Yeah, let that butt sway."

Joanne came back in, and she had Idiot Bob in hand.

Bob stopped and stared.

Joe stood still and stared.

We girls giggled.

Joanne: "What do you think, Bob?"

Bob: "Wow."

And we all felt it then. In an instant, Bob had stopped seeing Joe as a man and started seeing her as a woman.

And, perverse me, I pushed it. The music was going good and I said, "Dance with her, Bob."

Joanne clapped her hands in glee. This was her manly man hubbie, a homophobe from way back, and now he was trapped.

"I don't…I think—"

"Oh, Bob. You big sissie. She's a beautiful woman, and I just gave you permission to dance with her. Now take her in your arms."

Joe, for her part, opened her mouth in shock. Now not just to look like a woman, but to be treated like one, to be danced with, to be taken in the arms of a man…yet, I say it again, she was drunk.

Hesitantly, but with a vigor I found disconcerting, and would find troublesome later on, Bob took Joe in his arms and danced with her.

At first they sort of shuffled, arm's length. But something was happening to Bob, and he pulled Joe closer, and then they were body to body, and yet Bob kept his head back and stared at Joe, and his face was a picture of raptness which I didn't understand.

Then Bob started moving his head closer, and his lips started to focus on Joe's red lips, and I finally got the message.

"That's enough." I parted them, slightly in shock. Bob was actually going to kiss Joe?

And Joanne seemed a bit…weird about that.

On one hand she had encouraged it, and she hadn't spoken up, I had. She had seemed fascinated by the scene.

I think that was the point that I realized that things were happening here that I didn't understand.

That night I showed Joe how to make love like a woman. I dressed her in a bra—man, those boobs were world class—and garters and peignoir, full make up, and then I kissed her. And kissed her, and kissed her.

She was breathing hard, panting like a dog, and I cupped her mons and felt how wet her panties were.

Then I laid her down and nibbled on her chest. I loved those nipples and I palpated those mounds, and she began arching her back and moaning.

"Oh, baby," she said.

I just smiled, kissed her some more, and put my fingers up her pussy.

She went wild. She began to buck and squirm, and I could feel her moistness, and the heat, and I knew she wanted it.

"Oh, this is different," she moaned.

I went to my drawer and pulled out a dildo.

"What's that? You have one of those? What are you going to —"

"Shh," I whispered. "This is where it gets good."

I pushed her back on the bed, and—interesting, I was actually physically stronger than her now—and I pushed her knees apart.

She actually struggled a little. Well, heck. She was a guy, and about to be penetrated. No wonder, eh?

I began to lick her, slurping my tongue up her sweet labs, I made sure she was wet and ready, then I placed the dildo into her junction.

"Oh!" Her eyes were wide.

I pushed it gently, and it slid in nicely. Apparently my little Joe was hot to trot, and quite well lubricated. Shortly she was biting the sheets and groaning and twisting her hips all over the place.

"Yeah, baby," I pushed it in hard, then let it slide slowly out. The interchange of hard and soft drove Joe wild. She tried to grab it herself, but I was able to fend her off and stay in charge.

"Please! Please! Do me!"

"I am, baby. I am."

And she groaned and held to my wrists and even felt up her own tits. She pulled those nips and started to spasm. I knew it was happening, so I turned on the vibrator.

"OOHHH!" Joe wailed, her body thrashing on the mattress, totally out of control.

"OOOHHH!"

And I reamed her out, circled the base of the vibrator and felt the tip circling within her, and her hips bounced and tilted and she had a massive orgasm. Not bad for it being her first female big O.

The next day was Monday, and I went to work with Joe. It wasn't just that I knew she needed help in adjusting, it was a feeling that I had, something deep inside that told me to be careful, to watch out, that there were things happening that I didn't fully understand.

We were in the truck, and she drove, and it was fun watching her figure out how to drive with high heels.

And there was still a bit of 'man' to her. She drove like a man, cutting people off, hogging a lane, telling somebody who wanted to get in line to 'fuck off.'

It made me frown, but I think I realized that it was okay. After all, we had just started her journey.

We stopped in front of the office trailer and got out, and the looks started right away. And it wasn't two minutes before everybody in the company was in the office, ogling Joe.

I explained the situation. Joe was still getting his feet wet, and everybody took it all right. In fact, they took it a little too well.

Suddenly I felt very small, being surrounded by all these big, hunky type construction workers.

And they were all crowding around Joe, staring at her, making crude remarks.

"You got some nice ta tas, Joe."

"Does this mean you'll be drinking wine instead of beer?"

"You got a nice ass, Joe."

It was like a gang bang. Not that I've ever seen one, or been in one, but it was like I imagined it would be. Guys crowding around, getting closer and closer, and then, I imagined, they would be pulling out their dicks, stroking them, getting ready for a little action.

I cut into the crowd. “All right, you guys. Show and tell is over. Back to work.”

It took a second, which surprised me, but then they all left, but with back glances and…and something in their eyes.

Lust? Was that lust?

So I stayed close to Joe, and she didn’t mind it, and we took off at noon. At that, it was a hard day. At least for me. It seemed like every guy wanted to come up and talk to Joe. And they were so damned familiar. Yes, she had been their male boss, but it was almost like they were trying to work up the courage to hit on her.

And Joe infected every last one of them.

We walked into a trendy restaurant. The kind that Joe hated when she was a man, but now her eyes lit up.

“Wow!”

That simple word made me smile.

And she ordered, get this, a veggie wrap!

“Joe?” I asked him when he made his order.

“It just feels right. And I’ve got to watch my figure. And can I have water with a slice of lemon in it?”

I watched, amazed, and felt like a pig eating my turkey breast.

And, when we left the restaurant I am pretty sure that Joe had infected over a 100 people.

A 100 people. Waiters and busboys, people at nearby tables, people passing by as we waited for a table. Even the fellow who parked the truck.

But, of course, I didn’t know it at the time. And I wouldn’t know it for a few days. But my first hint came that very night. But it was a strange hint that I only figured out after a few days, while putting pieces of strange behavior together.

"Bob wants to dance with Joe again."

"What?"

"He says he can't get it out of his mind."

"Really!"

We were standing on the shared lawn between our driveways.

"And here's the bad news. Last night, Joe couldn't get it up."

Joanne is one of those people who seem to want to talk about their love lives constantly. I guess it makes them the center of attention, or something.

"Happens to everybody at some time or another," I shrugged it off.

"Not to Bob. He's a male nympho. You hold up a toilet roll and he gets a boner."

We giggled at that. Then we heard: "Let go of me!"

Shocked, we looked at each other, and then ran for my house. That was Joe.

We burst into the kitchen and Bob was trying to kiss Joe. He was holding him in his arms, and Joe had his hands up, but Bob was so much stronger. He didn't use to be stronger, but he was now.

"Help me!" Joe yelped at us.

I cut in between the two…uh, between Joe and Bob. Joanne grabbed Bob by the collar and pulled him around. "What the fuck do you think you're doing?"

"I…I don't…" confusion left his eyes. "Joanne? What's going on?"

"You were trying to molest Joe. What the hell were you thinking?"

"I was? I don't…I didn't?"

I held Joe, who was sniffling in my arms. Funny, for the first time in my life I felt like a protector, and it felt good. It gave me a sense of power, made me feel strong and really worth something.

"You did! We just came in and…" suddenly we were all silent. I think it hit us that Bob really didn't know what he was doing.

"Take him home, Joanne."

"Come on, Bob," she held his arm and dragged him.

Bob looked like he wanted to cry. Like he wanted to apologize, bu that he wasn't really sure what for.

And that was my hint. But, like I say, I didn't really understand it for a few days. Until Wednesday, to be exact.

Six in the morning on Wednesday. It had been two days since Bob had gone out of control, and I was still puzzling over it. I was awake, Joe was sleeping next to me, and my mind was still turning over the odd situation of Bob and Joe.

Sure, he's a guy, and Joe looks like a…heck, he *is* a girl, but why did Bob overcome all societal conditioning and suddenly start forcing himself on women?

I mean, Bob's an idiot, but…but what was really going on?

KNOCK KNOCK!

I jumped up, I didn't want to wake Joe, and ran for the kitchen door. The kitchen. It had to be Joanne.

"Hey, girl, come on in."

Joanne entered the kitchen, and she looked a mess. She was bedraggled and miserable and looked like she had been crying.

"Oh, Jesse!" and she hugged me and started crying anew.

I let her cry for a moment, hoping it would just cry out, and then I put her at the table. "Hold on, coffee, and then we'll talk."

So I made some brew and poured a couple of cups, and the whole time Joanne sniffled.

"So what is happening?"

"Bob's turning into a girl!"

"What?" I almost spit out the coffee in my mouth.

"He couldn't get it up the other day. The next day he seemed a little smaller, but I figured…I don't know what I figured, but now his dick is real small, and it doesn't get hard, and I can see him changing."

"See how?"

"His hair is longer. His lips are fuller. It's like fat is moving around on his face, and his waist is smaller, and…and….I could swear he has little boobs!"

"Oh. My. God!" And it started to hit me, I started to put it all together, the way Bob had been acting, the way the men had crowded around Joe at the worksite, what Joanne had said about Bob getting a sudden case of Erectile Dysfunction…could it be? Were they? Were the men turning into women? All of them?

And on some, deep, dark level of perception I understood it. But it would be some weeks before it was scientifically proven true.

In every man there is a bit of woman. In every woman there is a bit of man.

But in Joe there was no man. All the Y chromosomes had been knocked out. Deleted. And that made him…a perfect woman.

Heck, I was imperfect. I still had bits of man in me. But Joe…

he was a better woman than me. And the men were attracted to him. And it was like a survival thing, they all wanted to have babies with Joe, and make the race perfect, but what nobody realized was that Joe was a carrier, so that even as the men were attracted to her, they were infected, and their Y chromosomes were being deleted.

I didn't fully realize that, the morning that Joanne talked to me over coffee, but I intuited it, pieces of it, and things were already coming together in my mind.

Joe, a woman, a perfect woman, a carrier, and if he wasn't stopped it could spell the end of the human race.

No more men.

Nothing but women.

OMFG!

PART TWO

I have never been a Lesbian.

Nothing against them, I just preferred men.

And I could make love to Joe, though she was a woman, because there was something in me that still saw her as a man.

Even though there was no man, no Y chromosome, at all, in Joe, my residual mental image of her was as a man.

I don't know why I explain that right now, probably for the same reason I did nothing about the situation once Joanne educated me.

I wasn't a coward, I understood the ramifications, but it was like being hit by a truck, sometimes it takes a couple of minutes to get back up on your feet.

Thursday, however, I swung into action.

First, I called the doctors and told them what was happening. They wanted to see Joe right away, but I wasn't ready for them to take her away, lock her up in some facility and poke her with needles for the rest of her life.

Second, I called lawyers to see what our rights were. Turns out, Joe and I had lots of rights. We had the right to sue, might come in handy, and we had the right to tell the doctors to go pound sand.

But, and here's the big one, if a state of emergency was declared we would have no rights. Which meant they could take Joe, and I, and lock us up and stick needles into us for the rest of our lives.

Third, based on what I had learned from points one and two, we ran for our lives.

I know, that's a little dire sounding, and it really wasn't that bad.

We loaded up our car, hid it in the airport parking lot, long term parking, Ubered to the work site and took one of the company trucks. Signed it out to one of the fellows who was on vacation.

When the FBI finally figured out what we had done it would be too late. We would be long gone, or, maybe, back home.

You see, I knew this COVID SC was going to happen fast. It had taken Bob two days to present symptoms. And I knew from talking to Joanne, over the next few days, and from what Joe had told me, that full change actually happened in about a week.

And Joe had infected probably 120 people, the restaurant and the guys working for him, and Bob, of course. And those 120 people would probably infect another 100 people each within two days. So by the time the FBI, or CDC, or the WHO, or whoever, got serious in their investigation, a full week would have passed. Or 100 X 100 X 100 X 100 X 100 X 100 X 100. Or 1 with 14 zeros behind it. Or 100 trillion people. Or, since there weren't that many people on earth, the whole earth would have been infected.

Or, to put in very slightly different terms. Within a couple of weeks 3.8 billion men would have turned into women.

We drove to our cabin in the hills. We stopped and shopped, we made sure we had plenty of propane, though it was summer and there was no big requirement for heat, and we made sure we had books and videos and extra clothes and everything, and then we did something sneaky.

When we arrived at our cabin we passed it by. We knew the Joneses lived two cabins down, so we went to their cabin. The FBI would take apart our cabin, and we could watch them from across the bay. The Joneses were on a world tour, so we were good.

And, as I said, I talked to Joanne.

Sure enough, some guys in hazmat suits came by and took everything out of the house, then surrounded it with yellow tape and armed guards.

Joanne gave me the daily report, and she even went out and talked to the men in hazmat suits and tried to get more information.

But they weren't very forthcoming.

And, a day later, Joe and I watched the 'Invasion of the Haz Mat' suits across the bay.

We had binoculars and we sat on the deck and watched the men take everything out of that house.

And, by the next day the shit storm had hit the world.

I mean, how can you hide the fact of 3.8 billion men turning into women from the world?

How can you stare at a TV screen and watch the male announcers get a little softer in appearance and manner, and then have the whole news thing taken over by women, and not be suspicious. I mean, every man in the world going on vacation at the same time?

"You can come home now," I was on the cell with Joanne. "Tape's down, but you 're going to need new furniture."

I smiled. I knew that would happen. I just didn't know it

would happen this fast.

I brought up the subject with Joe at dinner that night.

"We can go home. Joanne says it's safe."

Joe was different.

He had changed into a woman, and that had made her different, but there was something else going on with her.

"What?" I asked, as she hemmed and hawed. "What's wrong?"

"I don't know. I just feel…I don't know."

"Well, don't you feel like going home?"

"I do." But there was a big 'but' in there.

So I took her to bed. Well, isn't that the way women have manipulated men for the history of the human race? The only problem was that Joe wasn't a man anymore.

"Would you like me to do you tonight?"

"Yeah. Sure." But there wasn't a lot of enthusiasm.

I strapped on the dildo. Tell the truth, I liked the dildo. I used to love taking it, it was a good change up for a big, old flesh weenie, but now…now I loved giving it.

There was nothing better than kissing Joe's soft body to a nubbin. Of sucking on her big breasts, they were bigger than mine, and feel the electricity shoot through her. Of sliding that pole, Joe liked a big one, right up her love alley.

And her lips were so soft, and it was such a delight to hold myself over her, to brush her hair and kiss her cheek and nuzzle her neck.

And when she started to squirm and spasm, Oh, Lordie, it was a heaven I had never known.

And I freely admit, here and now, that I was into control. I loved controlling her. Bringing her to the Big O and pushing her over.

This night we spent a long time just making out on the front room couch. We sipped wine and each other, and we felt each other's tits, and I was feeling about as warm as warm could be. And I knew Joe was feeling the same way.

"Come on, babe," I led her by the hand through the cabin to our bedroom. It felt so good to hear her little feet pattering behind mine. And as I laid her down and fell on top of her I felt a surge of horniness that threatened me with a premature orgasm.

But I held off, and I went between her legs and spent a lot of time licking her, and then finger banging her. She was lusting and pulsing and her face was perspiring with lust when I crawled up and began to insert my fake penis into her.

Joe arched her body up to accept the dildo. Her lips spread and I pushed the point into her. She accepted the tool, and it slid down into her depths.

"Uh, yes!" she hugged me, and we played with each other's breasts and we kissed and loved and, she had a glorious orgasm.

Then it was my turn. In the darkness Joe put on the strap on, I could see the glint of light reflected in his eyes as he watched me. And I knew something was wrong.

Yet, when he fucked me, I couldn't tell that anything was wrong.

It was the same Joe, be it in a different body. The same mannerisms, the same way of eating me, of suckling me, and yet I knew something was wrong.

The next day we drove back to town. First we trundled our

belongings back to our own cabin. the furniture, and everything else, was gone, so we just put everything on the floor and left it.

In town it was obvious that panic had struck. Cars were abandoned here and there. Grocery stores were out of toilet paper. We just barely managed to get our grocery shopping done, the store was that empty. At that, we would be eating our meat from cans for a while.

Finally, we arrived at home.

Home sweet home.

Emptied of furniture. And all the little things that people collect throughout their lives. Pictures, Christmas ornaments, scrap books.

Everything gone.

But Joanne and Bob were there, and they welcomed us home.

Bob.

He was a lithesome blonde. Joanne had made her up and dressed her, and she was gorgeous.

And when Joe and I got out of the car she ran around to Joe, held his hands in a very feminine way, and just stared at Joe.

And Joe stared back.

Joanne and I stood together and watched them.

I felt a sinking in my heart, and I had the feeling Joanne was feeling the same.

Our men were women. And they were more attracted to each other than to us.

Still, what could we do about it? And that was when I started to realize that the changes women were going through were tougher than that of the men.

Men change into women, and they have to learn. But women

are left with the debris of the change.

What do you say to the man, who is now a woman, who is no longer interested in you?

And it was true. Observing the looks in Joe's and Bob's eyes, both Joanne and I knew that they were more interested in each other.

"I have some people you need to meet."

I looked at Joanne.

"This is Jesse Hardy. Her husband, Bob, was the first to be infected with the COVID SC mutation."

The room filled with ladies gave me a polite hand clap. We were all in Joanne's garage, which was bigger than any room in her house and so accommodated our numbers.

Our husbands, not just Joe and Bob, but the husbands of all the ladies, were in my house. Sitting and standing and talking and…and who knew what.

In the eyes of every woman in the house was a hurt. A betrayal. A loneliness that only a woman abandoned can understand.

"Okay," Joanne said. "We can meet and greet afterwards, but right now let's have reports.

A thin girl, Elsa, stood up. "Apparently not every man is changing into a woman. The actual statistic is about 90%, which is still considerable. The population of the United States will likely decrease severely, no estimates as of yet."

And that was her report.

Another gal stood up, Chantel, a chunky girl with heavy tits and a swollen face. Swollen with crying as much as anything else.

"The roads are still working, a lot of truckers are women now, but they keep driving. The real problem seems to be on the home front. Men change into women, panic, go through all sorts of emotional BS, and they have to be coddled into working and holding up their end."

She sat. And I wondered: *their end of what?*

And there were more reports. Talks about police protection, fire services, and even a rather lengthy bit of wind about politics.

And, of course, the Dems accused the Repubs, and the Repubs accused the Dems. At which point I stood up. And, because I was the wife of Patient Zero, everybody paid attention.

"I think we all better get over it and realize that there are no more Dems and Repubs. That's yesterday. Today we have a different society. We have a spattering of men, and we have old women, and new women."

The girls looked thoughtful, so I decided to keep going.

I don't know about you, but my husband is…falling out of love with me. I don't know why specifically, but it seems he likes the company of new women better than old women. This is going to be the new dividing line. And I want to pose one question, it's probably ill thought out, might be totally inconsequential, but…are the new women going to be in charge? Or the old women?"

"Men are in charge," said some poor twit. There was bitter laughter at her comment, however, so she didn't say anything else.

Elsa stood up and said, "How does that effect sex."

And now we were all silent.

Finally, unable to endure silence, I stood up again. "Let's analyze the possibilities.

"There's a few men left, but not enough to go around.

“And then there’s woman on woman. Which doesn’t seem to be new woman on old woman, or old woman on new woman. Elsa, your question is good, but it is still going to resolve with a political decision, or maybe some kind of sociological resolution.”

More silence. And, finally, we resolved to discuss the issue at the next meeting. Until then, have some donuts or go collect your husband, such as she is.

The men, when we did go ‘collect’ them from my house, looked guilty. Like they had been doing something they were not supposed to do.

Still, they were relatively docile creatures, so nobody cross examined them, or shamed them, or otherwise mistreated them.

I just know that when I saw Joe she was bland and cheerful, too cheerful, and I knew she had been with somebody.

The next meeting, a week later, was much the same as the first. The number of men changed into women was down a bit, down to about 85%, but we all agreed that the extra 5% was probably old men, past their prime, into the male ‘change of life,’ as it were.

The interesting thing was that children were changing, and this almost without exception.

And, a side note, scientists were looking into possible breeding programs, which opened up the door to designer babies and such.

And that one twit, who had spoken so stupidly last week, wondered if they could make a dog. She would much rather raise a dog than a child.

I kid you not.

But she shut up again, she was only good for one stupidity a week, apparently, and the meeting went on.

"My name is Janey. I just wanted to say that it looks like the new women are banding together."

A bunch of raised voices and Joanne had to slap her shoe on a table to get proper silence reinstated. "What do you mean?"

"I don't mean politically, like we've discussed, it's more like they have some sort of deep feeling for each other. I've caught my husband standing, holding hands, staring into the eyes of other new women."

Some of the girls scoffed at that, some were upset, and some said nothing, just thought out loud.

It made me think.

But, like most meetings, in the end it was just a bunch of talk, and we all went for donuts or husbands, as was our wont. The next meeting was scheduled for a week hence, and it was to be held in the auditorium of the local school. Changes had been happening so fast, and there were so many old women now. But before the next meeting I had my own little crisis, and that crisis would drastically effect the world.

Wednesday. Joanne and I went out shopping. Afterwards, she wanted to go visit a friend, and I didn't, so she let me off at the corner and I walked 100 yards to my home.

It was dark in the house, but I didn't think anything of it. Joe might be over at Bob's holding hands and gazing into each other's eyes. I had caught them before, and I was sure to catch them again.

Then, feeling a bit perverse, and curious, I slipped through the front door and listened.

The mutter of voices down the hall.

I tip toed down the hallway…to my bedroom.

Well, Bob and mine.

And I listened.

"Oh, baby, put it there. Oh…yes! Now wiggle."

Heavy breathing. I could feel lust emanating from the room, a palpable wave of emotion that was all consuming.

"Here, one on top."

"Yes, oh, this is a good dildo!"

They were fucking, shamelessly, just hiding in a corner, apart from the world, and I felt so betrayed, so left out. I had done everything for Joe, and now he and Bob were doing for themselves, and I was lurking in the hallway, tears streaming down my face, wishing it could be me that under the dildo, or over it. Being the penetrator or penetrated, it made no difference. I just didn't want to be lonely.

"Oh! That's it! Now fuck me!"

I could hear the bed springs creaking as their weight went up and down. I could hear their voices, gasping in pleasure. I could even hear the moist suckiness of the dildo as it went in and out.

"Oh, I love you!"

And that was what did it.

I went through the door, straight arming it to the side where it bounced off the wall. I stood glaring at the two…women.

Bob was on the bottom, her face turned towards me. She was shocked and shamed and embarrassed and trapped.

Joe was on the top, half risen in shock, and her face was the same, humiliated and sad.

I said nothing. Nothing needed to be said.

I turned and walked out of the room.

I heard their voices whispering behind me. I heard the creak of bed as they got off, and the scamper of their little girl's feet.

I sat in the living room and waited. Bob went into the kitchen and out the side door. She was like a little elf, kicked out by the big monster Santa Claus.

Then Joe came in. Her head was hanging and she was ashamed.

"I'm sorry."

"For what?" I asked bitterly.

"For…you know…we're married."

"Are we?"

"When I was a man I married you. For better or worse. I guess this was the worst."

Interestingly, this was the most Joe had talked to me in weeks. And it was intriguing. I wanted to see where it would go.

"Do you want a divorce?"

"Oh, no! No!" And she looked really frightened. Her eyes grew enormous, and I could tell this was actual fear.

"So you don't want to divorce, but you want to have your cake and eat it too."

I was dreadfully aware of how trite this was. How cliche ridden. The only thing that was odd was that it was between a woman and a woman, and not a man and a woman.

She fell to her knees then, and tears filled her eyes. "Please. I'm sorry. Isn't sorry enough?"

"No." Cold bitch, I. But she deserved it. And there was something here I couldn't figure out.

"So why are you fucking Bob?"

"Because…I can't help it." Tears were coming out of her eyes now.

"But you won't stop."

"I can't!" and she actually wailed this answer out.

I didn't say anything for a while, then, angrily, I snapped, "Go clean yourself up. You're disgusting."

Her tears had been lessening, but my words snapped her back into her crying. She ran from the room, sobbing, like a 15 year old girl.

I thought for a long time then.

I was married, and he became a she, and now it was different. No brainer there.

She couldn't keep her hands off the little girl next door. Or, for that matter, off any little girl. I didn't know, but that might be the truth. To watch a bunch of the little sissies interact, it certainly seemed possible.

Sissies. Huh. I had just called my 'man' a sissy. Yet, wasn't she? There was a whole lexicon here that needed to be analyzed and fixed.

Why was she so scared of me leaving her? With her looks she could probably even get one of the last few men with dicks to take her on.

Joe appeared at the doorway. She was cleaned up, and she had re-applied her make up. She was wearing nothing, just her boobs sticking out, and her little patch of heaven below. Snuffling, she asked, "Can you come to bed?"

I blinked. I had done this same thing to Joe. I had lost an argument, and won it in the bedroom, and here it was being done to me.

She saw my quandary, she came to me, timidly, hesitantly, and touched my hand.

"Please Jesse. I need you. We need to make this all right."

On one hand I wanted to slap her, to yell at her, to scream out that I wanted a divorce.

On the other hand, she was so pathetic it was adorable. In that moment, Bob aside, she lived for me. She wanted to please me. She wanted my love.

How could I say no to such adoration, misbegotten as it was?

I stood up and she grabbed my hand with both of hers. A thin grin bubbled out on her face, an embarrassed grin, yet, a hint of triumph?

She tugged me, pulled me down the hallway. She was acting giddy, and she got behind me and pushed me down on the bed.

I had no expression on my face; I felt like somebody else was having this done to her.

She took off my clothes, whispering all the time. "I'm so sorry. I never want to hurt you. I just couldn't...you're so beautiful.

My clothes off, she launched her body on to mine. She was slightly smaller than me now. Maybe an inch smaller and 20 pounds lighter. Physically, I was dominant.

She kissed me, and I felt the slither of lipstick on my lips. I felt her hands groping my pussy.

I felt myself giving in. This pleasure was all for me, and how can any saner person say no to pleasure?

Then said, breathily, "Wait. I'll go put on the strap on."

She got off the bed and I followed her shadow in the darkness. I could see her fitting the dildo on, adjusting it, then she was back.

She climbed up, kneed her way between my legs, and suddenly, I didn't want to be fucked.

Oh, I wanted to fuck. She had me so wet and horny, but I didn't want to be fucked, I wanted to fuck. I wanted to drive that delicate creature down under me. I wanted to open her, separate her from her senses, make her scream with pleasure until she was stupid.

"Give me that," my voice was harsh, grating, and she quickly handed me the strap on.

I stood up and stepped into it and began adjusting the buckles. "Lie on the fucking bed," I snarled.

There was an anger in me, but not with her.

Was it with myself? Was I angry for falling in to this trap?

I didn't know. I just knew what I was supposed to do.

"Get up there and spread your legs."

She should have run from the anger in my voice, but she didn't. It seemed to actually make her hornier, hotter, and she scooched back on the bed and opened her sweet thighs.

I climbed on to the bed, knee walked between her legs. In the dim light I could see her eyes, glinting with fear and happiness.

Fear and happiness, both emotions, contrary emotions, and yet it seemed to satisfy her.

I put my hands on her thighs and pulled myself the remaining few inches. She groaned as my hands dug into her legs.

"Oh, please," she whispered, a guttural prayer to the God of the dildo."

"Please my ass," I snarled, and I sunk it into her.

Oh, she was wet. The dildo slid in like it was greased, and she arched her back and gave a cry. And I knew, she wanted this rough.

She wanted to be taken. This was a battle here, and I had somehow been selected to be the winner.

I fucked her brutal then. I rammed it in and out, and I grabbed her tits and squeezed them until she cried.

Yet it was right. It wasn't mean, it was the pecking order, and I was meant to be the top pecker. And she…she needed to be put in her place.

For long minutes I abused her with the dildo, and she whimpered and cried and loved every second. And though I was being mean, and though she loved it and wanted more, I didn't know what to think.

But then, I wasn't supposed to think. I was supposed to ravage, and let the Gods sort out the remains.

So I delved deep, I dug out her soul, I brought out the whimpering, little submissive that she was designed to be, and though I wondered, I didn't hold myself back.

Then, when she was crying, yet holding on for dear life, I drew out. I flipped her over and took her from the rear. I held on to her ass and rammed her between the cheeks, and she howled.

But I repeat, it wasn't pain, it was the pleasure of submitting, of giving up. She had been a he, and he had never submitted. Therefore, this was crucial to her understanding, and to our relationship.

We had made love before…but this was me FUCKING her.

She cried, and yet she wiggled back up against me.

I slapped her ass, and she bucked and wanted more, looking over her shoulder with begging in her eyes.

And, finally, butt fucking done, I only had one tool left. I pulled out and I began pushing my fingers into her. Three fingers, sliding smoothly in and out. And, as she got used to it, I used four fingers. And, finally, my hand slipped in. I fisted her, and now I turned gentle.

I knew this hurt, and I knew it was necessary, and that she was giving herself to me in the most intimate manner. She would never be the same after this, she would be totally female, and she wanted me to take her.

This was how I would beat Bob, and any of the other sissies who wanted to supplant me.

And I think, somewhere in there, I realized a truth. A truth I would bring to the next ladies meeting.

But right now that truth couldn't be verbalized, it could only be imparted on my knuckles and in her pussy.

Interestingly, neither of us had an orgasm that night. She was submitting, not looking for sexual pleasure. And I was doing my duty. A duty I had been remiss in, and I had to rectify that mistake. I had to make her mine.

The contract between us hadn't changed. And she had been acting like a 16 year old girl. I had to put her in her place, teach her to be an adult in her relationships. We had swapped roles, but the contract was still there. We had put ourselves together for better or worse, and this was the worst.

And the best.

For it was the sealing of the deal.

This was the signature at the bottom of the paper.

This was our souls bonding.

Finally, I took my fist out of her, and I lay, exhausted, and stared at the ceiling.

She had started crying somewhere in there, but not tears of

pain, but of happiness. She had been put in her place.

She turned over and snuggled up against me. I could feel her small hands holding on to me. I could feel her lips pressed against my rib cage, and the flow of tears down my flesh.

Most of all, I could feel her, no longer conflicted, now decided. Happy.

The very next day I told Joanne what I had done. I spoke aloud, and Joe was humming happily as she did the dishes and made sure we had enough coffee. She didn't mind that I described how I had beaten her ass and shaped her to my will.

In fact, I think he liked it. It was like a compliment to him.

"I fucked her senseless. And then I turned her over and fucked her ass. And I wasn't gentle.

Joanne looked puzzled. "I don't understand."

"And then I rammed my fist up her pussy."

"What?"

"I know, it sounds brutal, but it was necessary."

"Why?"

"Because Joe was alpha, and there was too much alpha left in her. I had to drive the alpha out of her. I had to show her who's boss."

Joanne said nothing for a while, but as I continued explaining, she got a far away look in her eyes.

Bob had strayed. Bob needed to be returned to the fold. Bob needed a good fuck. A fuck that showed the sheep who the master was.

I smiled. First Joanne, then the world.

Joanne and I went to the meeting that weekend, and we were smiling. And the other ladies all noticed.

"What are you two goin on about?" asked somebody.

"I'll tell you after reports."

Reports, and the percentages of men who retained their dicks was better.

And scientists were gleefully talking about artificial insemination, and how there was plenty of sperm to go around, and…yes, designer babies was possible.

And there were more female cops now, and they had better manners, were more compassionate and less likely to use their billy clubs.

The military was being redesigned as an 'emergency corps.' Women who traveled the world and helped out int he emergencies.

And the news went on and on.

And, finally, it was my turn.

"Ladies," I gave a big grin. "There are three races now. There are the males, the old females, and the new females. And we are the old females, and we need to consolidate our position if the races are to progress."

"What do you mean?"

"How are you…"

And so on.

So I told everybody what I had done with Joe. how I had made the old marriage contract work by becoming the alpha, the one in charge.

Let me tell you, there were a lot of thoughtful ladies as I wound up my talk.

And I said: "Think of it this way. Men have X and Y

chromosomes. New women have only pure X chromosomes. Old women have X chromosomes, but there is a smattering of Y in them, and this Y has remained intact. The COVID SC has not taken the Y out of us, and that is good. For if there is not a bit of man in a woman, and a bit of woman in man, then we would not understand each other. We would be a species eternally at war, and that until one or the other was destroyed.

"The new woman, however has absolutely no Y chromosome. The new woman is perfect. A perfect X chromosome.

But the Y chromosome made men dominant. And the X chromosome made for perfect submission. The new women are waiting for the Y to rule them, to give them their place and purpose in the world. Thus, you must do as I have done. Take your old men, your new women, and teach them who is boss, who is in charge. Until you do that the new women will wander and search, and they are only looking for somebody to tell them what to do, to take charge of them.

End

A Note from the Author!

I hope you liked these little gems.
Please take a moment to rate me five stars.
That helps support my writing,
and lets me know which direction I should take
for future books.

Thank you

Grace

Six volumes! Over 40 stories!

Five Star Gropper Stories on Amazon!

Full Length Books from Gropper Press

A classic of feminization.

Alex is ensnared by an internet stalker. Day after day he is forced to feminize. His neighbor finds out and the situation becomes worse. Now his wife is due home, and he doesn't know what to do. What's worse, he is starting to like it.

This book has forced feminization, forced crossdressing, gender transformation, sissy, teasing and denial, erotic spanking, pegging.

Sissy Ride: The Book!

Randy catches his wife cheating, but a mysterious woman is about to take him in hand and teach him that when a woman cheats…it is the man's fault.

This story has female domination, spanking, male submission, male chastity, pegging, cross dressing, feminization

The Big Tease!

Full Length Books from Gropper Press

Full Length Books from Gropper Press

The Feminization Games

Jim Camden was a manly man, until the day he crossed his wife. Now he's in for a battle of the sexes, and if he loses… he has to dress like a woman for a week. But what he doesn't know is the depths of manipulation his wife will go to. Lois Camden, you see, is a woman about to break free, and if she has to step on her husband to do it…so be it. And Jim is about to learn that a woman unleashed is a man consumed.

This story has female domination, forced feminization, cross dressing, chastity belts, pegging, shrunken manhood and orgasm denial.

My Husband's Funny Breasts

Tom Dickson was a happy camper. He lived a good life, had a beautiful wife, then he started to grow breasts, his hair grew long, and his body reshaped. Now Tom is on the way to being a woman, and he doesn't know why.

This book has forced feminization, cross dressing, hormones, gender transformation, pegging and breast growth.

Full Length Books from Gropper Press

The Stepforth Husband

Rick Boston and his beautiful wife, Jamey, move to Stepforth Valley, where Rick is offered a job at a high tech cosmetics company. The House of Chimera is planning on releasing a male cosmetics line, and Rick is their first test subject. Now Rick is changing. The House of Chimera has a deep, dark secret, and Rick is just one more step on the path to world domination!

This book has female domination, feminization, cross dressing, hormones, gender transformation, forced transgender and pegging.

The Broken Man

Kyle Talon loves his wife, and he'll do anything for her, including getting into the trunk of a car driven by a beautiful woman. What Kyle doesn't know is that the beautiful woman is taking him to a ranch where men are subjected to unbelievable perversion…and they all love it. All except Kyle. Kyle still loves his wife. Silly man.

This book has bondage, female supremacy, male chastity training and erotic punishment.

BIG COLLECTIONS!

The Electric Groin!

Save money

SEVEN sexy stories

A sorority that feminizes, 'Tootsie' goes all the way, National lipstick day and all the men in Hollywood start growing breasts, learning to be a man by being a woman, and more, more, more.

The Secret is Out!

Save money
SEVEN orotic stories

Men with breasts, COVID mutates men into women, a man doubles in size and turns into a woman, and much more!

BIG COLLECTIONS!

The Girl in Me

Save money

SEVEN erotic stories

A woman gives her man boobs…a scientist figures out how to lose the Y chromosome…a young man will get free college, if he lets them give him boobs…and all sorts of stuff!

Quivering Buns

Save money

SEVEN erotic stories

Men turning into women because of the vaccine...a woman makes her husband wear a chastity device, then they swap bodies...feminization training…feminized by his sister…and more, more!

BIG COLLECTIONS!

Tainted Love!

Save money
SEVEN erotic stories

A curse makes him lose his package and grow boobs…the latest medical device has side effects…a man dominated by a gang of women…and much, MUCH more!

Stories to Pump your Heart

Save money
SEVEN erotic stories

A nephew changed into a girl… emasculating a cheating husband…a feminized cop…sentenced to feminization…and a LOT More!

Big Novelettes

The Day the Democrats Turned the Republicans into...Girls! ~ A note from Grace...I got tired of all the politics on TV, everybody yelling at everybody, and everybody knowing they are the only ones that are right...it's enough to make a girl pick up an erotic book. You know? So, are you ready for the 'transgenderment' of half the country?

This book contains forced transgender, forced feminization, power exchange, gender transformation, bisexual, lesbian, breast growth.

The Day the Democrats Turned the Republicans into...GIRLS!

Grace Mansfield

The Lactating Man ~ Jessica is about to have a bay, the only problem is she can't produce enough milk to nurse. Solution? Her husband, Robert, is about to go on the wildest trip any man has ever gone on.

This book has feminization, cross dressing, hormones, breast growth, lactation, small penis, pegging.

Big Novelettes

The Were-Fem ~ Rodney is a hard working lad who stumbles upon a beautiful girl in the forest. The girl turns out to be a demon, and Rodney is cursed. By day an honorable man, by night a man sucking demon.

This book contains supernatural sex book, erotic punishment, gender transformation short story, forced transgender, demon sex, blackmail, deals with the devil.

The Half and Half Man ~ Jesse is forced to have his hands manicured, which causes an orgasms. Now he is faced with full feminism. Will Jesse survive the trip?

This story contains androgynous models, feminization kindle, transgender story, submissive husbands, humiliation, shrunken manhood, pegging.

Big Novelettes

Feminized for Granny ~ Underwear is disappearing from Joanna's department store. She catches the culprit, and a spanking reveals that Eric is a cross dresser. Joann realizes there is something very hot about cross dressing, but how far can she push Eric?

This story has female domination, forced feminization, crossdressing, submissive male story, erotic sissy, brassiered, humiliation.

Feminized Cop ~ He wasn't big enough to be a real cop, so he became T-Rex, a feminized cop. He infiltrated a dangerous gang and got the goods, but now he has to get out.

This story has feminization, crossdressing, transvestite, gender transformation, castration, erotic police sex, transgender.
This story has female domination, forced feminization, crossdressing, submissive male story, erotic sissy, brassiered, humiliation.

Big Novelettes

Feminized in 100 Days ~ Tom loves his wife, but he doesn't feel worthy. She is so beautiful and powerful. Tammi learns how Tom feels, and comes up with a plan to make Tom feel beautiful and worthy, and It only takes 100 days.

A wonderful tale of erotic sex and the exchange of power.

This story has female domination, feminization, crossdressing, submissive male story, erotic hormones, teasing and denial, female led relationship.

Dominated for a Week: He was Caught and Punished! ~ Brandon is a kinky, little boy. He wears dresses, has a chastity device, and lives for when his wife is working as a stewardess. Then he is caught, and five women take control of him. He doesn't know who they are, but his wife is due home any time!

This story has crossdressing, feminization, chastity, orgasm denial, male submission, lingerie, female led relationship

Big Novelettes

My Wife Dominated Me: He asked for a little, she gave him a lot! ~ Jerrod and Janice have a strange relationship, he gets to make love to her when he makes a million dollars. What he doesn't know is that the end of one agreement is the beginning of another, and she has incredible plans for him!

This story has crossdressing, feminization, chastity, orgasm denial, male submission, lingerie, female led relationships.

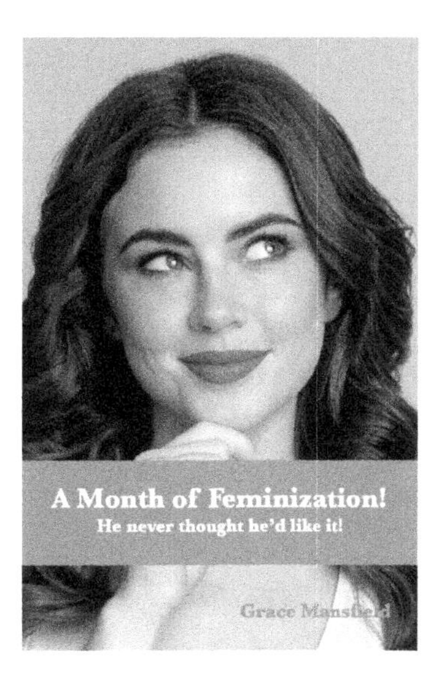

A Month of Feminization: He never thought he'd like it! ~ Roger received a mysterious present, now he's locked into a chastity belt, and somebody has hacked it! His wife thinks it's funny, her friend thinks it's hilarious, then his wife goes away and the fun starts. Will Roger ever be free from the clutches a mysterious internet hacker and...his wife's best friend?

This story has female domination, feminization, teasing and denial, male chastity, orgasm denial, power exchange, blackmail.

If you liked

'The Great Gender Revolt'

you will really love...

'I Changed My Husband into a Woman'

A full length novel by Grace Mansfield

Here is an excerpt...

"What the fuck!"

I roused myself from a deep and very deserved sleep, only to see Roscoe standing next to the bed, looking down at his feet and cursing.

"Wha..." I mumbled, pulling the covers over me and trying to look like I was still asleep. In truth, though I was tired, I was as awake as I had ever been.

"Did you do this?" His voice was going up. "Is this your idea of a joke?"

"Shut up," I whined. "I wanna sleep!"

"No! Wake up! Why'd you do this?"

"Do what?" and I finally rolled over and made my eyes sleepy and tired.

Oh, baby, was I acting. And I was acting in front of the fellow who had created a half a dozen Best Actor Oscar winners. This was going to take all my prowess to pull off.

"My toes! Look at my toes."

I blinked, and edged towards the side of the bed so I could look down to where he was pointing. And I exulted. He had felt he had to explain that it was his toes, so he was just working off emotion and blaming whoever was closest. He didn't have any clue as to why his toes were red.

"What the fuck!" I opened my eyes wide and stared at his tootsies.

"Why'd you do this?"

I looked up at him and put a tiny edge of anger in my voice. "I didn't do that! Why the hell would I paint my sissy husband's toes red?" Very important to get the word sissy into the conversation as quickly as possible. "Do I look like I'm the kind of girl who'd marry a sissy?"

He kept trying to look fierce, but I could tell that my arrows had hit the mark. In some odd, almost invisible way he shriveled. He withdrew slightly into himself. I had met the challenge and acted my way out of being the culprit.

"Okay, okay," then he tried again. "You did this because I jacked off on you the other day."

"First, I just said I didn't do that!" I pointed at his toes. "And, I already got you back, and, husband of mine, practical jokes aren't my forte." At least they usually weren't. I was enjoying this; I was thinking of a career change. Sandy Tannenbaum, Practical Joker Extraordinaire!

"So who did this?"

Now I looked at him suspiciously. "There's only two people in this room."

He sputtered in outrage, so I kept up the attack. "So why did you paint your toe nails red?"

"I didn't!"

"There's nobody else here!" I was pushing him now. I had been accused unfairly (he thought) so I had to act the outrage. I narrowed my eyes. "Are you going pervert on me?"

"I didn't do this!" he wailed.

"Well I didn't, and I didn't figure on waking up next to Bruce Jenner."

Oh, Jesus!" he almost ran to my make up station and started looking for polish remover. "Where is it!?"

I got out of bed, and went to him. I didn't want him making a mess, so I handed him a bottle of polish remover. He grabbed at it like a sailor grabs a life preserver after jumping off the Titanic. He sat down and lifted his foot up to the edge of the chair.

"Hold on," I said. I took the remover out of his hands. "I don't want you making a mess. Come here."

I led him into the bathroom. "Put your foot here," I pointed to the john. He placed his foot on the toilet and I sat cross legged in front of it. I giggled.

"What?" he groused.

"It is sort of cute. Hubbie gives himself a peddie. Make a good TV series."

He let his breath out in disgust. "I'm a man's man, not a girly man."

Yeah, that's right, you like to get young girl's pregnant. how manly. But I didn't say that, I just thought it, and kept manipulating him.

"Well, you might say so, but Roscoe Junior says otherwise."

Now, truth, he wasn't really all that hard, just sort of a morning half woodie, but I reached up and grabbed his meat and in a second he was throbbing in my hand.

"Hey!" he said. But he wasn't really protesting. What man would object to a pair of sexy hands fondling his man pole? "Take the polish off."

"Oh, okay." but the damage was done. He was now erect, and associating that erection with nail polish. Manly man. Huh!

So I hummed a tune and stripped the polish off and returned his toes to their 'manly' state.

"Okay," he said. Standing and looking down at his repaired

manhood, uh, nails.

"Not even a thanks?"

"Thank you," and he did sound abashed. "But I have no idea how... somebody must have broken in and done it."

"While you slept? They painted your nails and you didn't even wake up?"

"Well, I was pretty drunk."

I'll say.

"Not that drunk," I lied. "You never get that drunk."

"Well, yeah. But somebody did it." We left the bathroom then and re-entered the bedroom. He walked over to the double windows, which led out to a small patio. He tried the doors. "See! they're open!"

"We're on the second floor."

"He had a ladder."

"He?"

"Well, you don't think a woman did this?"

"Those nails were done pretty well. Men don't know how to apply polish that well." Then I cocked my head and it was obvious what I was thinking.

"Don't look at me that way! I didn't polish my own nails."

I shrugged. "Okay. So Spiderman left off fighting crime for one day so he could paint your nails."

He made a grimace.

"Or maybe somebody just walked in because our door is unlocked." I swung the bedroom door opened.

"Well, I don't..."

"Forget it, Roscoe." I use his name when I am angry with him, or irritated, and he took notice of that. "just admit that you did some sleep walking." Then I giggled, "Or sleep toenail painting."

"Oh, shut up." he brushed past me and headed down the stairs. It was a mark of how irritated and upset he was that he had forgotten to get dressed.

"Ahem!" I cleared my throat.

He turned at the top of the stairs and looked at me. Oh, the look on his face. Irritated, confused. Priceless.

I looked at his groin, placed an elbow in a palm and wiggled my index finger in the air.

He looked down at himself, mumbled a curse word I dasn't dare repeat, and stomped back into the bedroom.

Made in the USA
Las Vegas, NV
20 April 2022